SUNCRANES

AND OTHER STORIES

SUNCRANES

AND OTHER STORIES

MODERN MONGOLIAN SHORT FICTION

TRANSLATED BY

SIMON WICKHAMSMITH

COLUMBIA UNIVERSITY PRESS   NEW YORK

COLUMBIA
UNIVERSITY
PRESS

Columbia University Press gratefully acknowledges the generous support for this
book provided by Publisher's Circle member Bruno A. Quinson.

Columbia University Press wishes to express its appreciation for assistance
given by the Pushkin Fund in the publication of this book.

Columbia University Press
Publishers Since 1893
New York   Chichester, West Sussex
cup.columbia.edu

Library of Congress Cataloging-in-Publication Data
Names: Wickhamsmith, Simon, translator.
Title: Suncranes and other stories : modern Mongolian short fiction /
translated by Simon Wickhamsmith.
Description: New York : Columbia University Press, [2021]
Identifiers: LCCN 2020049781 (print) | LCCN 2020049782 (ebook) | ISBN
9780231196765 (hardback ; acid-free paper) | ISBN 9780231196772 (trade paperback ;
acid-free paper) | ISBN 9780231551816 (ebook)
Subjects: LCSH: Short stories, Mongolian—Translations into English. |
Mongolia—Social life and customs—Fiction.
Classification: LCC PL418.2.E5 .S86 2021 (print) | LCC PL418.2.E5 (ebook) |
DDC 894/.23—dc23
LC record available at https://lccn.loc.gov/2020049781
LC ebook record available at https://lccn.loc.gov/2020049782

Columbia University Press books are printed on permanent
and durable acid-free paper.
Printed in the United States of America

Cover image: Dae Sung Lee, from the series *Futuristic Archaeology*, Erden, Mongolia, 2015
Cover and book design: Chang Jae Lee

CONTENTS

A book whose covers and final chapter are missing, and whose pages are worn and frayed, makes for a singular gift. But in 2006, on my first visit to Mongolia, a friend presented me with such a gift, discovered in one of Ulaanbaatar's used bookstores. It was a rare treasure, the collected works of the influential revolutionary writer M. Yadamsüren (1904–1937), published in 1970 and never reprinted. At the time, I had little idea about Yadamsüren's life, had barely heard his name, and had only an inkling of how important his few short stories had been to the development of literature in Mongolia during the 1930s. When I read his story "The Young Couple," I sensed in it the Mongolia I was right then discovering. It was sharp and fresh, and somehow both traditional and very modern, a love story set among Ulaanbaatar's urban laboring class, but with elements of suspense and friendship and a modernist view of nomadic life seen through the eyes of the country's new and revolutionary urban youth. I began to explore Yadamsüren's work and that of his contemporaries and those who followed him, and to translate the pieces that accompany "The Young Couple" in *Suncranes and Other Stories*.

Even today, there exist hardly any volumes showcasing translations of Mongolia's literature in English, and this collection marks the first commercial publication in the United States of Mongolian prose fiction. For more than a century, influenced both by a long tradition of narrative epic poetry and Buddhist teaching stories and by Western literature in Mongolian or Russian translation, Mongolia's writers have been reflecting in their fiction the country's nomadic culture and the ways its revolutions, initially of socialism and centralized control and latterly of global capitalism and the free market, have transformed it.

These stories provide one possible route by which to understand these transformations. This exploration did not begin from a standstill, but was a continuation of the tradition of fables, tales, epics, and occasional experiments with Western models on which Mongolian writers had been raised during the first decades of the twentieth century. Since much of the population was at that point illiterate, many early attempts to spread the message of the revolution took the form of drama. These plays sought to convey to the country's nomadic herding communities the (supposed) stark differences between their old life of suppression and exploitation by the monasteries and noble families and the new utopia granted them by the revolution, that is, by the Mongolian People's Revolutionary Party and, by extension, the Soviet Union.

The starkness of this contrast was far more aspirational and ideological than practical. The situation that had prevailed before the Soviet-backed socialist revolution of 1921 was by no means ideal for nomadic herders but was a largely self-regulated system, according to which herding families had for centuries moved across the land in seasonal cycles, tending their herds and interacting, at markets, at festivals, and when they met by happenstance, with one another and with their wider community. With the revolution came a swift centralization of power, and a consequent focus on the nation rather than on the individual or on small, self-contained herding communities. Collectivization—a very foreign concept considering the self-reliance of these communities—became the goal, and five-year plans imposed by the government in Ulaanbaatar (following directives from Moscow) brought, over the course of several decades, levels of disruption and development similar to those felt across Soviet Central Asia.

The bedrock upon which the new revolutionary literature developed was the Buddhism that Mongolia had inherited from Tibet in the late sixteenth century. The vast corpus of Tibetan and Indic sources that informed Buddhist philosophy and practice filtered into Mongolia's religious and secular literature, and these teaching stories, legends, and mystical narratives provided copious material for Mongolian writers to adapt and draw upon in their own work. In addition, Mongolia's own indigenous oral literature, its stories, songs, shamanic prayers, and other examples of vocal and dramatic arts, all contributed to a rich and diverse literary culture. With increased literacy as a key aspect of the government's cultural plan, the state-run publishing industry began to produce journals that mixed literature with revolutionary ideology, as well as books of stories, essays, and poems whose revolutionary heroes enacted revolutionary themes. And in order that writers would remain in step with the Party, the publishing process came to be strictly monitored by the Writers' Union and by a censorship bureau modeled on the Soviet Glavlit.

Yet while the revolution had primarily been an attempt to oust the Chinese from Mongolia rather than to install a Marxist-Leninist system, among its political and social effects had been a determination to improve the education system and to select and train promising students in Western sciences and humanities. Eventually, in the early 1950s, Mongolia would begin sending its most promising writers to the Gorky Institute in Moscow, but during the 1920s, the focus was on building cultural and educational exchanges with Europe. In 1926, forty-five students, including two represented here, D. Natsagdorj and D. Namdag, were sent to study in Berlin, where the social and literary experimentation of the Weimar Republic presented new and challenging ways to think and to create. Mongolia also sent some young intellectuals, among them D. Chimid, to the Communist University of the Toilers of the East in Moscow, and through exchanges such as these, fostered an atmosphere in which some, albeit a very few, of the country's most promising young people could experience the kind of "advanced" culture to which the Party in Ulaanbaatar aspired.

The stories written during this period looked out from the traditional nomadic lifestyle toward a revolutionary and industrialized future. Ideas of how the improvements brought by the revolution could best be safeguarded by the kind of close personal relationships central to a successful nomadic society can be found in many stories, including M. Yadamsüren's "The Young Couple" and O. Tsend's "A Great Mystery." The tradition of reciprocal behavior, crucial for a steppe life that demanded unconditional assistance in times of severe personal or practical difficulty, became a powerful regulating aspect of Mongolia's socialist culture and remains a strong influence on the society even today.

The development of literature over the half century of increased Soviet influence, between the Stalinist purges of the late 1930s and the repercussions of Mikhail Gorbachev's policies during the mid-1980s, traced a similar path to that in other Soviet satellites. Mongolia's experiment with socialist realism began slowly, but by the time of the first Congress of Mongolian Writers in April 1948, it was the primary approach to literary creation. We can see, from works such as Ts. Ulambayar's "The Morning of the First," how socialist realism required writers to create believable and emotionally driven stories while promoting the concrete benefits (however exaggerated) of socialism.

The result was literature that, while ostensibly exhortatory and celebratory, was also negotiating the often fraught relationship between the Party's message and the lived experience of ordinary people. Indeed, one deliberate aspect of this negotiation was the assumption that those who had yet to recognize and integrate into their own lives the positive effect exerted by the Party could educate themselves and so become committed workers for the state, a powerful idea that had surfaced, even before the 1948 Congress, in Ts. Damdinsüren's "How Soli Changed" (1945). This story, probably the first example in Mongolia of literature extolling the virtue of labor, reveals how determined hard work could transform an individual, and so by implication the entire population, from a lazy and self-serving individualist into an exemplar of heroic and selfless revolutionary labor. In various guises and with varying degrees of subtlety, this took root as a powerful literary theme over the following decades.

The initial excitement of this new approach to literature and of the new society it described faded following the deaths of the Mongolian leader Choibalsan in 1953 and Stalin in the following year. However, despite a thaw in Mongolia akin to that engendered by Nikita Krushchev in the Soviet Union, by the early 1960s, the literary and artistic establishment was once again in a cultural lockdown, with political control being exercised through state censorship as well as through the far stronger motives of self-preservation. Very few were those writers who, like the poet R. Choinom (1936–1979), were prepared to give impromptu public readings attacking the government, and suffer the consequences: Choinom himself was imprisoned in the early 1970s and subsequently blacklisted, his work remaining unpublished until 1990, but others received less severe punishment for less severe infractions and were eventually allowed again to publish.

The program of collectivization, which finally succeeded during the 1950s in integrating the vast majority of the nomadic herding community into a system of state farms, meant that, while the majority of Mongolians remained living with their herds, far away from urban centers, their lives of seasonal movement, livestock husbandry, and relationship with the landscape through which they moved remained key subjects for Mongolian literature despite the new, and very different, practical and ideological context.

The natural world, then, pervades every story set on the seemingly endless steppe that stretches away from the capital of Ulaanbaatar: its menacing shadows in D. Natsagdorj's Gothic tale "Dark Cliffs" and O. Tsend's "A Great Mystery," its vastness and emotional depth in Ts. Damdinsüren's "Two White Things," and its place as a site where social (and socialist) relationships are played out in D. Garmaa's "The Wolf's Lair" and P. Luvsantseren's "Blue as Water." The vitality with which writers express the character of the landscape and the relationships between the people and animals that inhabit it is an indication, in stories such as G. Mend-Ooyo's "The Ballad of the Unweaned Camel," of their having (with a few exceptions) been raised as nomadic herders themselves.

But at the same time as writers were seeking new approaches informed by socialism to the traditional subject of nomadic life, the Party was seeking to forge closer cultural links with Moscow. With the friendship between Mongolia and the Soviet Union came the relative freedom of Mongolian writers to travel and study in the Soviet bloc, and this in turn brought a greater familiarity with European literature and literary developments. Many writers, fluent in Russian, began to translate not only Western classics but also the literature of East Asia. The journalist and poet B. Yavuuhulan (1929–1983) translated into Mongolian Russian translations of Japanese haiku, and so the haiku, and its succinct brevity, became a cipher for Mongolian poets of cultural exploration and modern thought. And yet, the way poetry looked eastward from Russian, and latterly Soviet, literature was not replicated in prose fiction. Rather, it was ideologically safe Russian authors such as Mikhail Sholokov and an assortment of European and American writers whose works were deemed suitable for translation—among them Jack London, Edgar Allen Poe, and Guy de Maupassant—who came to exercise thematic, and occasionally stylistic, influence over Mongolia's growing number of prose fiction writers.

These cultural connections, together with the broad economic and political support, were withdrawn suddenly in 1990 following the democratic revolution, which had taken place over the previous winter, and the disintegration of the Soviet Union, and Mongolia was left in a state of financial and social turmoil. The sudden relaxation of censorship and cultural restrictions brought to the fore a small group of writers in their early twenties who looked toward Western literature and to the experimentation that had been under way in contemporary Russian literature, such as the nihilistic *chernukha* style, in which the vision of a socialist utopia was replaced by a "realist" portrayal of drugs, violence, and prostitution. Foremost among this young group were S. Anudar, whom one of his contemporaries described as the only truly avant-garde writer in Mongolia at the time; L. Ölziitögs and G. Ayurzana, who subsequently married; and P. Bathuyag. The few stories Anudar wrote prior to his death at the age of twenty-two were about his own disaffected generation, abandoned by the Soviet Union with neither money nor jobs, and with time to squander.

The world of crisis inhabited by Anudar's characters, though, gave way to a normalcy in which Mongolians have turned increasingly toward Euro-American, and more recently Korean and Chinese, cultural models. There is still lyricism found in the likes of B. Zolbayar's love story "Beside the Water," but with growing urbanization there is greater interest in portraying Ulaanbaatar's young and upwardly mobile population, searching for a place to live in H. Bolor-Erdene's "Room for Rent" or dealing with trauma in M. Uyansüh's "The Composer," and apparently less interest in the lives of herders and in nomadic traditions.

The tattered collection of Yadamsüren's writing with which this collection began tells another story of Mongolia's democratic era. Many of the texts translated here have, like Yadamsüren's, not been reprinted in the thirty years since the fall of the Soviet Union, but rather crowd the shelves of secondhand bookstores. These bookstores function like repositories of a not-quite-lost past, but this is a past that not everyone in Mongolia wishes to remember. In reading the stories set during the period of Soviet influence, we should remember that they represent life as it was lived at the time, but that this life, and what normalcy it represented, was defined by unspoken forces of constraint and restriction. Conversely, the stories written during the last thirty years have come to reflect the changing aesthetic of Mongolian culture, a kind of oneiric absurdity, or perhaps of magical realism, in which Bolor-Erdene's dark ghost story, P. Bathuyag's fantasy of human flight, and the ordinary bizarreness of adolescence in the stories by L. Ölziitögs and S. Anudar attempt to make sense of the new social order in whose development these writers have found themselves complicit.

The central focus of Mongolia's youngest writers—those under thirty—is not on socialism (except as history), but rather on how to forge a life in a developing democracy in the center of Asia. Mongolia looks north to Russia and south to China, but it looks culturally also to European and American models. How these influences will play out over the next two or three decades, as these writers become (in their own way) the establishment and begin to influence those writers who are only now learning to read, will, it is hoped, offer the next generation of readers, and translators, fictional worlds as unusual and heartfelt as those offered here.

A NOTE ON MONGOLIAN NAMES

M ongolian names have two parts, the patronymic (or occasionally matronymic: a grammatically genitive form generally reduced to an initial) and the given name. For instance, the writer D. Natsagdorj's father was called Dashdorj, and so Natsagdorj's name in full was Dashdorjiin Natsagdorj. This book uses the standard model, and renders names (at least on first appearance) as, for instance, "D. Natsagdorj."

1

SOMETHING WONDERFUL

S. BUYANNEMEH

O ne day in June, when the clear, bright sun was declining into the west and the color of the sky was bright blue like lapis lazuli, a pure wind came in from the northwest, bringing strips of clouds edged in white and grayish-blue that, as though preparing for battle, made to cover the form of the golden sun. Then, with the light at the sun's bright center shining all around, there fell from the dark clouds a gentle drizzle of flowers; the sun blazed red, and across the world there spread a red glow, and something wonderful occurred in the human world.

As this pure rain of rustling flowers cleared away, the sun's jewel-like rays transfixed the misty air and melded with the vapor, and a wonderful rainbow of five colors spread out against the silvern blue sky; and so it was that the colors of the vast and broad world took on a most lovely appearance. At that wonderful moment, somewhere to the west of Bogd Uul and to the east of the spring at Songini Burgast, near an ancient elm at the edge of a patch of sunlight, on a square stone platform on the wide banks of the Tuul, an old man with gray hair, around sixty years of age, sat resting. In his right hand he held a rosary, in his left hand he held a staff of willow wood, and his mind was contemplating samsara and nirvana; he was seeking eternal spiritual alchemy. He felt himself to be in the Buddha's realm of Sukhavātī, and there came to his ears the gentle soughing of the wind and the rippling of the waters, and suddenly he opened his eyes. There, to his right, a cloudy mist was slowly advancing, and when the sun touched the gentle drizzle falling on the hilltops, the sky was transformed, with a red glow covering the earth and the five colors of the rainbow stretching above the earth. To his mind it was even more lovely than the Buddha's realm, and it seemed to the old man that he was dreaming, or else experiencing a vision. He called out, "Children, are you there? Am I in the world, or am I in Sukhavātī?" Two little boys were playing among the stones near the stone platform, and when he called to them, they answered him, "Father, father, you're seeing things, we're over here. How could this be the Buddha's realm?"

Straightaway the old man recognized the children's voices.

"Is that so?" he said. "Look at this. What beautiful colors there are in this heavenly land! This world is filled with rays of red light, so I imagined I'd reached the Buddha's realm." When he looked beyond where the boys had been playing, it was even more beautiful. The boys forgot their play; they stood open-mouthed, staring at the sky in delight, and in their imagination they were playing out there in the sky. As they watched these distant images, from between the clouds, arrayed like flowers of five colors around the red-hued sun, a large creature suddenly emerged, and while its physical form was like a bird's, from between the four great wings upon its back there came rays of red light. It moved along, clear as a daytime star, and the force of its sound was like an earthquake. Closer it came, flying away from the sun, and the two young boys saw it and rushed around in amazement, calling out to the old man, "Father, father, please look. There's a huge bird, it's the size of a large *ger*, it came from where the sun is, from between the clouds of five colors. It seems like there's red light coming from its body, and it's so noisy! What kind of bird is it? Come quickly—look, look!" The old man was amazed; he said, "Where is it, where is it?" and when he looked where they were pointing, because truly it was such a wonderful bird, he quickly said, "Children, children, pay close attention. This is certainly a heavenly *garuda*, one of the Buddha's messengers. Through the beneficence of the buddhas in whom I place my trust, this bird has appeared to us!" And the two boys looked on with unblinking eyes.

As the bird flew directly toward the east, suddenly they saw a multitude of things falling behind it, and the little boys shouted out, "Father, father! There are droppings coming from the bird." The old man stood up quickly and said to them, "Look around. You will receive a great blessing if you gather up the droppings. Go, go and look!" The two boys went to look, and they found that what had fallen from the sky was not in one place alone, but in every direction. All of a sudden, there were what appeared to be larks fluttering toward them on the breeze, and the two boys were jumping around happily, shouting, "Something's coming toward us, something's coming toward us!" One of these objects came straight at them and fell into the old man's skirts. The boys said, "Father, father, they're not droppings falling from the heavenly bird, they're books, books! One's fallen into your lap!" The old man was startled to hear the word "books" and especially so when he heard that they were falling into his lap, and when he took the books and looked at them they were in fact rectangular sheets of paper, and because they were inscribed in gold, and in Mongolian script, he suddenly realized that they had been scattered upon the world from the land of the Buddha. The three of them quickly got down on their knees, folded up the sheets of paper, and placed them between the covers of a copy of the Sūtra of the Golden Light, which the old man carried inside his *deel*. They could not have been happier if they had found a precious jewel. And the old man, who carried a staff, now even forgot that staff as he headed home clutching the book in his hands. He moved quickly, as though flying on his two feet, thinking, *I should show this to someone who can understand it*, and the two little boys barely managed to keep up as they ran behind him.

The old man and the two boys hurried back to their ger, and in some confusion the man spoke to his wife and told her to light incense and candles. She did so, and they reverently placed the sacred texts on the altar. While the old man was explaining to his wife how these texts had fallen from Heaven, a man came in from outside. "How are you, Dorj?" the old man said urgently. "It's lucky you're here! I just found a book that fell from the sky. Would you mind reading it for me?" Dorj said, "Well then, what kind of book falls out of the sky?" The old man told him what had happened and handed him one of the texts. Dorj took it and read in a loud voice:

This eleventh day of July is the great and joyful day on which the Mongolian people's government has been established. The significance of this day is that the true Mongolian people, who have been oppressed and exhausted in the pastures, have now attained their freedom; the door has been opened for them to advance along the bright path of culture, and they have found the path of escape from centuries of wandering among dark mists. For this reason, not only will we the people observe this day forever with our minds and in our hearts, but every year without fail we will all commemorate this day as a blessed memory, and take note year upon year of our advancement. . . .

As they listened, they realized that it had been the flying machines of the people's Party that had scattered these texts upon them all, and that this was the day when the people's liberation had been proclaimed. And every year without fail, on that same day, they organized events to commemorate this proclamation.

1925

2

THE SHELDUCKS

D. CHIMID

Following the cycle of the seasons, many flocks of shelducks bring their young to the streams and rivers and pools and lakes of the Hangai ridges for a cool breath amid the heat, enjoying themselves and singing out, loudly and elegantly, *kang huwang.* The people never treat them badly; they refer to them as "monk birds." They have an elegant outer hue of whitish yellow, and when they look at you, they really do seem like noble monks. As soon as it turns cold, a little before winter, they all settle themselves in warm spots, and in this way the shelducks live their lives in the demigods' ocean of happiness without being encroached upon. Here is a short poem that relates the constant yearnings of the heart:

In the clear wind,
above all animals,
amid the lonely skies,
along the path of peaceful happiness,
their eternal destiny
is an easygoing joy.

For many generations
they have enjoyed all they have found.
Born without guile,
they reside at the peak,
and for their artistic singing
they are worshipped.

Attracted as well
by their fine outer colors,
the earth rumbles
with their calling song—
with just a single word, people
everywhere admire them.

The shelducks in the north do whatever pleases them, they relentlessly move in and entrap those whom they encounter with the melody of their voices, and so eat up their food.

One day, there were some small birds flying in the eternal blue sky, and they were saying, "Let's fly north of the ridges of the broad mountains and salt marshes and enjoy some tasty food just like before." Catching hold of one another's tails, they formed a circle, making noise to protect their food, and taking turns to eat. A shelduck saw this, and he thought, *Oh, I have come from far away with a desire for good fortune, and I will dominate these wretched creatures, these little excuses for birds. I'm quite far away, but I have dominated them from ancient times, and with the power of my pointed beak and sharp talons, and with my superiority, I have threatened those who are so meek, and so I shall seize all those wretches and dominate them myself.* And he went in among the little birds and paraded his arrogance.

"Why are simpletons like you sitting around, so unconcerned, when I'm right here? Previously you would have fled for your lives. At one time, if I had developed my nest even just a little, because I consider you good-for-nothings no better than the dust on my claws, it would most definitely have caused you great suffering. And moreover, you should tell me why you are dragging the reputation of the 'monk bird,' the name that so many have given us, through the mud!" There were many of the little birds listening to what he said, and they said quietly to one another, "For a long time, we have borne a grudge against them because they have been overpowering us and stealing our food and eating it, but now we have strengthened our force and created a just system by uniting with our younger brothers and sisters, and our fear has passed." Then they attacked the shelduck from front and back, from above and below, pecking him with their beaks and grabbing him with their claws, ripping all his feathers and tearing his flesh. And immediately in his fear his heart started to pound and he broke out in a cold sweat, ashamed that his fame as a superior creature had been sullied, and he went off to grieve in isolation while thousands of small birds cried out with pride, like the howling of hungry wolves.

One of the little birds, their leader, whose name was Shining Tailfeathers, spoke up for all of them: "Listen, comrades! Let us each attack with resolve, like thirsty cattle. I want to say two or three words to you all. Take heed of what I say!" Cheering loudly, the small birds immediately ceased their noisy attack, and while they listened attentively to his words, they surrounded the shelduck on all sides.

Shining Tailfeathers flew slowly over the other small birds. He shouted, "Hey there, comrades! If we consider the shelducks, who, honored with the name of the noble monks, are a hindrance by being so covetous and our seniors by dint of their association with the pure sangha, we understand they possess beautiful words and skillful voices. While they are revered and trusted by many creatures, we little birds especially have slipped into showing them great respect and treating them accordingly in how we address them. We know now that their large form and fine colors are like paint that can be blown away on the wind, their skillful words are like dirt that can be washed away in water, and so it is fitting that we should forbid such shows of respect toward the shelducks and cleanse the indirect errors of those who follow after these dissolute birds. Now, through the great custom of showing compassion to all creatures, we will temporarily defer the prosecution of this matter, and we encourage the shelducks to understand that there will be a severe and suitable punishment for them, the justice of winged creatures, if they continue to beat our ears and poke our eyes. We will inform them that, from now on, they may choose—or not—to disregard their previous ways, by which they sullied the respect of so many and continually nourished themselves through destruction and through their theft of others' property. So how about having this shelduck sign and confirm that his kind will now turn away from this activity, and send him back to the flock to establish a just system? If the shelducks exhibit the same kind of behavior as before, dominating and controlling everyone and taking for their food the seeds and grains of poor ones such as ourselves, then no matter what happens, may we not let it pass: we will use force to pacify the enemy, subjugate them, and eliminate them!" He spoke with a passionate anger, and for a long time the little birds cheered vociferously and shouted "Hear! Hear!"

As all the little birds raised their voices, sounding like the voice of Heaven, the shelduck listened from where he was lying prostrate and thought, *How very strange this is.* Observing Shining Tailfeathers's speech and increasing anger, he raised his little body to see what was happening. In great fear and in a distressed voice he repeated, "Please have mercy, please have mercy, I'm not going back to my old ways, I'm not." And then, "What gracious and compassionate birds you are! I will firmly protect the pure discipline of the wonderful wisdom that you, my younger brothers and sisters, have taught me. In senility and in the worldly mists of foolishness, I have grown ignorant and feeble minded. Now I understand, I know that yours are good and pure thoughts, and so may your reputation, my younger brothers and sisters, always be praised for its wisdom and merit!" And this he repeated steadfastly.

The small birds brought many from among their number to establish the balance of power. They handed the shelduck over to his own, and he explained the situation to the leaders of the shelduck assembly. After that, the shelducks behaved with civility and not as they had done before, and their previous behavior grew rare. In general, when they saw a large number of the little birds, they straightaway hid in fear, and whenever they saw even a few of the small birds, they puffed themselves up only very slightly. What's more, it is said that the number of supporters of the Party of the small birds increased.

1927

3

DARK CLIFFS

D. NATSAGDORJ

S ummer nights are short, and by eight o'clock, the sun had already risen. Almost as soon as I had awakened, I struck a match, lighting my cigarette. That day, while I had been lying down, recovering from my sickness, I had been thinking about some things, and as I took my journal from beneath my pillow, a few indistinct letters appeared, written in pencil. I looked through the book, turning the pages with my fingers, moistened with saliva. I was not clear as to why I had noted down the words *Saturday, August 30, Dark Cliffs, Nina*. I had completely forgotten what I had been writing about. I read it slowly one more time, and when I reached the final letter, it suddenly flashed into my brain: *Nina was the name of an old girlfriend of mine*, I had once embraced and kissed this girl in the shade of an oak tree. I brought that moment to mind, and the more the past and the present revolved in my thoughts, the more I was lulled, carried, and pulled into a state in which all things were parallel dreams, and when the ash fell from my cigarette onto my chest, I came back to my senses and returned to what that note might signify.

Before thinking about what it meant, though, I thought about this name that I had written down. *I met Nina seven years ago, she was a lively young girl, I fell madly in love with her; later we were distant, like the mountains and the ocean; as the gap between us grew, our minds and our hearts were at odds. I don't know what happened later, I tried to find her a few times. I was distressed when I couldn't find her.*

But this morning, unexpectedly, as I was looking through these notes, I had seen her name among a few letters whose meaning I didn't grasp, and they had lit a candle for me. I was thinking back now and realized that *these letters were reminders she wrote in my journal when she left me, but I still could not understand their meaning.* And now, unexpectedly, the thought occurred to me that Nina was no regular person, that she was a noble young woman and that what was written here was certainly meaningful. I was thinking, *If I discover the meaning, I will definitely discover Nina*, and I took a cup of tea and drank, still lying down, and began to consider again the meaning of the note. At this point, my cook was looking very serious. He asked me,

"Hey, boss, what is it? Are you sick?"

"Not really."

"Oh, I was worried. You look bad."

"I'm just tired."

I lay there, looking away, the blankets pulled up over my head, thinking. My cook said, "Fine," and he went away. About an hour later, after turning things over in my head as best I could, I suspected that this *Saturday, August 30*, referred to some kind of meeting. And because this *Dark Cliffs* is a place, it must have been the place where we were supposed to meet. I thought it through one more time, I didn't reject the idea, and I looked at the calendar and found that that very day was Saturday, August 30. I stood up quickly and said to the cook, "Saddle my horse," to which he, looking at me with wide eyes, whispered in reply, "What's happened, boss?" and went out to saddle my horse. When he shouted, "Your horse is saddled!," I immediately grabbed a whip, hurried out, and mounted the horse. But I really didn't know where I was going, nor where in the world was this Dark Cliffs. I waited, frustrated, gazing blankly between the horse's two ears. My cook was nearby; he said to me, "Why don't you go? What have you forgotten?" But my horse stood still; his legs were tired, but, because he was fundamentally a proud horse, he felt obligated to move about. I loosened the reins and he walked off toward the southwest. I considered him a top quality mount, so we went in precisely that direction in which he was headed. As we went along, I turned right and left, looking at what there was to see, and all of a sudden we had covered a few dozen miles with absolutely no success, and had come to a deserted spot devoid of both man and beast. I was utterly parched, and despondent. The horse was sweating, but not unduly tired; we headed into the wind, it rushed against our chests, I followed some leads and came to a salt marsh rich in sea blite. There was nothing to see in any direction, but there were dark clouds in the distance and it felt like rain. The wild salt marsh to which we had unexpectedly come was not a pleasant place. I stared in vain. The autumn wind rustled and blew, and my mind grew exhausted. Had the idea of looking for Nina, and finding her, been an onrush of dreams? Had it gone astray on those southern slopes? But my horse started, his ears were alert, his nostrils flared, he was looking here and there as though there was an animal running about. In any case, we galloped closer and there was no fox or wolf but a dog, wagging its tail in a friendly manner, trying to get us to move off to the right. It might have been a local dog and, because it appeared to be well bred, I followed thirstily after it, believing that we would certainly reach some human encampment. We moved away from the salt marsh, over some small hills to where the land was rather different. This was a landscape of grass and plants, and to the northwest, beyond a high mountain, I could make out the flow of a long river. The dog moved slowly, and as we rounded a knoll, a dark ramshackle *ger* came into view.

There were no livestock outside, but there were clumps of feathergrass. A man came out and called the dog to him. My body, which had traveled the wilderness for a half day, felt as though it had been on the road for many months, and because I was exhausted and dispirited, seeing the ger was as pleasant as meeting Nina. The man went inside with me and sat down in the northeast, with one leg stretched out and the other drawn up, while I sat cross-legged on an antelope skin in the northwest. Then we exchanged pleasantries with each other. He was over thirty and wore a *deel* of suede, fastened with a leather strap.

The way he spoke sounded very unfamiliar. Someone was lying between the doorjambs to the southeast of the ger, covered in a deel made of hair. A gray-haired head was sticking out. The man gave me a dish of marmot meat, with a can of tea that was put among the ashes to keep warm. The tea was cloudy, like puddles on the road, and the meat had a musty smell, but I was hungry and thirsty and so I ate and drank. Nina came to my mind, and when I asked the man about the place I had noted down as Dark Cliffs, he said, "I was raised here and have grown old here and, being by nature a hunter, I know the places nearby pretty well." (This made me happy.) "But I have not heard of a place by this name." I felt discouraged at this, and now I had no idea where I should go.

The golden world is broad and wide, so who might know where this place called Dark Cliffs was? Even if I looked in every direction for a hundred, for a thousand years, still I might not find it. I felt devastated about Nina, it pained my body. I sat for a while like this, staring blankly, my face brooding. But was it a buddha to whom the gray-haired old woman, who rose now from where she lay, barely lifting her head, performed an offering, or was it a shamanist spirit? Whatever it was, as she prayed before it, the man said, "Granny, Granny." And then I was surprised, and I wondered who this old woman was who was performing her evening prayers, and I thought I should be off. But the old woman took something from the offering and, giving it to the dark-skinned man, said, "Son, this is something from our ancestors' time, perhaps it is the place of which this young man speaks." (At that, my ears pricked up, my eyes stared, and I took a breath.) "They say it's something rare." The man took it and, looking at it, said, "Old woman, you're senile, and now you're misleading him." He placed it on the table; I hurriedly took it, it was a piece of rock and it was heavy, it slipped from my hand and dropped to the floor. I saw it split into two parts, so it was a regular stone after all. When I took it and placed it on the table, the evening sun touched the western horizon and in its light, the piece of rock that had split away gleamed, and suddenly my interest was piqued. I would travel to the place from which this stone came. It had come from the peak of a high mountain, located a few hours from here; it was a creature that somehow had come from the depths of that great river, risen up the mountain valley, along the mud and marshes that lined the forests, and, from time to time, when there were no tracks or paths, it had encountered nothing living except some ravens.

Now that the sun had fully set, I stopped analyzing the rock. In fact, since any stone must roll downward, in vain I made my way upward. I was already in a deep forest. The overcast day now turned to rain. In the violent winds, with the branches of the trees shaking, the voice of the thunder rumbled. At every step there were muddy marshes and gullies. Here and there a wolf howled, and I was frightened by the noise of cracking and splitting. I hurried on and my heart and my mind grew excited. My body was broken. Earlier I had not known in which direction to go, but now I didn't even recognize the directions.

I had already forgotten what I was aiming at, the object of my search; I chose to keep myself safe. I held great store by basic wisdom, and although I had received such an education, silly things like demons and hell kept coming into my mind. As the rain fell, the thunder resounded. As the land became more difficult, so my fear became greater. Were I to go on, there would inevitably be rough ground up ahead, but were I to return, already I had lost my way. I checked in every direction, I was shocked by how dark were the cliffs that so utterly enclosed me. I concluded that this must be the place called Dark Cliffs, but how could dear Nina be in such a place? I dismounted and sat down. As I waited for the sun to rise, I jumped and startled ten thousand times from shock and surprise. All of a sudden my horse shied at something and neighed loudly at Dark Cliffs, and at that moment I realized there was some creature close by, but I passed out in fright before knowing what kind of creature it was. After some time, I came around and as I looked, I jumped up, I didn't know whether my head was in somebody's lap, or if I was sleeping or dreaming, or whether I was at home, and I saw my darling Nina standing nearby, and the jade face of a lovely young girl illuminated Dark Cliffs.

. . . I understood that my note had been about you, my love, but I didn't know where you had gone and I tried to find you. And I came to you believing that this horse was also your father's horse . . .

Great men seek adventure, thus you came to meet me here at Dark Cliffs. Now we can make love. We exchanged such words and hugged each other, passionately kissing. Then I woke up suddenly, finding out that it had been just a dream, and there was I, kissing my notebook in which I write poetry.

It is frightening and dangerous at Dark Cliffs,
but the jade girl is intrigued.
Poetry fascinates the world, and,
like Nina, it captures a young man's mind.

August 24, 1930

4

THINGS THAT HAD NEVER BEEN SEEN

D. NATSAGDORJ

The lovely River Ider came from the lovely ridges of the *hangai*, dropping down from the high mountains; its flow ever quicker, it rushed along like music. It was truly a pleasure to sit nearby and listen. Why had people passing by on the road not previously noticed it? This pure clear river had flowed the same for thousands upon thousands of years, but the history of humans and animals dwelling upon its banks had changed over and over. The surrounding mountains were hard and high, the protruding and overhanging rocks magnificent, the forests dense, the waters gurgling and babbling.

The scattering of waterfalls down the gorge came together in the River Ider, and drinking their waters awakened the senses within. In the first ten days of the first month of summer, when nature had not yet quite come forth, once the yellow rays of dawn had struck the withers of the eastern mountains, the cuckoos on the peaks sang out, and the boys watching the horses were pleased to hear their song; the birdsong gave them pleasure. The morning sun poured out in its rising, lit up the hollows where the river had its source, brought a pure air: truly the

18 summer's breath could be sensed now, and white hoarfrost

glistened among the flowers and the grasses, and in the forests a green haze settled, drawing the minds of the nomadic herders.

On such a lovely morning, on a terrace on the southern side of the Ider, there are a few smart-looking white *ger*, blue smoke pluming through their roof rings, and livestock scattered all about.

Soon, four or five hundred sheep emerge from the encampment, quickly herded westward out to pasture. Beside a ger off to the southwest, a young man mounts a horse, which has been tied up to harden it; he gallops in behind the sheep, shouting as he drives them forward.

To look at him, he might be twenty-three or twenty-four; his face is bright, his eyes burn, he's a strapping young lad. He's dressed in a blue cotton *deel*, tied with a yellow-green silken belt; he has no queue, but wears a Russian-style felt hat at a jaunty angle. The little black horse is spirited, it can barely keep still. The young man, Bold, strikes the horse's rump with his whip, *tass tass*, jerks the reins, and walks him in behind the sheep.

He goes out onto the hillock to the west, and the sheep move too, greedy for the new-sprung vegetation, not raising their heads from the earth. Bold dismounts on the slope of a nearby hill, lets his horse rest, and goes and sits astride a rock, looking around, wondering at the turning seasons.

He lifts his head. The weather is calm in every direction, the horizon perfectly clear. The animals are clustered here and there, following the untrodden grasses and the clarity of the water.

In the magnificence of the four seasons, with the coming of friendly summer, human civilization and the natural world truly do awaken. Bold likewise is cheered; he breathes the pure air and fills his chest; he looks out at nature, at the hills and the waters; he enjoys the wonders of the wild steppe and gazes out over the southern valley. Oh, how lovely is the broad landscape, which captures the hearts of Mongolian nomads.

Why is he doing this? Well, he was in school abroad for some years and came home via the capital, and now he will soon be going back to take up an official position in Ulaanbaatar. So today, depending on the benefit of the sheep, he has gone out to meet with the wild and peaceful landscape and is yearning to talk with his old friend Balgarmaa with the language of heart and mind, and to discuss his decision with her. Bold spends some time captured by the hills and the waters and some time happy at Balgarmaa's coming, and whenever he thinks of taking Balgarmaa to the city he feels happy, he can barely keep still, and now there appears from the south a person riding a horse, trotting toward him. He looks carefully and is in no doubt that the elegant rider is Balgarmaa. Bold is thrilled and, given that the sheep are at rest, he decides to go meet her; he's hurrying to stand, pushing himself up with his whip, when suddenly behind him there's the sound of a gunshot, and then twice more, and when he looks around there are three people on horseback, riding in from the north.

Bold wonders whether these might be thieves or bandits or hunters, and as he goes to mount his horse, the three men come trotting up. "Stop, put your hands up!" they shout, as though angry. Bold is shocked, but he doesn't let his fear show. "Who are you?" he asks. "What's with the guns? What do you want with me?" He looks them over. One of them is an earnest man with a dark face, and although he's wearing a yellow silken deel, he's also got on a young woman's brocade waistcoat like a stiltwalker; he has gauze offering scarves of every color around his neck like a wandering mendicant, and he looks at Bold like a ravenous wolf. He has a blade hanging at his waist in a red sheath and a gun over his shoulder; he's not a regular type of person. There's another dark man, in a blue pongee deel and wearing a round hat, and what with all those red buttons he was clearly an official before the revolution. He has a Vintov over his shoulder, and pinned to his lapel he has a ribbon with Tibetan writing. To look at him, he's a religious man. The third man is young, with a white scarf tied around his head. Over his shoulder he has a gun, the bolt newly locked; he holds a whip and gives the appearance of a highwayman. The horses under these three men are all sweating profusely. The men are eyeing Bold suspiciously, and the one who looks like a monk says, "You think you'll interrogate us? We'll interrogate you! What's your name? Where are you from?" And the one with the red buttons lays into him, "Hey, take off your hat. Let's see your head. You've got short hair. What's your organization? Speak!" The third one scolds him, "Why don't you have a queue? How come you've no food for our horses?"

Bold is amazed, he looks at them and says, "Look at how you're dressed, you're wearing things I've never seen. When I listen to what you're saying, you're like feral beasts—what kind of men are you?" Immediately they have their guns pointed at him, they're saying "We'll take him, bind him, kill him, and rob him," and they take Bold and tie him up with their leather tethering reins, and the young man's face grows dark, his heart is pounding, he wonders what's going to happen to him. And they interrogate him again, their horses growing tense. "Where is your horse?" they ask him. "Where is your home? Is your collective close by?" Bold has already realized who they are, and because he is a bold young man, he doesn't answer them, and they put him on his horse, intending to take him to their headquarters and take one of the sheep for food. But as they make ready to head westward, Balgarmaa rides up and interrupts them; she comes to Bold, who looks at her silently.

The three men ask Bold the young woman's name, and because she's frightened to ask who they are, he answers only, "I don't know, I don't know." For a while, they violently criticize them both, but then they grow a little calmer, they say, "Come along with us, you can be the general's wife." But Balgarmaa holds tightly onto her reins at their unpleasant behavior and stands a short distance away. Bold is nodding quietly, and Balgarmaa immediately understands; she whips her horse and so escapes. The two men who are not holding Bold chase after her, but because Balgarmaa's horse has only just been ridden out, she disappears in a flash. It's already past noon, and there are clouds massing together out of the broad morning sky, and it looks like rain; there's a sharp cold wind blowing. Bold is led away by the three men; the leather rein digs into his flesh and his face grows more and more distressed. He worries that he has no idea where they're taking him or what they'll do with him, and he keeps looking at them. He's listening to what they are saying, they're talking about this general, that general, this holy man, and that goddess; they're saying how it would be good to kill him, it would be right to kill him, and it's distressing for him to hear such things. As the sun descends into the west, they go up a hill and soon reach the place where they're holed up.

The golden finials of the small temple's meditation hall glisten beautifully in the evening sunlight, and although they strike the minds of devoted worshippers, who might imagine there might be foul assassins there, killing animals and people nearby?

Next to the temple, among a few gers with prayer flags fluttering over their doors and pennants bearing the image of the sacred parasol, a few hundred people, both lay and monastic, are walking around, and gathering in groups here and there.

As they pass by the ger farthest to the east, they can hear the sounds of clanking chains, and people moaning sadly, and others having their faces slapped with shoes and crying out. Bold has never seen people doing such things. His eyes shift around and his mind races; to him it's like a folk tale.

They reach the ger farthest to the east, and a couple of men come and take the horses. They take Bold from his horse and bring him to where a group of about ten people, young and old, are sitting with their legs bound, and they fasten his legs with iron shackles and leave him there.

Although Bold has never seen them before and doesn't know who they might be, he greets his new companions and asks them how they have come here and why, but many of them are unable to say anything. A few of them quietly tell him that they are waiting to die, that they'll be tortured for a while and then killed. Bold is shocked and when he asks more detailed questions, one of them, a dark man of about forty years old, says that this is the place called the Ministry of Ochirbat. To look at him, it would seem that he's talking about the worst hell. "My son has a position in the city," he says, "so I was arrested and have been interrogated here for four days."

After a few days their captors go out and lay waste to the people and animals nearby. Bold has never seen upstanding monks who attack like wild beasts, as though they know nothing except slaughter and plunder. There's a young man of about twenty-seven or twenty-eight, the monks call him "General," they give him blessings with their cudgels and, because he's not waiting to be called up for military service, they say they'll slice through his sinews and kill him. Bold asks about the wounds on his left cheek, but he cannot say much, except that he was beaten the previous day with a shoe. Seeing them and listening to what they tell him, Bold feels pity for them; he is distressed and can barely comprehend the monks' brutality. And then from the ger to the west come the three men, along with three or four others, their eyes bulging, their teeth bared, and the men who took the horses are saying, "I'm going to kill this one. You kill that one"—truly they are like the carnivorous Mangas. But there's a young woman floating among them too, wearing a green deel and a gauze offering scarf, and listening to what they say; she's the one they call the goddess. She comes to Bold, who's standing, legs apart, and prods him with her Mauser, saying with a laugh, "I'll kill this one tomorrow."

Who could have known that morning that this evening Bold would find himself at the point of a gun?

When the sheep still haven't come back at noon, nor by evening, the people at Bold's ger grow concerned and wonder whether he might have lost his horse, or what else might have happened. But at sunset, when Balgarmaa returns and inquires whether Bold has come back, they grow worried and they listen to Balgarmaa's account of what has happened, and why he might not have come back. Bold's father and elder sister immediately saddle horses and set off to look for him.

They sit and talk about whether these men might be bandits or robbers, and Gongor taiji, from an encampment to the east, is sitting with them.

This fellow's one of the old feudals; last winter and this past spring he spent time on the monastic estate at Tariat, where he met with an important monk, and although he knows a little of the smell of counterrevolution, he's somewhat afraid and sits there, listening silently, and when he hears this about Bold, a light shines in his brain, he can't contain his happiness, he says, "I have an idea, I'll go and get a divination done by the monks," and he puts on his old-fashioned deel, surreptitiously puts his badges of office inside it, and rides quickly off toward Tariat.

Although it's already dark, Gongor travels imagining that light from the stars is indistinctly glistening, and his heart races when he thinks how, when the old regime rises again, the nobility will be rich and the common people will be oppressed. He's not out to help this Bold; rather he's salivating thinking that when Bold is destroyed, the old women in the ger will be crushed and he'll get to pocket the money, so he bends forward and urges his horse on at a fast trot. Among those left confused in Bold's ger, Bold's mother rushes out when someone shouts, "Hold the dogs!" and a man named Baldan helps Gongor from his horse. The horse is sweating heavily, it's panting hard, and Baldan says, "How are you, sir?" and Gongor goes into the ger and exchanges greetings. While he's drinking a mug of tea, he tells them, "Counterrevolutionaries have rushed in and pillaged the cooperative to the north. The chief was captured. I ran away. They were saying that they'd kill the ones they capture. They said they'd torture and kill him. It's been a few days since they set off for the northwest."

Everyone, old and young, is upset at this. Bold's father cries out, "My son!" and falls in a faint. Near the fire, Balgarmaa is upset and weeping. Bold's father talks with Baldan about how they could now flee, he's so worried for his son. There is weeping and distress inside the ger, nobody can find a solution, and Baldan says, "What's the point of weeping and being distressed? The people's army is coming from the city, so if we're ready to show them the way, perhaps we'll be saved. My horse is tired, his eyes are bad, you are old, and there are no children around, right? What about Gongor?" He discusses with Bold's father, and Balgarmaa, who's sitting weeping by the fire, says, "I'll go." Immediately she stands, but they protest, saying, "It's getting late, you don't know the land, you're just a child, what can you do?" But Balgarmaa argues back, "If not me, then who's going to go?" and then she leaves.

Once Balgarmaa's outside, it's already fairly dark. Her gray horse pricks its ears at the white light disappearing from the horizon and shifts about. She releases the hobble, and as she mounts, the horse is pawing the ground; as soon as they are out of the encampment, Balgarmaa trots out toward the southeast.

She disappears just as, like an eyebrow, the new moon appears. With the night wind gusting against her, Balgarmaa shivers inside. As her mind moves, so Bold appears and then disappears. But oh, how likely is it that she will find him?

She enters a thick forest leading up onto a high pass, and in the pitch darkness the ground is uneven. Now and again there are sounds; over and over her horse startles. Among the dense trees the path slips away from her; each direction looks the same. She wants to help all those people, but she is food for the wolves and other wild animals in this empty place and is constantly on edge. And then from among the trees there's the sound of a gun, a bullet whizzes past her head, her horse shies and she can barely hold him, and then she comes face to face with two soldiers, and they load their guns and shout at Balgarmaa, "Who are you?" They are from the People's Army, and Balgarmaa expresses her happiness and relief. She's surprised by how imposing they are, and they take her into custody and lead her to the military headquarters, in accordance with army regulations.

That night, under interrogation, Balgarmaa gives a true account of what has happened, and at dawn, amid her impatience to get on the road with the army, Bold's face appears to her and she keeps wondering whether he has lost his life. Once she has told the commanding officer the name of the place to which they took Bold, she forgets her fear and listens for the sound of guns on the battlefield.

How are they going to arrange this? Who knows what's going to happen? These ten or so bound men have received a harsh sentence and slept fitfully through their final night in this world. After this, their children will be left all alone, and they give a pained sigh, long and hard, thinking about their parents' compassion, and in the rising of the clear morning sun, the light touches them.

The so-called generals and their like sleep soundly in their temporary billets; they rise like hungry wolves and set off in groups of two or three, as though to kill a sheep. Each brings one of the captives with them; they take out a knife and drive it into the man's sternum, the cartilage rustles on the sharp blade, they shout coarsely, they extract the heart and finish with a great shout.

Not only is this impossible for a human being to watch, but it is unbearable for the mind to contemplate, and so we shut our eyes and wonder whose turn it will be next.

Like savage beasts they wander around looking for someone, and Bold watches the others with grieving eyes. It would be better for them to torture and slaughter him now, and he says "Take me!" but they lead another man away. They ask, "Is that what you want?" and the other man is staring and trembling, he asks to be shot straightaway. He's a strong type, like a rock or iron, yet he can't bear it, and a couple of men say to him, "Oh no, we'll torture you and then kill you." They restrain him and slice quickly through his skin and his veins and sinews one by one, and by four o'clock he's crying and screaming, and they leave him half dead, and at six o'clock the two of them take a little rest.

Oh, they don't describe this as the hell realms, but this is their beginning. The monks say such things in order to help the six levels of sentient beings, who have all been our mothers. The ten or so bound men are desperate for their lives, but because they are stuck there, in the darkness of night, they relive the terrifying torture of the day, and they cannot get it out of their mind and it tortures them again at night.

However much they suffer, by dawn each man has inevitably suppressed it with sleep and is at that moment of peace, when suddenly a few gunshots ring out, and everyone wakes up and listens, and from around the nearby mountains the lovely sound of the artillery of the People's Army resounds sweetly in the ears and lifts the heart. The bound men are happy, a resolve is born—even if we are killed, they say, the time for these evil bandits to die has come.

The so-called generals and their like get up and rush around in confusion.

The rank-and-file soldiers get ready. The old nuns and monks get together in a straggle and they take their shoddy bayonets and their bows and arrows of reed and horn, their clubs and cudgels; they make incantations over handfuls of earth, which they put into their pockets, and a few hundred people with a few guns set off to confront the armor of the People's Army. It's ridiculous.

An airplane flies over. Frightened and confused, they fall to their knees. A tank comes past. They run together and perish here and there. For a moment, it's like another world. A red flag appears fluttering on a mountain pass to the north, and for the bound men the sun rises, they raise a cheer for the People's Army, the souls of the cruel oppressors flee and the standard of the People's Army advances.

Balgarmaa gallops ahead of the revolutionary army; she's proud and happy, but she's concerned that she doesn't know what's happened to Bold. She keeps her eyes skinned and if she comes across a corpse, she checks it, and she comes with a few soldiers to where the bound men are. Then, with tears in her eyes, she drops down and hugs Bold.

The soldiers unbind him, and as they are tending to him, Balgarmaa unties his horse.

One extraordinary morning and evening have passed, and the People's Red Army has crushed the enemy. Bold and Balgarmaa have seen things that they had never seen before, and on the way home they gather the sheep, and return home in happy conversation.

And the River Ider continues to flow as it always has.

1933

5

THE YOUNG COUPLE

M. YADAMSÜREN

1. An Invisible Electric Shock

As soon as work was over, there was a large number of women and men moving about in every direction, heading home on horseback, on foot, on bicycles, and in cars, looking forward to hot tea, a freshly prepared meal, and a comfortable bed. At six o'clock, they were all worn out and focused on this one thought; they came home, undressed, stretched their legs, ate and drank quietly, and regained their strength.

Upon coming home after work, young Jaltsan, however, hung around his door with its black lock, waiting to open it, and when he had opened it and come inside, the covers from which he had risen that morning were all bunched up on his bed; there were rolled cigarettes strewn here and there, and deels and boots scattered in the corner of the room; he salvaged some shirts and a pair of trousers from the bed and stuffed them underneath. The half-closed window allowed a hazy light to shine through, a couple of flies had fallen to their death into a half-consumed cup of tea on the table, and Jaltsan turned about and then, motionless, grew disinterested as he took in the truly feckless state of his youth, and in the absolute stillness he was utterly alone. As he sat briefly on the edge of a chair, he poured the remainder of the cup of tea out the window and poured another cup of cold tea from the pot and, as he sat sadly amid the utter silence, his exhausted body, unwilling to rest, conversed with his mind, and he placed his writing box down on the table, took out his bicycle, gave the door up to the lock that was await-ing it, and took a right down the street.

As he rode toward Bank Street, there were people on horse-back, on foot, in trucks, and on bicycles weaving in and out, a single movement of constant sound, a blend of noise.

A moment before Jaltsan entered into this, he was flooded with a silent melancholy. He was scared of the cars, he avoided the bicy-cles, and he threaded his way through them and entered a coop-erative café. He saw the customers, they were all well behaved, sitting in pairs, laughing together, ordering food, and eating. Young Jaltsan sat down at an empty table, ordered food, and watched what was going on; he was disturbed by the springtime. As he sat there, clanking his cutlery and fiddling with the table-ware, suddenly from behind he heard a clarity and lightness of step, and he turned around and looked, and a lovely young woman floated past and sat down, alone, at a small corner table.

Straightaway young Jaltsan opened his eyes and wiped away his grief. He was revived, and he began to look thoughtfully at the lovely young woman.

This young woman had a fine body, straight and tall; she wore a deel of thin Chinese silk, and a simple green jacket cov-ered her shoulders, as was the current fashion.

He looked at her legs in their white silk stockings, watched the step of her white leather pumps; truly she outdid the Euro-pean girls in her elegance. Her blackish hair was not so much black exactly, her bright and agreeable face was round and evenly proportioned. Her lips were full and red, her cheeks were nothing but apples. Her alert and playful eyes, black as cherries, struck at his young man's heart like a magnet. She was almost laughing.

It seemed as though her eyebrows were painted on, incomparable, like shards of the nighttime moon. Like a flower in a bouquet, only just bloomed, her mouth was open and straight, her two lips preserving the grace of laughter.

Jaltsan watched her and a fire of desire blazed up in his heart, the lights of his eyes danced a dance of love, and the cords of intention knotted at the center of his heart. The pert young girl, meanwhile, had already divined from his eyes what was going on in Jaltsan; she had transformed him and had awakened a gift in him, and her face reddened and the beating of her heart grew faster.

Jaltsan was also a fine-looking young man, and he shone with a youthful splendor that was not lost on the eyes of young girls.

Between such young men and young women there runs an invisible electric shock. As they come to know each other they desire each other, as they touch each other they tremble with excitement, the warm hearts in their bodies are wounded as they come together: how might the people in the restaurant have divined the unconscious blaze, the unspoken movement between them?

As they sat in their seats and ate their food, some of the diners were picturing themselves walking in Moscow. Some were criticizing the government. Some quarreled about what was happening at home. Some looked for money, and others planned the next day's work. All the people who sat eating in this building, beginning with Jaltsan and the young woman, were thinking about specific issues, and although the concerns of the world were gathered together into their thoughts, how might these thoughts be opened up?

When one looks closely at the human mind, it's really rather ungainly. It has no form that can be touched and no sound to listen for, but how amazing that, at a single moment, it can create and destroy a thousand situations.

And what might this be? It is the neural center of the brain that produces an image of the physical world.

But as we critique the mind of the masses, we have forgotten young Jaltsan. We should turn now and look at what is happening with Jaltsan and the young woman.

While within themselves, they desired to do as the rain, moving across the clouds to replace the moon, nonetheless while they finished eating, their eyes secretly made subtle contact but one time, and the situation was grasped and the expressions on their faces spoke together, and then each went their own way home. *Why should I hurry home?* Jaltsan wondered, and he took the opportunity to silently follow behind the beautiful young woman and to find out where she lived. But she appeared to have hailed a car. Jaltsan thought quickly; he approached the driver and asked him whether he could take him eastward. The car had a flat tire, he could not but sit shoulder to shoulder with the beautiful young woman, and he smiled as he thought how their eyes would weave together, the warmth uniting their two bodies, their minds in intimate conversation.

As he spent a few moments like this, not unreasonably, like a fly coming down with warm wings, suddenly a drunk driver sped by at about 40 mph, scattering oil and dust, and quietly he cursed the wretched car, and bowed down before the beautiful young woman who dwelt in his heart.

"What on earth?" he said. "Almost ran us over! Driver must be drunk."

Jaltsan seized the opportunity and grasped the beautiful young woman in the car.

"Okay, take it easy. If you panic, you could get run over by a car. And if you die, how many men apart from me will weep?"

The young woman was afraid to move, her eyes flashed with intelligence, she didn't know where she was going. But she squeezed a sweet smile from between her lips.

"Oh, don't worry. Will you cry if I fall?"

Jaltsan couldn't believe that a way had opened up. His deep black eyes moved his heart and he revealed a smile.

"Not only if you fall, I'd cry if I didn't see you for a long time." The girl seemed pleased by this and smiled, but she meant to give the impression that she was embarrassed.

"You're sick," she said, and Jaltsan parried back,

"Sure I am. No better doctor than you, but I have a sickness you can't cure."

And the girl, quite softly, with words like clear and gentle music, spoke from her heart, which was utterly one with her mind.

"Don't say such things. . . ." Her eyes did not shift markedly from Jaltsan, she looked at him and smiled. Jaltsan clearly expressed the desire of his heart in his eyes and, though he would say it again, however intolerable it might be, the girl called on the driver to stop, and she got out. Jaltsan followed her, paid the fare, and exchanged some private words with the fellow who had come to change the flat tire, but the girl was some way away now, heading east. He rushed off on his bicycle and caught up with her; she looked back and her kind eyes smiled and flashed a wound through Jaltsan's chest, scratching his heart as she approached a small red door. Jaltsan called out too late, "Let's go out together," and although he had no idea who might be in her house, nonetheless he had initiated a nice conversation. He was frustrated and annoyed, though, because he had not asked her name, nor inquired about her family. He stood and watched the golden disc of the sun, bright still in the clarity of evening, smiling upon the Tuul as it headed into hiding beyond the Chingelt ridge.

Jaltsan stood there a while. He made a mental note of the street and the door, and he got on his bicycle and rode home. Alone, he was overwhelmed by the thought of how he desired the beautiful young woman, and how he had failed to ask her name or get information about her family, and it pained him that he had not found time to talk with the driver. He'd been delayed by the removal of the faulty tire. *Otherwise*, he thought as he flew along on his bicycle, *it would have been easily changed as soon as I'd left the car.* And straightaway he thought happily, *How lovely it was that I met you.* As he rode on, he was barely able to keep from thoughts of misery and joy and anger and pleasure and haste and yearning and, as he came home, he held the big black lock, took the key from his jacket, opened the door, and went inside. He sat down at his desk and, thinking about the lovely young woman, he took a pen that was at hand and focused his mind and, on a sheet of paper, he wrote a poem.

> Wandering mindlessly along, I met a fine person.
> We came close to chat, sent the wind's flame to sleep.
> As I thought of her and yearned, the golden sun setting,
> the cold wind remained, and there I faded, all alone.
> Though I think and think again, of where
> I might meet her again, how difficult it is to find her.
> The bitterness of desire covers up my dear heart,
> and I would cast away all thought of food and sleep.

When he had finished writing, he couldn't stop himself from getting up, and he left the apartment and spent some minutes wandering back and forth outside the small red door, but since there was no noise to be heard he went straight to a restaurant, where he ordered dinner to kill time, and a bottle of beer, and he sat there, eating and drinking with scant satisfaction. In fact, Jaltsan already had an untouched bottle of vodka before him, but that day he had no taste for it, and he instead drank several beers.

He really did look like a vodka drinker. When he was sad, he would take solace in vodka. And when he got drunk on vodka, he became greedy. But young Jaltsan did not keep on with this sad state of affairs; he would meet with the beloved young girl. But what of such loose talk? The young man had but a single thought.

Then Jaltsan drank his beer and ate his way through the food, and he went outside, still the same, having failed to decide anything. He didn't care to go home yet, but with nowhere to go, he hung around the market, passing by the small red door now and again, and then he turned and went home. That night, when his usual bedtime came, Jaltsan was taking another walk around the market in an attempt to get away from the city's bustle.

Once again he turned his bicycle around and went home. He took his key from his pocket, opened his door, and went inside his apartment. He carelessly pulled back the bedclothes, half undressed, and lay down on his bed. Although Jaltsan's body was at home, lying down on his bed, his mind had gone back and was outside that small red door, and he thought ten thousand times about the day's events. A thousand times before, he had wanted a family, but he had spent his days slackly, not following the true path of love; he had been like a man passing through relay posts, and he regretted all that he had done wrong by this person or that, and now that he was thinking about that girl, how could he possibly get any rest? Vainly he tossed and turned, and before the light of dawn he fell into an inevitable sleep, but his weary body found no peace in the ensuing brief slumber. As he slept, moreover, his overexcited brain did not cease from desire and, as he dreamed his dreams, he rested soundly, taking joy in emptiness, drawing amusement from his dreams.

2. An Unknown Response

Suddenly, amid this sound sleep, there was a bang, and Jaltsan woke with a shock. On the stylish table beside his bed, motionless, the little brown clock that had unkindly broken Jaltsan's delicious morning sleep announced that it was seven o'clock.

Jaltsan nonchalantly opened his eyes and stretched his arms. As he raised himself from sleep, he was quickly overtaken by the events of the previous day and, as he considered the various ways he might encounter that lovely young woman, he quietly hummed a tune and dressed himself.

There was a knock at the door, a man's voice clearly calling, "Anyone there?" And while Jaltsan wondered who it might be, he answered and said, "I'm coming," but then the door opened and he saw a man entering. Jaltsan was happy to see his good friend Myagmar, and he said,

"I put off going to that girl's place, and by some good fortune Myagmar comes along. Now then, let's figure out a plan and go make friends with her." He offered Myagmar a seat and, taking the opportunity of their close friendship to have a chat, laid out to him what he needed. They discussed the matter, for instance whether he should use his free time that weekend to meet with the girl and get a response. They decided to go to Myagmar's home and ask his wife Udval about the girl's family, and what her name might be. They set off and came to Myagmar's home, and because Udval was not at home, they had no choice but to sit and talk together. They made friends with the time, playing chess while they waited for her. When Udval came back after midday, Myagmar and Jaltsan questioned her closely about where she had been, and they kept on at her, asking without letup about the girl's family and what her name was, about her apartment and the street where she lived. Udval thought a while, and they pestered her again about the street where the girl was living. She clearly knew and couldn't stop laughing, and Jaltsan, gasping for breath, hurried to utter a word and "Yes, yes?" he said, "Speak, speak!" Udval took a breath, silently she produced a smile, and she spoke.

"I came back just now in a truck with the young girl you're asking about." She smiled again. "You're too late. She's gone to Shar Höv."

It was as though Jaltsan did not understand her words.

"Is that true?" he asked, again and again, "Is that true?" And the discussion among these three, which had blazed up like a fire, was suddenly like water turned to ice, and it faded away into complete silence. It was Myagmar who was the first to break the silence.

"Whose daughter is she?" he asked. "Where has she gone in the countryside, and why?"

Now Jaltsan took over.

"Will she be in the countryside long?" he pestered. "Is she there with her husband? Do you know? Tell me something good about her." And the sound of talk resumed. Luckily, Udval knew everything about the young girl's situation, and in great detail.

She explained quite clearly.

"That girl and I spent a day getting to know each other, we've become friends. Her name is Adilbish. She lives at home with her father, mother, and many brothers and sisters, but she's someone who speaks her mind. She's not married, and she says that she's looking for a man who suits her, who's not dissolute, who doesn't treat women with old-fashioned disrespect, who's dignified and doesn't hang around with reprobates. She's gone now to Arhangai, to take a few months' rest in the country. She said she'll be back soon."

As Jaltsan listened to them, his spirits rose higher and it came to his mind that he would send a letter addressing his previous encounter with the young woman, and so test the situation. This is what he resolved to do, and he frittered away the time, speculating idly as to whether the girl would or would not be interested in him. So that evening he came home and wrote his first letter to lovely Adilbish, confessing the truth of his heart to her.

Will you deign to notice me, my sweet Adilbish?

I have been thinking to introduce myself to you for a short while, and because my mind is true and because my resolve is clear, I am writing directly to you my own true thoughts, although these cannot be expressed in even the most beautiful language.

Please forgive me if what I say here seems artless. I sincerely trust that you will let it pass, and not turn away. And if I may speak openly, and without embarrassment, I discovered in your face of jade that first day, that it could outcandle a candle:

Your sweetness brings my desire gushing forth,
your gentle ways attract my love.
Your voice of melody gathers my thoughts,
your lovely gaze shakes my heart.

The true thoughts of my mind, struggling toward you with not a single instant of respite, their power being unwavering, they request that I renounce immorality and write to you in good faith.

And the time of pleasure already having come, when our two bodies are joined as one, this is a joyous fate, described as faultless since it is felt by good people to be a suitable response. It pushes me again and again, and so I shall straightaway abandon my clumsy shyness and careful reserve, and resolve to think our two minds compatible, like a fish and the water. I'll place my heart into your hands and from my heart, which awaits with unease your consenting reply, I again and again send my deepest respect.

Jaltsan

When Jaltsan finished writing the letter, he read it over and over. He thought about his first meeting with this fine person and considered his future meetings with her, and was deeply frustrated at his inability to herd his scattered thoughts together, as with shaking hand and anxious breath he sealed the letter.

Then Jaltsan left his home and went to the home of his acquaintance Urtnasan, who was a driver, and who delivered mail along the western streets. By chance Urtnasan was outside his house, by his car, and they greeted each other and talked a while, and Jaltsan took out his letter and handed it over, saying,

"Could you be sure to deliver this letter, and if you can't deliver it yourself, could you have someone reliable do it, as quickly as possible?"

"Yes, I can do that," Urtnasan said, and he took it and went off. From then on, Jaltsan stayed at home, agitated and concerned, wishing the unknown response into his hands. *Shouldn't someone tell you when Urtnasan's delivered the letter and what answer there might be? In any case, you can always wait until he gets back. It takes two days to travel between Arhangai and Ulaanbaatar, so he won't be back much before five days, and if it rains and the road becomes impassible, it's not clear how long it's going to take.*

In fact Jaltsan was disappointed that his years of pleasure had been short, and he was unhappy that his hours of suffering were long. How would Jaltsan's mind manage successfully to endure five days of such suffering . . . ?

Besides, he was exhausted for five days counting the seconds into minutes, totting up the minutes into hours, totting up the hours into days, and so the final day arrived, and it was a longer day than the previous four days, and when the fellow for whom Jaltsan had been waiting didn't show, how could he not be at his wit's end? He went back again and again to Urtnasan's home and looked carefully for his truck, and waited eagerly for the driver. How could Jaltsan have spent five days wearing himself out?

And why had Jaltsan waited so eagerly for the driver?

As we know, not only had Urtnasan spent these five days traveling to and from Arhangai and running the errands that had fallen to him, he also hadn't brought Adilbish back with him. We also know what state Jaltsan would have been in, however quickly Urtnasan might come. All that notwithstanding, it was not even clear whether Urtnasan himself had delivered Jaltsan's letter.

But while Jaltsan was aware of all of this, how would he deal with Urtnasan's not bringing back a response? Is it not frequently the case that the human mind, while truly wise, seems stupid, and although clear, seems obscured? People are, therefore, unable to constantly be alert in the control and guidance of their minds, and although they create nothing amazing, neither do they suffer disgrace. What is there to be done?

So Jaltsan could no longer wait for the driver Urtnasan, and when Urtnasan didn't materialize, he was so frustrated that he decided to go and eat supper and then return.

During this time, Urtnasan returned, and his wife, Gerelt, prepared food, and she asked him whether he was tired and so forth, and so those two young people talked together and brought happiness to their warm minds of desire, and their gentle glances ensnared their bodies, their loving words foretold the night's action, and so they came together with loving minds and took care of their bodies. She was concerned to offer him food and drink, and he rummaged around in his suitcase and produced the present he had brought for her.

On these occasions, these two young people would sit together in the warmth of their love, holding each other, and kissing and embracing each other. As they talked together, Gerelt casually noted,

"There's a young fellow called Jaltsan, he keeps coming around asking for you, says you were delivering a letter for him."

Urtnasan was amazed at what she was telling him, about how Jaltsan had come around so many times. "I passed Jaltsan's letter via the local community leader. Why would Jaltsan need to meet with me otherwise? Why is he around here to ask about me every day?"

There are one or two reasons he might want to come here, he thought, hiding his anger, *but someone might have told him lies about me.* He said to Gerelt,

"It seems that I shouldn't have met with Jaltsan. I wonder why all this has happened?"

Gerelt stood up. "Who knows? He keeps asking for you, and I'm thinking to tell him, 'You can go and find other people to ask, please don't come back here.' Someone's been telling him something."

Urtnasan's suspicions grew ever stronger and he figured, *She's saying exactly what I'm thinking. He had some kind of plan before and he managed to hoodwink me,* and while this dark poison bubbled within him, Jaltsan suddenly entered. Since it was just past nine-thirty and evening was drawing in, Jaltsan's entrance further poisoned the doubt in Urtnasan's mind and lit the fires of his anger.

But as we know, in fact, Jaltsan was quite without guile and now, while he repeatedly explained that his mind had been focused on getting to Adilbish, that it was impossible to find a way, it seemed dreadfully hard for his words to sound credible.

Besides, because Jaltsan himself was not at fault, as soon as he saw Urtnasan, he had felt really happy. And it was unclear why he was so happy, so Urtnasan could only conclude that his happiness was a cover.

Jaltsan sighed, and said, "Urtnasan, how was your trip? I was looking forward to seeing you. Did you deliver my letter? Did you get a reply? Where is that girl now?"

And inside himself, Urtnasan lashed out at Jaltsan, *So, then, did you really come because of the letter? But you didn't know I'd returned, and when you came in and we came face to face, the letter was just a cover*, but he didn't let it show, and he said,

"The trip was good. And how are you doing? I gave your letter to someone there. He'll pass it on. Because I didn't meet this woman, I couldn't get an answer. So why were you looking forward to seeing me?" As he coldly delivered his reply, he hardly looked at Gerelt and Jaltsan, but looked rather for some kind of signal passing between them.

But Jaltsan wasn't looking at anything else, he heard that it was uncertain whether his letter to Adilbish had reached her, and his face showed discontent, he didn't remember what more they spoke about, but he said, "Why else would I be looking forward to seeing you other than to find out whether you'd delivered that letter or not? Is there anything else so important? Whom did you get to pass it on?"

At Jaltsan's words Urtnasan's expression changed, his gaze became awkward, his doubt intensified, and he became full of anger. But he kept his composure and he said,

"It seems that you were hardly able to bear it, you were so looking forward to seeing me. You were very distraught by so insignificant a thing. I passed it on through someone important, so it'll surely arrive." And he smiled a cold smile.

Jaltsan didn't sense that Urtnasan's disinterest in this matter might indicate anything, and so he said nothing more.

"Well, if it gets delivered, that's fine," he said, and went out. And when Jaltsan had left, Urtnasan was annoyed and said to Gerelt,

"Please don't have anything to do with him. If you don't like it," he continued bitterly, "you'd better think about what you two were saying earlier." Gerelt was also quite without guile, and they talked for a long while, they spoke badly of each other without restraint, their argument was utterly out of character, and those two inseparable lovers for an instant became intractable enemies, they pushed each other away, and then, no longer fighting, they came back to each other, and they lay together.

Morning came, and because they realized that the argument might continue and their discussion grow broader, they brought other concerns to the table, and so argument and resolution became mixed together. And shabby old nuns and the wives of hatters passed hurriedly by.

And those old nuns and wives continued to scheme, claiming that Geshé Shirnen would perform a rite for repelling evil, and so patch up their good relationship.

The young people born at the beginning of the season most probably missed this slight misfortune that remained at the end of the previous season, but they took notice nonetheless of what they encountered.

Bad news travels fast, and Jaltsan was unhappy when he heard what had happened, and then when they broke up he was very distressed. He went over to Myagmar's; they discussed the news, but although he mentioned his thoughtlessness to Myagmar and Udval they didn't hold him responsible, and he distracted them from the issue of suspicion, back to how to bring peace and reconcile Urtnasan and Gerelt.

That what had happened in the meantime was all new to young Jaltsan was of help as the days slowly passed. Jaltsan didn't want to speak further about it, and after five days Urtnasan had gone to Arhangai and come back. In this slow movement, he came bringing a reply to Jaltsan's letter. One morning, Jaltsan got up and, as he was washing his face and hands, Myagmar came in smiling, and saying not one word of greeting, he said, "Your girl wrote a letter to my wife, and she put her answer to your letter in the envelope and asked her to give it to you," and he handed over the letter. Jaltsan quickly finished washing his face and hands, he snatched up the letter without a word, opened it, and, with Myagmar peering over his shoulder, they read the letter together.

Will you deign to notice me, noble Jaltsan?

Had I been looking out this past month for a letter, even had it been written by a fine man, I would have been amazed to be associated with the things described there. And had it come to me with the name and address wrong, I should have opened and read it, and should have asked forgiveness for my mistake. And had it been some insignificant fellow's idea of a joke, seeking to amuse himself by relieving an hour's boredom, I trust that I would not pass the time again amusing myself with so weak a man. And had I previously considered the thoughts of this insignificant fellow as weakness and had my ignorant mind been uselessly entertained by a bunch of artless words, I would have no other response but to laugh.

If you had written, after an hour's impulsive thoughts, suddenly and without controlling your joyous heart, I think that a noble man should have been more attentive and kept his wise thoughts under control.

Because of this, while the insignificant fellow might have his ignorant thoughts, and while there is something in the great attention shown in the letter which the noble man has granted me, which cannot establish any one of those four conditions outlined above, I trust that the noble man in question is fully in control. Meanwhile I will relax and await your letter, and I send you my greetings.

Jaltsan read quickly through the letter and was very happy to know that the secret thoughts of good people were in agreement, and he discussed with Myagmar how he should now respond.

And Myagmar said, "In the letter my wife received from Adilbish, she was asking in confidence all about you."

Surely this was a positive sign. Jaltsan decided that he should now use these circumstances and act quickly, and that he should write again, this time more intimately and more explicitly, and send her the letter she was requesting. He hurried to write his answer.

Will you deign to notice me, beautiful Adilbish, who dwells at the center of my heart?

As the colorful flowers on the mountains desire the gentle swirling rain, so my mind, which yearns for you, is struggling toward you with not a moment of respite, and my desire is to look out for your assenting reply and for the bright face that comes with it, and for us to enjoy ourselves together. I immediately began to seek the reply that for many days has still not appeared, the firm desire of my loving mind being truly in line with destiny, and, as the swallows flap their wings, as they take off into the wind of these days and circle in flight, my desire is set in the roots of my warm heart and urges forth the seed of happiness that flows within.

Soon the flower of happiness will grow and spread its petals like a lotus, and I fully believe that it will overwhelm the contemplative heart in a single lifetime. So how can my belief bring forth such doubt as to entertain any one of those four conditions your letter described?

When a great artist draws, say, a bird, he doesn't draw the flesh and bones differentiated from its form. In this way it goes without saying that a person manifests the truth in their heart no less than in their words. How does the old saying go? "Know how to ride the good qualities of a horse, understand how to make friends with the good qualities of a husband."

Suppose one of these conditions were to be true and our meeting were to be deferred, then I would be upset, and immediately my quick wits would range far and near, and I would keep pushing at all possibilities, so as to bring our two bodies together as one.

When I think about it, I feel that the gracious mind of a good person will look with kindness upon me and bring great happiness without keeping me waiting for a long time. With deep respect Jaltsan remains here, awaiting your swift reply.

When Jaltsan had finished writing this, they read it through and edited it together, and then Jaltsan sealed it and handed it over to Myagmar, entrusting him with its speedy delivery.

And so Jaltsan again entered into the distress of waiting for an unknown response. But this time, he was given special work and went to the countryside nearby for ten days, and when he returned, these days had passed by without the misery of delay.

The day following Jaltsan's return from the countryside, he was on his way to Myagmar's home to ask about the reply to his letter, when he met Myagmar. "This letter came for you," he said, "I was just on my way to deliver it." He gave Jaltsan the letter, but Jaltsan couldn't wait to get back home, and he opened the letter and read it on the street as he walked home. The letter said,

Will you deign to notice me, noble Jaltsan? I received the letter you sent and, when I opened and looked through the letter I was pleased and, having initially thought it likely to be a reproach, my mind was put at ease. Moreover, having twice read it through, I found that truly your words are clear and your request explicit.

I compared your true and undeceiving words with my own heart and read what you wrote with great interest.

I will honor from afar the dear heart that wrote those kind words, and I will not eschew reading several more times over these two letters. However, reading this letter with interest at this moment, when I think about anything important other than that day when we met face to face, I have no clarity.

Although, when I read these two letters of yours, I am encouraged, I have no way to wipe away the doubt of these conditions within my heart. Meanwhile, I will think of how we laughed that day, and how I passed the following days free from thoughts of sadness. But truly, without considering bitterness, how can I now be certain that we will meet? No matter—different questions will enter together inside the heart, and the mind will not flourish once it escapes the pasture. Moving secretly from the ordinary world, I wish to nourish the body and mind that is protected by the waters and hills of the countryside.

But you should know that I will be here for no more than three days and then quietly return to the city. I have read your letter with interest and my reply will seek my distant lover meanwhile and make itself known. Your One and Only sends greetings.

When he had read it through, Jaltsan thought, *Although this girl has written with a strong resolve, it is clear that she is swaying gently toward my own position, and replies that we might meet and speak face to face.*

So he set to thinking about such things as the need to provide without fail a means for her to come, and although he kept his happiness hidden, he had no idea how to organize it, and he went home without a word.

Myagmar asked him, "So what did she write? Why are you holding your tongue?"

Jaltsan told him the contents of the letter, and that she was likely to come soon, and that he was thinking how he might organize it. They discussed it together, and they decided that they would organize everything so that Jaltsan and Adilbish could meet and talk face to face as soon as Adilbish had arrived in Ulaanbaatar. The two young people spoke together about this and that for some time, and Jaltsan decided that there was nothing but to count the days until he and Adilbish would be together, and I should tell you that they left home now, laughing and exchanging many jokes and stories.

3. An Invisible Ambulance

Now that he knew his girl would soon be returning, the fires in Jaltsan's heart blazed up, and he could barely wait for the day when their two bodies would come together in conversation. He listened for news, he asked around, counting the hours, willing those five days to pass quickly and without delay, and as soon the morning came, and the hour, when Adilbish would come, Jaltsan was full of anxiety, his head teeming with thoughts of how best they might be reunited, of how best they might talk together. His confusion made him happy, his happiness made him confused. And so it was the morning of the sixth day of his waiting for Adilbish. The army *naadam* had begun, but Jaltsan alone failed to hurry to the naadam. As he sat tensely at home, there was a sudden low humming sound in the walls of his quite silent room, coming in close from far away, an utterly clear thread of sound, gently glistering like an unbroken pearl. It was a broadcast of the opening ceremony of the army naadam on the Ulaanbaatar radio station, intermittently broadcasting beautiful songs and music and poetry and celebration. Such wonderful things nourished Jaltsan's heart, swept away Jaltsan's sadness, called Jaltsan to notice, and Jaltsan found himself listening unbidden, and with pleasure. The radio station provided the listening public with a stream of interesting news and music, yet it announced to Jaltsan but one most alarming item. The final report, the final report.

It said that the driver of a mail truck—a 318—from Arhangai, carrying some ten or so people, had rolled and crashed the vehicle a couple of relay posts outside Lüngen, that a man and a woman had died, and a few people had been injured.

As soon as this news had been received, the announcement continued, an ambulance had been dispatched, and a shudder traversed Jaltsan's body and he went quite cold, concerned as to whether this vehicle that had crashed had in fact been the vehicle in which Adilbish had been traveling, and worried too, because there was no definite information to that effect, and he spent some time thinking about how he could find out what had happened. However, the thought occurred to him that he would go and catch up with the rescue vehicle, and he hurried off to Myagmar's house, and found them already gone to the naadam. He went straight to the naadam then and, wandering around among a few thousand people, he managed to find Myagmar and tell him the news, and the two of them went off in search of the vehicle. But how, during the naadam, could they hope to find the rescue vehicle, given that it was just a regular car? Jaltsan and Myagmar spent the day unable to find the car, and returned home that evening at the end of their tether.

Myagmar said, "How are we going to find this invisible ambulance? You should take my horse and set off tonight. A couple of relay stations won't finish him off. I bought him from the country just recently to ride at the naadam."

Jaltsan said, "What happens if Adilbish's injured and I've only one horse?"

Myagmar said, "If this happens, you're bound to find a way around it. In any case, it's important that you meet up with the ambulance."

Jaltsan agreed. He first packed the things he required for treating wounds in an emergency, such as a first-aid kit and eau de cologne, and he also took his sketching kit just in case, and— *I'm off* he called—he tied them together, and he made a point of packing the gold automatic pencil he had previously bought as a gift for his dear friend. He took a few journals and newspapers and, as he prepared his things in a little bundle, Myagmar brought the horse, and so they fixed the bundle behind the saddle, together with a raincoat. They shook hands and Jaltsan set off immediately, at full trot, pale white in the light of the moon that showed between the clouds in the dark of night, and soon he was out of sight, over the ridge of Songino Hairhan. It might have been summer, but the fresh night wind was chill, and the moonlight illumined what was close at hand and shut off what was distant. As the darkness set in, it seemed as though the shapes of vast mountains out near the lake were coming toward him, and the farther he galloped and hurried along, the deeper seemed the air, as though he were boring through a dark wall, and he didn't know what he might encounter. In the yellowing of dawn, as he traveled on, piercing the darkness before him, he saw, far off to the south, a cloth tent and two trucks, and he felt a surge of fear together with a surge of joy. *Why am I afraid?* he wondered, and managed to produce a long list of reasons. After thinking of only one or two, he was most distressed that he didn't know whether his dear friend was dead. Second, he was distressed when he wondered what kind of people were there and how he would meet with them and how he would start to speak with them. Third, he was distressed to imagine how she would be when they came face to face. Fourth, he was distressed by how, with just a single horse, he might offer help out on the open steppe if she had been injured. Fifth, he was distressed and thought to himself, *I really don't need to waste my heart on anyone else if Adilbish is actually not in that vehicle.* Such fearful and distressing ideas gushed all the while like spring waters, disturbing Jaltsan's mind. Yet if you ask, *Why then did he hurry happily onward?*, I would say that, while he kept his mind occupied with far too many fantastical circumstances to list here, he hurried happily onward so as to greet his lover in a warm embrace. Happily he hurried onward, that their meeting might immediately reveal and express the words of their hearts and minds, and might be the start of ten thousand years of pleasure. Happily he thought of how they would feel for each other, witnesses to the power of love, he having already dedicated from far away his body and mind, and already being on his way to his one and only. And so, his joyful heart being disturbed by these ten thousand ideas, Jaltsan at that moment could not but consider his happiness and fear, and although there was not a sound as he hurried toward the cloth tent, when he dismounted, lifted the tent flap, and looked inside, there were a few people sleeping there, at so many different angles that it was impossible to distinguish them. One of them quickly turned and rose.

"Who are you?" he asked.

Jaltsan replied, "I'm from the city. I heard that a vehicle had crashed here, I've come to get a friend of mine." The man was coughing and choking, he said,

"Who have you come to get? Yesterday a rescue vehicle came and took away some of the injured. Now there are only a few men and the driver remaining. We're waiting for the truck to be taken away for repairs. Some of the rest went off to an encampment south of here. These fellows are here mainly to help the driver." Jaltsan said,

"I've come to get a woman called Adilbish."

The man replied, "I don't know the name. One of the three women we had with us died, one's injured, and one's just fine. That's the one who's gone to the encampment. In any case, you could go meet her, and then you'd know." The wound stung in Jaltsan's heart all the more and, while he was anxiously wondering whether Adilbish was alive or dead, the man pointed out the direction of the encampment, and Jaltsan mounted his horse and hurried away in that direction.

The strong sun was smiling out its rays from beyond the eastern hills and tinting with pink the centers of the roof rings on the *ger* on the hilltops and on the lower slopes. The small drops of dew that had spent the day sheltering on the grassy hills were disintegrating and dampening the hooves of Jaltsan's horse. He dismounted on the near side of the southern scarp, from where he could see clumps of blue smoke puffing from the roof rings of three ger. The camp was full of sheep, roundels of white, surrounded by a herd of cattle of varying colors, lying prone and drowsy. Not far from the sheep, two horses were tied up and chewing lazily at the grassy hill. The poor countrywomen, having work to do around the clock, were already up at this hour, and Jaltsan felt uneasy at interrupting their work.

He went near to one of the ger and the dogs came rushing out.

Although people were continually coming and going along the highway where these country people were staying, who carried out their work, day in and day out, nonetheless their interest seemed newly piqued by the sound of their dogs, and someone came out of each of the ger and stood there, in front of Jaltsan and behind him, amazed. As soon as Jaltsan came close to the ger, the women and the children shooed the dogs away and looked Jaltsan directly in the eye. Jaltsan hobbled his horse and went into the ger to his right, and behind him came a swirling crush of women and children. In the back of the ger there were two children sleeping, their calloused brown feet sticking out from under tattered and threadbare deels. Off to the right, an old woman, no bigger than a child, lay on a cushion; she lay there, coughing as though in jest. There was a fire blazing, a deep roseate mirage, loose dry dung on a large dilapidated iron brazier, and there was tea on the boil. To left and right was a mess of black trunks with loose fasteners, and cushions and pillows and felt and skins, and between the rafters where the roof met the walls were squeezed bridles and hobbles, and on the doorjambs right and left there were stands holding rows of leather *airag* bags.

In the place of honor to the rear of the ger, in the middle of three red boxes, before a picture, in a sooty frame, of Maitreya Buddha, was a small brass bowl holding food offerings and a small copper bowl holding a candle. Directly above the buddha's picture they had stuffed a book called *The Fundamental Law*, which the smoke had turned to gray.

On a box to the left in the back was a red pioneer's neckerchief, and a book in a case, and against the wall, near a large and artless portrait of Lenin, which had been placed there with great respect, there was propped a framed picture of the revolutionary hero Sühbaatar.

Jaltsan went and sat to the right of the brazier and exchanged pleasantries with the swarthy man whose ger it was; they passed around food and tea and talked a while, and when Jaltsan asked after Adilbish, the man said,

"I really don't know anyone called Adilbish. Yesterday a woman and a couple of men came from where the crash had happened, and they went off by night from here, intending to go to the trade fair at the army naadam. They certainly went off during the night. They must be close to the river at Shar-Höv by now, but the owner of the vehicle, an old man named Tsogzol, knows what he's doing, so they'll certainly rest up in the heat of the day. If you set off now, you may not catch them by midday, but definitely by evening." While the older men were talking, Jaltsan hurried off in the direction they had indicated, following a lovely broad valley between the mountains and, though he sang merrily as he trotted along, moving quickly so as to catch up with the beautiful girl, still he took care of the horse, which had gone without stopping through the night, and from time to time, to preserve its health, he would slow the horse to a walk. Thus they journeyed through the day and, by the time the sun was setting, he passed by a little bubbling spring near to the terrace on the northern face of the mountain, where on a slanting area there were hot ashes, glowing red between the three stones from where a caravan had maybe only recently moved away. Jaltsan thought that this was certainly their fire, and he dismounted onto the earth of his homeland and loosened the horse's bit, thinking he'd let it relax a while and nibble at the delicious grass. He approached the stones at the campfire and there were bones and fat, as though from food just recently consumed. Jaltsan picked at what was left and lay down upon the silken meadow, and while he moved about, his elbow scrunched against something. He started up and looked, and there was a red packet of Mongol Coöp cigarettes, not the brand of cigarettes Adilbish smoked, though would that it had been, and it suddenly came to him that his seeking her was all in vain. Without thinking he opened the packet and saw that something had been inscribed and then crossed out on the cover, and he realized that it was in Adilbish's hand, and he took a joyful breath and read it carefully once again, and the two couplets she had inscribed and then crossed out were these:

The colored flowers of summer
adorn the natural world in different ways.
The sweet letters of a young man
transport my mind in different ways.

A third couplet had been started, but then abandoned.

Jaltsan's heart was filled with joy, but he thought, *I still have to establish that she's all right and not in danger*, and in his great happiness he kept his head, and decided that he could let the horse rest and eat no longer; he mounted immediately and raced off after his beloved.

4. The Ancient Poplar Was Not Scornful

Jaltsan rode the black horse out at an even trot, not too slack; he crossed a few low passes and over a slight incline, uneven and strewn with rocks, and came down a hollow in the hill to the east, the horse walking slowly, laboring for breath. A line of oxcarts came into view, and the shadows cast by the rainbow of pinkish rays from the low yellow sun struck the peak of the hill to the west, and seemed in places to grow in intensity. Ahead, the broad and spacious, mountainless steppe appeared far away. A wind blew gentle waves through the clear air, wafting the scent of juniper all around. As soon as Jaltsan saw the oxcarts, he galloped quickly toward them, assuming that there was traveling the one whom he desired, and once he had caught up with them, he saw that the carts were loaded with skins and wool and that there were a couple of boxes stacked upon the loads.

Jaltsan looked at this, and the closer he got the more he thought that surely such a cart would be traveling with someone from the city, and of the people sitting in the cart, three were probably from the countryside and two were old men from the city. On the very first cart, in a deel of Chinese silk covered in grease and perspiration, hunched over, and wearing an old gray hat full of holes, was a rather imposing old man of about fifty, who kept on shouting out—"Hey there! Hey!" Jaltsan came up close to the cart and the old man said,

"How are you?"

"Good—how are you?"

And so they exchanged greetings, and Jaltsan said, "Might you have a woman traveling with you?"

The old man said, "Yes, we do, she's riding my horse. She went off over the other side of this pass," and Jaltsan was so bewildered by joy that he suddenly set off, as though there was nothing for him to say in response to the old man. He galloped out from the pass and there was the beautiful girl who had been tiring his heart and mind, whom he had spent his days desiring, there was Adilbish, on a chestnut horse, walking down the track. She struck Jaltsan's eyes like a blazing fire and moved his simple heart, and he felt churned up inside; he was breathing heavily as though to expand his chest.

Jaltsan's heart grew lighter and, wondering what he should do, he quietly followed behind the one he loved, and gazed at her. So his eyes and his heart prowled; he hung back and watched. Adilbish was wearing a simple green crêpe deel, with a simple gray peaked hat aslant, and with her white-soled brown leather boots she kicked the stirrups at the side of the old man's saddle. Her back, straight as a river, moved gracefully, she sat slightly askew on the saddle, and she was singing "In the Shade of a Poplar Tree." Jaltsan bided his time for as long as he could and, when he could no longer endure it, he drove his horse forward, and Adilbish heard the hooves as he drew alongside, and she turned around but didn't recognize him. Jaltsan moved up beside her, and she could not suppress a cry as he embraced her and drew her from the horse and held her hand tight; his eyes could not look, so heavily was he breathing.

"So how are you then?" he said. "I've been pursuing you hard and now I've found you," and she could say nothing in reply, but she held the hand that held her all the tighter and her gentle eyes reflected him back to himself.

Adilbish's face was on fire, there were sparks in her eyes, the smoke of happiness completely covered her heart, and though in her confusion she was unable to ascertain why she was suddenly so overwhelmed, there were thoughts of joy in the depth of her warm heart, so that she could barely stay on the saddle, her lips sweetly moving like a bouquet of flowers.

"You're alive," she said. "But how did you get here? What an extraordinary man you are," and Jaltsan fixed his embrace firmer and gazed at her, unwavering, his black eyes like cherries as though to say, *I'm right here.*

Jaltsan stifled somewhat the beating of his heart and eased his mind of its urgent waves; he let the reins go loose, and the horse walked out quietly, and the two of them held each other and supported each other in their swaying movement, and meanwhile he told her the whole sequence of events, how he had become agitated at hearing the mysterious news on the radio, how he had found the horse and ridden through the night, and how he had now reached her. He told her too how he had found the lines of poetry where he had stopped and how his heart had leaped, and the more he opened up their old story, thinking and talking, and thinking about and adding to the story of their love, beginning from the day they met, how the yearning of true love had held sway over their hearts, and how he desired her forever and without respite.

And Adilbish spoke the unavoidable truth, seeking to confirm that theirs was but one desire.

Those two young bodies were together now, and since their minds were in rapture, all their faculties left them, and they took a solemn oath to remain forever faithful to each other, and with their loving and gentle words they nourished their will; their hearts opened as they talked together, so that I cannot really write the things of which they spoke so sweetly, what they learned about each other. Thus they went, and it was already evening and dark when the two of them dismounted near the road and sat down upon the gentle meadow, and while they waited for a northbound vehicle they talked, tasting each other's speech as though it were honey from a bee, and they held each other until they left, talking without end about more and more, and then when the vehicle inevitably arrived, they were like old friends as they chatted with old Tsogzol.

Tsogzol said to them, "Beyond this little ridge there's a spring. We can go over there and give the horses a little rest; we can have forty winks ourselves and then get up early in the morning and set off together."

They all agreed and went to the place he had mentioned, and there they set up a tent and a cooking pot with a ladle; they tied up the horses and the animals and prepared food and drink. Meanwhile, Jaltsan took off his pack and got out his notebook and pen, and the newspapers and magazines, and he gave them to Adilbish, and Adilbish was extremely happy. Old Tsogzol watched them reading the newspapers, and as he watched them with interest from nearby he thought how young people today were very open with each other, and that was nice enough, and these new ways he found interesting, and he said,

"So these fine books are really interesting to you young people, right? While we eat, will you read to me?" They smiled with pride as they read a few poems and, while they ate, a few people came and sat down around the fire, and as they all ate happily together, Jaltsan and Adilbish were the happiest, joyously talking and eating together, remembering that one day when they had sat eating together at the cooperative café. Then the travelers sent the horses and the animals back and checked the carts, and then they came back to the tent and slept. But Jaltsan and Adilbish went alone to the foot of the old poplar at the source of the spring and, wrapped in a single deel, talked through their powerful desire together.

But the ancient poplar was not scornful; heedlessly it swayed its branches and stood there, unmoving and concealing them, as though to grant its blessing.

And the moon did not beat the night's brow; as though cutting through heaven, silently it glanced between the clouds and merely smiled.

Old Tsogzol rose early and moved the carts and, among the sounds of the silent steppe, the travelers all got up. The two young people, who had come together where the ten thousand joys and pains of a single life meet, rose and sang the happiness of their full hearts, they took their horses and immediately prepared to leave.

In the yellow rays of dawn, the river of carts creaked along, the horses' hooves walking out, and on this summer morning of indistinct forms, a few travelers headed for the highway, moving each with their own thoughts toward the far distance.

5. An Old Man's Unforgettable Advice

They traveled slowly and without pausing along the road, and came to the city at evening when the sun was going down, and old Tsogzol went off to his home in one of the western suburbs.

Then the people traveling with them went their separate ways, and Jaltsan and Adilbish loaded their possessions onto Jaltsan's horse and went to Adilbish's house, where he met her parents and chatted with them, and when Adilbish went to take a hot bath, Jaltsan left to go home, saying that he would come back that evening.

Jaltsan went back via Myagmar's, where Myagmar and Udval had just gotten back from the naadam, and they sat together and talked about what had happened, and once Jaltsan had handed the horse back to Myagmar and had told them almost everything, Myagmar said,

"I tell you, you should go after her like a dog with a bone," and Udval asked them whether they'd have some airag, to which Jaltsan enthusiastically agreed; he said,

"Why not? With your airag, it'll be like a naadam."

Udval said, "A family we know was talking about the airag at the naadam. Yesterday they brought us a huge leather sack of airag for rounding up the local mares. But don't you have a new wife now?" She smiled.

"Hey Jaltsan," said Myagmar, "I thought there was something up with all this talk of airag. Just a little airag, it all mounts up—the naadam, your marriage. Let's stay in and have some fun tonight, we'll drink some airag and have some food, we'll sing along with the gramophone!" Jaltsan agreed and said that he'd bring Adilbish that evening, and when he came home, the black lock was hanging there, waiting for him still, yet when he unlocked the door and went inside he knew immediately that he felt no comfort there. That is to say, when two young people first come together, they fiddle about with ornaments and frippery and the sort of things that cultivated people don't bother with, and this inevitably results in pretentiousness, and so as soon as Jaltsan returned home, thinking to take a hot bath and get dressed up, there were no clean clothes, his room was untidy as usual and covered in dust, and it was evident that the place was a mess. And he noticed some slivers of bread on a plate, hard as wood, covered in moldering butter. There were no clean cups or bowls, a witness to the fact that he had not eaten any of the food he had made. Jaltsan was irritated that nothing had been cleared away; he rummaged in a trunk and got some new underwear, found a towel and quickly took a bath, washed his hair, and made himself presentable. He sprayed himself with cologne, he put on some nice clothes, and at sunset he came to Adilbish's house, where Adilbish too had taken a bath and dressed in clean clothes and put on some jewelry, and he desired her even more than he had before. So those two young people captured the wishes of each other's body, what can I say, they came together in desire and reached beyond each other's understanding. In short, then, Adilbish was happy to agree to the invitation Myagmar had extended to them, and the two of them now went out through that little red door, arm in arm. And as the young couple talked happily together at this beginning of their honeymoon, Adilbish said,

"Now we should get old Mr. Tsogzol and have him drink some airag and listen to the gramophone. People from the countryside like such things." Jaltsan agreed and the two of them went directly and invited old Tsogzol to Myagmar's home.

Soon Urtnasan the driver came with his wife, Gerelt, and soon the seven of them were loudly partying, drinking airag, eating meat, singing and dancing along with the gramophone to Mongolian songs. And since the young girl and the young man especially were newly come together in warmth and closeness, their friends said they'd go and chat about the naadam or entertain themselves somehow. But that pair were hot like embers in a fire, not an inch separated their bodies, they gazed tenderly at each other, as though their four eyes were joined together. Their manner, the way they talked, it all had a new refinement, a witness truly to a new transformation. The others were saying,

"The members of the Party's youth wing have arrived by plane. I'll definitely be getting out of school." Someone else was asking, "What's the deal if you're firing small-bore guns and hit with fewer than forty-five out of fifty bullets?" Another said, "The fitness academy in the city center is really fun." The women were talking about how it's not that hard to learn to operate the machinery in the garment factory, and it was a good idea to train in opera or theater skills. And some of the women, they were saying, make really good doctors. Meanwhile, someone brought a camera and lit some magnesium powder and took a photograph. Then they discussed which camera was good and which was bad, directing movies and whether to join the dawn bicycle-riders' club, and they talked about the writing and graphic design in the wall newspapers. Old Tsogzol heard what they were talking about with such intensity, and he was amazed at how interesting and novel it all was.

They imagined old Tsogzol's youth, in their theater of happiness and joy, they who so revered the new culture, and Tsogzol's simple heart felt stung by forty years of bitterness; he gave a long sigh and tears welled up in his eyes.

He trembled as he looked at the young people and, in a perfectly clear voice, sad and mournful, he said,

"Oh, my children! You were born at a good time, you are lucky. Your older brother here has reached the age of fifty-seven. I remember when I came of age at eighteen, and I have passed these forty years bearing the pain and happiness of the world. And I'm thinking to myself that, over these forty years, while I have had many happy days, I have also had many days of sadness. But now, if I look back and think about it carefully, as though waking from sleep, I have forced the myriad sources of sadness and bitterness into the darkness, as though under an inverted stewpot, and I cannot really make out what is truly different between sadness and happiness. If you ask me what it is that I do know, I know for sure that the monks who think that nothing has more water than the Tuul, that there is no mountain higher than Songino, that there is no vehicle quicker than a horse, that nothing burns hotter than wood, that nothing is more powerful than the Triple Jewel, and that nobody is more estimable than the ancestors, who if they're hungry moan about their fate, who if they're sick rely upon the monastic community, who go around reciting *Om mani padme hum*, and who earn no living for themselves—I slaughter a sheep to give to them and hope to get myself the head and the legs. I give a horse for the rich to break in and get a cup of airag in return. I'm sent as a messenger to one of the offices and get to hold the minister's cooking pot for warmth. I take requisitioned horses to the *taiji* and get my head smashed in, and when I pass days with nothing to do, then I rise thirsty, and I think that if I'm satisfied now, I'll be hungry in the morning. I'm suffering from seven types of pain, and I'm bound by the deceitful teaching of the lamas, who cheat me into foolishly praying for the nobles to oppress me in my work, into foolishly mistaking the rich people's exploitation of me for my own fate, and into foolishly believing that if I suffer in this life, I will be happy in future lives. So I am led astray, only to dive into a thousand situations in the ocean of bitter hardship. In this way, while I know that suffering is hard,

having suffered tens of thousands of hardships, I have not discovered the meaning of suffering, where it comes from, nor
have I found how to escape from it.

"Oh, my younger brothers and sisters! When I listen to all
you young people amusing yourselves and having fun, I recognize the shameful behavior of the old world.

"When I was twenty-one, although my relationship with
one of the younger nuns, a girl named Borloi, was innocent,
why should we not have been free together? We found a way,
and would meet where the sheep had been moved away from
the other animals.

"One day, I spent the day in the office of Galsan Meeren, I
was tired out from feeding dung into the fire for the cooking
pot; I found three lumps of sugar, a savory pastry, some slices of
torma, and I packed it all, covered in dust, into my belt and in
the end I went off to where the sheep were and gave it to Borloi,
and she lay down and placed her head of tangled hair in my lap,
and at that time I thought that a person's joy really might be
untamed. But as my dear Borloi pillowed her head, full of lice,
in my lap, I caressed her sweaty face with my gentle hand and
flicked the nits away, and as I sucked at the sugar lumps, love
rose in my mind and I was happy in thoughts of desire. In such
conditions your poor elder brother has passed through the seasons of the world and, as though blind and deaf, I have suffered
for many years." And so saying he gave a long, long sigh, and
the young people sitting around the old man were quite silent as
they listened attentively to him.

Suddenly, as the old man was speaking so mournfully and
with such sadness, he looked around with a gleam in his eye,
and the pleasure in his face returned and he spoke with a determined voice:

"The Party and the government of the people are able to
show the true qualities of pain and happiness. I have left behind
the poison of pain through the power of the state and I have

taken to the road of happiness. Today, as I am sitting together with you young people, who are growing up in this free country of ours, I will not stint in praising your abilities.

"Young people today have the power to bore holes in mountains, to evaporate water, to go beyond the clouds, and to pierce the moon; your intellect is sharp and your enthusiasm broad, and you can develop this culture, this society, to know the past and the future, to address the issues of the people, to equip yourselves with machinery; and when I see how this magical ability, glistening like a cleaned mirror, can unendingly do all things, my resolve rises unchecked and my mind is never properly satisfied," and he clenched his teeth bitterly, and continued.

"So I have been oppressed for forty years by the pitch darkness of an authority based upon monastic teaching, and I am truly aiming for the shining light of the people's government based upon the teaching of democracy, so that I can at least die able to read the newspapers, and content in my old age, as the broad voices of you young people thunder forth."

The voices filled the ger, they were all saying, "Yes, that's right, you really should study."

1937

6

WHAT CHANGED SOLI

TS. DAMDINSÜREN

A young Gobi man named Bat left his eighteen-year-old wife, Soli, and went off to do military service. Before he rode away, Bat stroked Soli's head and said to her, "It is hard now to separate from you. But after a few years I'll quit the military and come back. What's two or three years? Please look after yourself, keep our home clean, and increase our livestock." And Soli, barely holding back her tears, said to him,

"Please come back safely. I'll keep our home clean and increase our livestock, as you say, and," she added, "I'll keep my voice soft and our child will grow." Bat heard the word "child" and, surprised, asked, "What child?" But Soli, her face reddening slightly, said nothing.

Because Bat's heart was greatly affected by leaving his homeland for the first time to serve in the military, he didn't keep asking Soli what she had meant by that word. He grasped her small hand tight and said, "Protect your marriage vows," to which Soli said, "If you don't forget me, I'll not forget you."

And two tears dropped from Soli's black and shining eyes and fell onto Bat's hand.

Bat stood there, amazed and looking about, not understanding his sweetheart's tears. It wasn't so much that Bat didn't know Soli's character well, rather that she, who to him was like a precious jewel, didn't perhaps fully know his fine heart. Indeed, a loving heart is like a beautiful high mountain whose peak cannot be scaled, like a vast and deep ocean whose floor cannot be reached, it is a sacred jewel that no one can easily understand. Now, Bat was not thinking of his dear wife, but of the distant road he was to travel.

So Bat mounted his horse for the long journey and rode away to serve in the military. As Soli stood there, wondering whether Bat would turn and look back, Bat was on his stallion, struggling with the reins, unable to look back, and so it was that he disappeared into the swirling white dust.

As he journeyed, he looked forward to passing through Ulaanbaatar, and to his important post guarding the border once he had arrived. At first he thought about his home and his young wife, and wrote occasional letters to her, but as time passed he began to forget a little about her. He received a few letters from his wife too, but eventually they held no interest for him. This was because, except for saying, "I'm well. How are you? There's nothing interesting to write," every letter was ornamented with such things as "I'll tell you how your lover is, her body longer than our country's long rivers and whiter than paper, her speech dark and coarse." But now she wrote nothing about their homeland, or what she was doing, or what her life was like, nothing interesting about the families he knew, nothing about the increase or decrease in livestock. Her earlier letters were much the same as her subsequent letters. When Bat saw that the last two letters had the same handwriting, he thought that they had been written by the same person. And when he wondered who it might have been who had written them, he thought that the handwriting was rather like that of a dissolute fellow named Donoi. Bat thought, *My wife doesn't even know the alphabet, so she's been asking someone to write her letters to me. There's one young man in our area who knows how to write, and he's been scrawling letters like these, talking rubbish, quaffing tea until evening, and then he's been spending the night at our place on the pretense that his own ger is far off. Who knows what's been happening? But they've been sending me these pretty papers, all the while treating me with contempt!* And so he came to dislike anticipating these letters and reading them.

There was another thing. In the area where Bat was doing military service, there was a young couple. He noticed that when the man, Tsend, went off on a journey for a few months, his wife, Lham, wept inconsolably, drying her tears on a large cloth of what appeared to be calico. But when Tsend came back after two months, Lham was with another man. In fact, before the tears on her calico cloth had had a chance to dry, Lham had been embracing this other man. What crocodile tears were these? What kind of duplicitous love? Bat talked about all this with his military friends, and one of them told him, "That's how these young women are. Do you think that your wife won't hold another in her heart? Do you think that she won't let another man have her? You're wrong!"

As Bat listened to these words, his faith in his wife diminished, and as he thought about all these things, he became unhappy. But a person's mind does not remain sad forever. Just as flowing water wears away the edges of a rock, so the flowing time wore away the sadness of the mind.

Thus it was that Bat thought no more about Soli. He thought of her, of course, but he thought rather that Soli had not really been a suitable wife for him. Every day, Bat studied in school. One day passed, and he knew something that previously he had not known. But Soli didn't know how to write; she remained coarse and vulgar. Bat decided that as soon as he was discharged from the army, he would leave his wife and take up with a woman with whom he was better matched.

He shared this idea with Dorj, who was from his own home-land and who had served some years in the army. Dorj said to him, "It's a nasty business, divorcing your wife." Bat said, "I didn't start divorcing her, it's Soli who began it herself. My wife's name is Soli, it's not a good name. Her mother had five girls, but when the sixth was born, she once again was wanting a boy, and so she called her Soli—*change!*

"Those last few girls, they felt like burdens to their mother and father, they got names like Boli—*stop!*—and Soli. They wanted to change their daughter Soli into a boy, for her to be changed into a boy. What use do I have for a wife who doesn't even know the alphabet?" And Dorj, shaking his head, said nothing.

Dorj's time serving in the military soon came to an end; he was discharged and went home. Bat didn't send a letter to his wife through Dorj. Bat didn't get letters from anyone, nor did he write letters to anyone, and so a few years passed.

All alone, Bat carried out the work that had been assigned to him. He earnestly did his best to protect his country. He was constantly vigilant in protecting the borders, and because he had several times acted with great merit, he was awarded a medal for bravery in combat from the government.

When the time came for him to be discharged from the military, he was discouraged by not having a place to which he might return, and so he remained in service voluntarily. He was promoted to junior officer. Bat thought that he would not leave the army and go back to his homeland, he would go and serve somewhere else. Soon another two years had passed and, as the autumn of the third year approached, he was undecided whether this year he would leave the military or not.

But at that point, Bat came across an article about a fine Gobi herder named Hishig in a magazine for young women. In the pictures, the herder was dressed in a brocade deel with wheel patterns; she wore a fur hat, and on her chest was an award for labor, and a medal given to state-honored herders was pinned to her lapel. Regret and lonesomeness were not clearly represented in this woman's magazine. But this young woman's chubby face, the bright spark in her eyes, moved the heart of this soldier. One of the soldiers said, "She's a fine young woman," and some of the others agreed. And when Bat read the brief account of the young woman's life, he found that she was from the area next to his. Over the last few years, this young Gobi herder had risen quickly to become a fine model herder.

Bat led some of the soldiers in discussing this young woman. One of the soldiers said, "If this girl's not careful, what with this picture being published, she's going to be really happy." Another said, "Not only this girl, but her mother and father, her family, her husband, and everyone she knows are going to be happy." Bat said, "Never mind that, the people of our homeland are going to get happy because of her, they're going to be really fortunate to see this girl's photo," to which the first soldier added, "Sure." The second soldier said, "If a picture of any one of us soldiers' wives were published in a newspaper, how rich would we be?" The first soldier said, "That's quite right. Which of us is married?" and they both said, "It's Bat— Bat's married!"

Bat furrowed his brow and said, "You can't compare my wife with this girl Hishig. My wife let her skirts fall. It's been many years since I heard anything about her. I figure I don't have a wife anymore," and his friends looked at one another and nobody said a word against him. One of the soldiers read from the article about Hishig, "Hishig and her elder sister are herding two hundred head between them," and then he said, "So this young woman Hishig, she must either be unmarried or have a husband working elsewhere." The other soldier added, "Or else her husband's working and has forgotten all about his wife." The first replied, "What kind of foolish creature would forget about such a lovely wife and abandon her?" And the other said, "There are many such foolish creatures in this world. Some men go off to the military and forget all about their wives." Someone else added, "One such fool is sitting right here!" and pointed to Bat. "Ask him if he's written many letters home." And then, "You've got a wife. I've not taken a wife yet, I'm not like you. If I had a wife, why would I not write her letters to ask her how she's doing? It's a foolish man who takes a wife when he's young. A wise man completes his military service, gets an education, reaches twenty, and then when he's mature he takes a suitable wife and creates a stable home." To explain himself, Bat said, "There are differences between a good wife and a bad one. It's a fool who abandons a good wife, it's a wise man who abandons a poor wife. My wife, Soli, and this young woman Hishig are as different as day and night. Would you compare the surface of the shining sun with a plate of rusted brass? Soli is like a strip of dried jerky, but this one's a fine plump woman, she's like cheese curds." The soldiers laughed and said to him, "This picture is blurry, it's black and white, it's not clear." One of them said, "I would be wrong to abandon my wife and talk badly of her," and another said, "Let's talk about something other than problems with wives. What say we get together and write this Hishig a letter?" and everyone agreed to his suggestion. Bat began the letter: "To the excellent herder Hishig, a few of us soldiers, who are guarding the borders, have gotten together to write you this letter. We're called blahblah and soandso and we're from thisandthat *sum*. We found the news and pictures about how you have successfully herded and increased your livestock very interesting. We're all from the same region, and we'd like to tell you how happy we are for you. We're heroically protecting our nation. You and your sister are enriching our nation and increasing our livestock. So you're making our nation all the stronger. If you have the opportunity, we would be very happy to receive a reply from you." And they all signed the letter.

About a month later, our soldiers received a reply from Hishig. She extended her thanks to the soldiers and briefly mentioned how she had been working hard to herd her livestock. After they had received the letter, Bat thought, *I'd like to find out whether or not Hishig's married. If she's not, then after I'm discharged from service, I'll definitely strike up a relationship with her*, and he wrote her a letter that he alone signed. In the letter, he wrote, "To the excellent herder Hishig, thank you very much for your reply. We're from neighboring regions, and so we have a connection. I've been wondering whose daughter you were, but couldn't find out," and so he continued, and when Hishig replied, she said, "I'm one of the girls you used to know," but she didn't mention whose family she was from. And so Bat and Hishig continued to exchange letters.

The time was drawing close when Bat would leave the army. He wrote to Hishig that, if he were to be discharged, he had no home to which he could return.

In her reply, she wrote: "To my elder brother, a man in our revolutionary army should not have no home to which he can return. If you have no mother or father, no brothers or sisters, then please, when you are discharged from the army, come straight to my home. I will honor you as my own elder brother. This is because you are a man who has served in our revolutionary army. When you come to our home, you will not be at a loss for a horse to ride or a saddle to use. I have a few good horses. You can ride them at your leisure. I will erect a fine white ger for you, and you will take a fine wife. My elder sister and I will be happy to have you come." When he received this letter Bat was overjoyed, and as soon as he was discharged from the army he went to them. It was significant that she had said how he would take a fine wife. She had written that she was living with her elder sister, and it seemed from her words that neither had a husband. He thought, *That young woman will definitely agree to be my wife.*

So Bat's time in the army came to an end and he was discharged. He galloped home, passing through Ulaanbaatar on his way. He didn't go through his homeland, but came through the sum where Hishig lived. He met nobody in that sum whom he knew.

When he asked a courier, "Where's that young woman Hishig's place?" the fellow said, "You mean that fine herder Hishig?" and pointed toward her ger. It occurred to Bat that this fine herder Hishig was famous in her homeland. The courier asked Bat, "Do you want to ask her advice?" Bat replied, "What do you mean? What advice could a man ask of a young woman?" The courier was amazed: "You're from far away, right? You don't know about Hishig. Herders from our region come and ask her advice about herding livestock and about how best to move them seasonally. Even local and regional officials come to ask her advice. Just recently, the leader of our sum came and spoke with Hishig about his work. Now they're asking her to advise the herders' committee in the western sum. You should meet her, you should go immediately. Ride over straightaway."

As Bat galloped across the thick grasses of the lovely steppe, there appeared two white ger. These had to be Hishig's, there was furniture outside. Near the ger were pastured many sheep, cattle, and horses. Bat imagined that Hishig's must be a very rich family. But in a distant hollow there appeared two further ger. Bat was astounded, for these must also be Hishig's, and he decided to ride up to the two nearer to him. As he approached, a fat brown-and-white dog came rushing out, barking. The dog came up to Bat and kept barking, pressing in on him as he removed the saddlecloth. Bat approached the ger. "Hold the dogs," he called loudly, and a young woman came partway out of the ger, said "Hey, what's up?" and went back inside.

Nobody came out. The dog was barking. After a few minutes, he again called out, "Hold the dogs," and a child of about five or six came out and chased after the dog, and the dog ran away.

Bat dismounted and, that he might know who lived there, gently asked the child, "Who lives here, boy?" The boy said, "My mother." Hishig had a son, then, and Bat wondered who the father might be. He asked, "Is there nobody else living here?" and the boy said, "My father." Bat was shocked to hear this; he felt as though his body was shaking.

Bat stood there for a while, wondering whether or not to go inside, and the boy said, "Are you afraid of my father? There's nothing to be afraid of. He's always lying in bed."

Bat asked him, "Is your father sick?" The boy thought for a bit and said, "I don't know if he's sick. I'll go find out," and he ran toward the ger. Bat stopped him: "You don't need to do that, you don't need to do that." Bat was very concerned then, he was thinking that he might have come to another family. He said, "What's your mother's name?" And the boy said, "I don't use her name, it's the Mongolian custom. My mother's washing her face," he said, answering Bat's question with all manner of formulas. He'd come to another family then. Or else, thought Bat, somewhat discouraged, perhaps that Hishig, whom he so desired, was an older woman with a sick husband and a young son. But it was already wrong for him to have come to this family, and he went inside with little enthusiasm.

A single young woman, wearing a green silk deel, was standing in the ger, quickly tying her blue crêpe belt. She looked as though she had just been changing her deel.

When the young woman said "Hello," it seemed that she could have been Bat's ex-wife Soli. At this remove, she seemed strangely other. Soli had been eighteen, a skinny young girl, and now this one was chubby with a pinkish face. Shocked, Bat wiped his eyes and again and again looked at her; he stood there dumbfounded. The young woman said, "Well, Bat. How was it doing military service? Don't be bashful. We're doing well."

And she said to the boy, "Come and greet your father," and as soon as the little child heard the word "father" he brought a picture of a man from under his mother's pillow and asked her, "Is my father well? Is he sick?" Flustered, she said, "Don't be crazy. This is your father. Come and meet him," and she pushed the boy toward Bat.

When the boy came close, Bat took him and kissed him, and when he looked at the picture it was of him, and he thought, *I came to Hishig's, but I've mistakenly ended up at Soli's.* Then the young woman said, "When you went off to serve in the military, I was pregnant, but I kept my word, I kept our home clean, I increased our livestock, and I raised our son. Now my husband who changed his mind and forgot about his wife and child is going to abandon us." And Bat thought, regretfully, *What a foolish creature I was to have abandoned such a fine wife and my son. What luck to have come to the wrong family.* He said, "Let me explain to you, my beloved Soli," but his wife grabbed him and said, "I know a little about your explanation. You didn't like the name Soli. And you didn't like your coarse wife either. I heard a little from Dorj, when he was discharged from the army, that you would have liked a wife who could work and who knew how to read and write. So I left behind my coarseness and, over several years, I have made an effort to become an educated wife.

"In our country, the road has been opened for anyone, man or woman, to advance themselves and become educated. I left my region and moved to this sum and involved myself in education and work, and now I can write well. I read books too. I changed my name to better suit your thinking. I am the Soli whom you discarded. I am the Hishig, the bounty, whom you loved." And Bat said without a thought, "I was shocked to hear the name Hishig. I don't like Hishig. I like my Soli. Hishig led my thoughts astray, she was the one who drew me away from my dear wife Soli," and the child took the picture and said again, "Mother, is my father sick? Is he well? And Bat's wife said, "He really seems to be sick." And to Bat she said, "I changed my name to suit your thinking, and became Hishig, I became a bounty. I am the Soli whom you discarded," she repeated, "I am the Hishig, the bounty, whom you loved." Bat immediately understood, and roughly grabbed his wife's hand. "I was a thousand times wrong to abandon you. If you'll forgive my mistake, I will love you and live with you. I want to have a fine and educated wife like you."

Hishig said, "You went to serve in the army and protect our country. I have to forgive your mistake because, hot in the heat and frozen in the cold, you have righteously protected our nation." Bat was beside himself with joy—"My wife and my son!"—and he hugged and kissed them. The award for labor glistered on his wife's lapel, and his combat medal glistered on his own lapel.

The child looked at Bat. "Are you my father, then?" he asked, and Bat said that he was. "Do you know how to ride a horse?" the boy asked. "Yes, I do. Didn't you see me ride in?" And the boy said, "I'm so happy. The kids are constantly teasing me. They say their fathers ride around, but because my father is in a photograph, he cannot ride, he just lies on the bed beneath my mother's pillow. Now I have a real father, and he can ride a horse, and they'll not be mean to me anymore," he said.

Bat stroked his wife's head and his son's; he said, "We're the happiest people in the world today," and Hishig just said, "Yes," and looked at Bat and smiled. When Hishig smiled, she bared her straight white teeth. But from her dark eyes a single tear fell. This was a tear of joy, Bat understood, a tear of love, and he knew the truth of the old saying, "A single tear of love is worth a thousand gold pieces."

7

TWO WHITE THINGS

TS. DAMDINSÜREN

I n the heat of summer, white snow silvered the majestic ridges of the Gobi-Altai. Other than a few pasque flowers, on the northern side, there were almost no trees or plants, and the rocky peaks and ravines loomed gloomily above. Watching the high and protruding peaks, anyone would be distressed and sad, naturally fearful at what might appear to be a pale old man who, angry at his younger relatives, was getting ready to lay into them.

Majestic though the landscape may have been, the hardships of the road were too much. Because the road was so difficult, the locals didn't use carts but traveled with their possessions loaded on the backs of their livestock. There was also no way to cross the mountains, and it was still really tough to traverse the many hollows and hills of the southern slopes. That year, I traversed the many hollows and hills of the southern Gobi-Altai, using official transport to carry out my duties. Steep ridges alternated with deep gullies, like fingers on a hand, like wrinkles in clothes. I had barely managed to clamber up one ridge when there appeared a deep gorge ahead of me. And barely had I stumbled through the gravelly stones in the deep gorge when

76

another steep ridge hove clearly into view. So it was really tough, going up and down in this way among the cliffs, following a narrow trail.

It was a summer of severe heat. The golden sun glistened amid a sky of deep blue. But beneath the sky were the Altai's uneven rocky cliffs, and they troubled my mind.

My body was weak from the hardships of the road, and I was exhausted. The land was an undulating movement of steep cliffs and ravines, and I dismounted and made my way on foot, ending up completely shattered. I went along the edge of a dark precipice, my heart pounding, my head dizzy. My guide was an experienced old man; he went trotting on ahead, quite unconcerned. I had to make a point of not getting left behind. But I was not going to tell him that I was afraid of the mountains. And I was not going to tell him that I could not deal with the horse I was riding. And yet, I had learned little by traveling the mountains, following the ravine edges up and down. And because I was worn out, I gave up dismounting whenever we came to difficult terrain and instead tightly gripped the pommel and pushed forward. I saw the brown stones reddened in the sun, and the dark-colored mountains, and my eyes grew tired. There was nothing that was in any way pale. In desperation, I thought, *Please let there be a single blade of green grass, just one white rock.*

And as though answering my thoughts, straight ahead of us and down, at the foot of a precipice, there flowed the glistening blue waters of a spring, like a length of sky-blue silk, its banks skirted by meadows of patterned green velvet. I thought it could be the topaz treasure, as big as a horse's head, hidden in the mountains, that the elders would talk about.

In the spaces between the brown mountains, a fine picture came together of blue waters, green meadows, and white rocks, like a pattern of spirals. My sad spirits were lifted, my depression relieved, and even my body felt lighter. I couldn't get there fast enough. There were rocks, though, and if we stepped hastily, we could fall. But if we went around the edge, I imagined that we could reach the water and the stones.

I called over to the old man, "Let's go down to the water."

He glowered and waved his hand, as if to say *We can't go down there*, and he only mumbled something, an unclear response. He might have been reciting a mantra, for all I knew. I felt it useless to further press this nervous old man. I thought I would head down on my own, but because I didn't know the route, I would have to wander along behind him. We had just about made it along a hazardous path when out of the corner of one eye I noticed those three beautiful things. More precisely, there were two white things, one of which was round and the other rectangular. The round thing was near the water and the rectangular thing was at an angle, and a little farther up. As my view became better, it was as though the light was reflecting off these two white things. I thought this was really quite significant. I had no doubt that these were jewels. The old man said nothing, and I thought that he was trying to frighten me, that he would have us pass by without seeing the jewels. Or else he would perhaps be wondering whether this was an area inhabited by fearful demons. I really wanted to go there, so when the road had become a little easier, I asked the old man,

"What are those white things? Sir?"

And the old man's face became angry and he said quietly,

"Wait, son, just wait. We mustn't talk about them now. I'll tell you when we're hidden from them." And he returned to reciting his mantras.

I lost hope of this old man leading me down there. And I hesitated to insist on going alone.

We went on a little while until the two white things were hidden from view. The path had become considerably easier; now we were riding next to each other. My guide looked about and, realizing that he was not within view of the two white things, stopped his mantra and told me about them.

This is what he said.

"Where I'm from, there was a young lad called Gombo. He had an inheritance from his father, as well as some livestock. His mother herded the cows and the sheep. Gombo herded the horses himself. But whatever he herded, he would mistreat it. Every one of the horses he rode ended up run down. When a horse was finished, he traded in the sheep and the cattle for another horse to ride. Gombo was a beast with the whip. When he rode, he would continually whip his horse's head. His fortune in having a horse ran out because he treated them so badly. Nothing he rode would last long. Whenever he managed to get a new horse, certainly it would be eaten by wolves or die from some disease. My relative Jambal had sold him an old white horse. Gombo mistreated this horse too; among other things, he beat it with his whip. When Jambal saw this, he berated himself, *Why on earth did I sell Gombo this horse?* So he asked Gombo to sell it back to him, but Gombo refused. Gombo had no other horse to ride, so why would he give this one back? And soon this white horse died. The whips couldn't stand up to Gombo's use. Fine-quality bamboo whips normally last for many years, but after just half a year, these Chinese bamboo whips would snap in Gombo's hand. He was a wretched man. Gombo could find nobody who would sell him another horse. He asked around for a couple of days of rent, but nobody would even rent him a horse to ride. Who was going to say, "Sure, I'll sell you a horse to torture!"? So Gombo, without a horse to ride, went around on foot for many years.

"At naadam time, while the young men were galloping around on horseback, Gombo would be walking around on foot. It seemed he might be learning his lesson a little.

"Some years later, Gombo suddenly got himself a silver grey horse. Nobody knew where he got it from. His story was that he had bought it from a caravaner who came in from some distance away. It might have been true. This silver grey found grass to eat from the barest of earth; it found water to drink from the driest of puddles; it was an excellent horse, unusually hardy. And Gombo was full of himself, riding this silver grey horse.

"The local elders said to him, 'Now you have a good horse. Treat it only with love.'

"But I also said to Gombo, 'For a man, there is nothing much better than a horse. You have learned your lesson by walking about on foot. Now it's time to use your brain. Don't go hammering at that horse's skull with your whip as you did with the others. Look after this horse well.'

" 'I will,' said Gombo. 'I will.'

" 'I'm thinking about mending my ways,' he said. He promised, 'I'll take care of this silver grey horse as though it were my eyes.'

"And it did indeed seem as though Gombo had mended his ways. The horse looked sharp, its legs were all in great shape. Everyone said that Gombo was treating the horse with care. To begin with, his mother hid his whip from him and wouldn't hand it over. Gombo traveled here and there about the empty countryside on horseback. But when he was with other people, he didn't abuse the horse; rather he treated it with great care. We were impressed; we said he had really mended his ways. But suddenly something nasty happened. One morning, apparently, Gombo said he was going to tack up the horse, but for whatever reason the horse never got tacked up. Gombo suddenly became angry and beat the horse's head with his thick whip. He became disturbed and struck the horse in the eyes, ripping one of them right out. Gombo was very ashamed. He said, 'This is the fault of my unlucky right hand,' and he struck his right hand with his left. What good did that do? The silver grey ended up losing an eye. When the whip made an appearance, the horse would become frightened. And Gombo rode the half-blind horse for one or two years more.

"One summer, six or seven years ago, there was a naadam. Some young men were coming, single file, along this narrow track. Second in line rode Gombo on his silver grey horse. Third was Buyan, a young man from my homeland, carrying a horse-catching pole with a noose on the end. At the edge of the path, unable to sling the pole over his shoulders and drag it behind him, he was riding along, holding the pole in his hand on top of the horse. As soon as the shadow from Buyan's lariat touched the head of Gombo's silver grey, the horse shied as though it had been struck in the head. It couldn't see the edge of the path with its blind eye; it slipped and fell, along with Gombo, to its death. My God, they say that they fell with a clanking of stirrups, down down among those hard rocks. Many years have passed now, and Gombo's skull and the horse's are lying there glistening. That's what those two white things are. Interestingly enough, Gombo fell to his death quite some way from where those two skulls are now. His saddle and clothing were quite some way away. But they say that the two heads rose up, above the ground. The horse's skull sought sanctuary from Gombo's skull and, being the bone of a well-bred creature, it fled upward. Gombo's skull moved to a place nearby, or that's what people say. It could be true. A bad man is poison even after he's died.

"This place of water and withered grass was previously where people dwelt with their animals. After Gombo's death, people stopped coming. If anyone or any creature came close, they would be harmed. I feel really nauseated here; I'm telling you, I think it's his bad bones." That's what the old man said to me.

And then he began to trot forward. I followed him, he said not a word, and we reached the next relay station. Listening to what he had said, I thought that these strange white things had been both sad and edifying memories of what had happened. After that I became wary of whipping even my horse's thigh.

When I watch people mistreating their livestock, it calls to mind the brown rocks, narrow paths, and dark precipices of the Altai, and those two white things. Although from time to time what the old man told me is of use, the main point for me is not whether or not it was true. What he said clarified for me what great love herdsmen feel for their livestock.

1945

8

THE MORNING OF THE FIRST

TS. ULAMBAYAR

Young Bidyalah rose from her bed and sat among the blankets. She looked over at the window, thinking, *Maybe dawn hasn't yet come. If only morning would come soon.* Beyond the window, covered by the pitch darkness of the night, the lights from a line of cars filed along the road, occasionally illuminating the inside of the building. When they touched Bidyalah's face, the young girl blinked her eyes in the glare, and she went over and turned on the electric light. It was just past three o'clock. She wondered where so many cars were going so late at night, but more than that she thought about her father, who had been gone for two days in Altanbulag. And now she thought that he would be rushing onward, with lights glittering just like these.

At this moment on the night of the thirty-first, Bidyalah's father, Namsrai, was driving a fully laden truck, and as he hurried along without sleep on this damp autumn night, he was thinking that he would reach the town that night.

By delivering the load that night, he imagined he could deliver his projected quota for 1949, the second year of the five-year plan. *I'll have managed to complete the quota for one year by* 83

August, he thought, and as he sped ahead, the road in front of him was a glistening line, just like a mirror, and he saw the hoarfrost on the heads of the tall grasses along both sides of the road.

His daughter Bidyalah was not thinking about her father much; rather she wanted the sun to rise and the morning gradually to appear.

She went back under the covers and closed her eyes. But sleep had already deserted her. There had been no obstacles when she had been comfortably sleeping. It was strangely quiet, with only the sound of the clock on the wall, gently tick-tocking as though to say *sleep sleep my girl.* She lay there for a while. Then she got up again—*Nobody's going to criticize me for getting up early*—and went to the window. Luckily for her, the dawn was breaking. *Yes!* she thought, and she got dressed, and opened the small book cupboard that her father had made. She took out several picture books, published especially for children, and as she turned the pages, she was thinking, *When will I be able to read all these books?* What a pity it was that she couldn't read the letters. The previous year, her father had taken her to enroll at the school. But the teacher had asked,

"How old is your daughter?"

For the first time in his life, her father had told a lie.

"This year, she'll be eight," he had said.

"What's her name?" the teacher had asked. And when he heard that she was called Bidyalah, the teacher knew that she had been born during the war.

"Your daughter is seven years old this year. She cannot enter school. Bring her back next year!" There were many people who had enrolled their child in school by exaggerating their age. It wasn't a good thing, but people said that a child so young would find it hard to understand the lessons. The year she was born, her father still hadn't known well how to read and write.

When the people who had thrown the good luck party for the child's arrival had demanded, "Give her a name!" her father had taken a book from nearby and, reading from the contents, had come to the line "Our cause is true, and we will be victorious," and that was the name she had been given.

If her father had given her not that name but another, what would have happened? *It was only because of my father that I couldn't go to school this year*, she thought, and as she considered what had happened the previous year she was almost in tears. And then, as the morning she had so desired appeared, the light of the sun broke beyond the window and the legs of humans and animals began to move. Bidyalah washed her face and hands, and putting on her clothes, made herself ready. She looked at herself in the mirror, clutching the leather case that her elder brother had bought for her in Nalaih.

It seemed that her case was too large, and yet it suited her well. She watched as the local children went off to school, some with their elder brothers and sisters, some with their fathers and mothers, and she was almost crying.

She didn't think about how, at that moment, her father was delivering his load, nor that her mother had not quite finished her night shift at the factory, nor that her brother was driving a coal train along the railway from Nalaih; rather, she thought about how she had nobody to go to school with her. It seemed as though the children had all gone past. She was left behind, and they were all running here and there inside the school building. The gate of the enclosure opened and the little boy from the next-door enclosure came in. This child thought of Bidyalah as the strange student who had come to school the previous year. "Your mother called us, and asked me to go to school with you," he said. "So let's go to school!" He led her outside; it was as though he was saying, *Now you're not a little kid, wearing your little cloth satchel and following the schoolchildren in tears. Now you're a student.* The young girl went to school with the boy and entered through the large blue door. As she walked across that first threshold onto the glittering road, who could grasp just how happy that little girl was?

Erdene-Bulgan, 1948

9

THE SAIGA

CH. LODOIDAMBA

The sharp springtime sun had risen quite high, a bluish haze covered the surrounding area, and everything on the broad steppe glistened like a mirage.

The female saiga had spent a few days on the eastern edge of the salt marsh, moving downhill from the spring into a patch of feathergrass, accompanied by her fair white calf. The calf bucked and played, rejoicing at everything as though he was the only one there; his mother paid careful attention to every slight noise, unsettled as she was on the steppe, noticing whatever her gaze locked on, as though to say, "What's that? What's happening?" Her colostrum had not yet dried up—was her infant's belly full of her nutritious milk, or was he tired out from playing? Was this the teaching of their hard life, lived for many many centuries? Who knows? But soon after he had gone into the feathergrass, the calf disappeared into sleep.

In fact, by day, the female would hide her calf away in the feathergrass or in a bush while she ate her way through some fresh vegetation. Should any danger come at this time, she could rush quickly away with the strength of her legs, and then wander back and give her milk to the sleeping youngster she had left behind; it tasted of her happiness at having dispatched the danger, and of flourishing life. And then, once she'd hidden her calf, the saiga would prick her fine ears and jump about and play.

If a dancer had seen her then, they would never have been able to embody all the elegance in the saiga's fine movement.

She kept playing, leaping about for a while, and then a strong scent hit her nose, and she ate from a sprouting bunch of young wild leeks.

But then a car, in which sat a driver as well as three fellows off on a jaunt, trundled along the road that ran past where the saiga was, casting up the dust.

Inside the fast-moving car, the stench of alcohol mingled with the bitter smoke from cigarettes, and because all apart from the one sitting behind the driver were drunk, their eyes turned glossily at nothing in particular and their heads tossed and swayed, as though nodding along with the regular movement of the motor.

If the person sitting next to the driver had not lit his cigarette, the car would have passed by without the saiga and her calf meeting with bitter pain. But he did look at the driver, to ask for a light, and the saiga, eating there all alone, appeared right in his gaze.

"An antelope!" he shouted, and straightaway they sobered up.

"Where?" they shouted in reply, and looked across the steppe with dozy eyes.

"Might have been a saiga and her calf," said the man sitting behind the driver. "We should kill them right now."

"They'll be easy for us," said the driver, "trotting out like that. If we shoot, we'll have them. Get ready!" He turned the car around and set off at speed toward the doe, who had been startled by the noise.

The man sitting behind the driver said, "It's our responsibility to put the law into practice—but equally so if we don't put the law into practice."

"Sure," said the man sitting next to the driver. "We'll be upholding the law," and he gave a cheerful laugh.

"So let's chase them," he said, and because the calf was sleeping on that side of the road, the doe ran from the approaching danger; she galloped quickly down the open steppe, her fine ears shooting back and forth as she darted about.

The car headed quickly after her, the men's guns poking through the windows.

The saiga doe soared on her swift and trustworthy legs; it was hard to tell whether her feet even touched the ground.

But it was not so much that, at that moment, those behind her were pursuing a creature of muscle and sinew that would finally tire, but that they were riding a swift steed who did not know exhaustion. The enemy, overcome with greed for hunting the antelope it was anxiously pursuing but which it had not yet fully dispatched with the bullets from its gun, was moving along at fifty kph, not getting farther away, but gaining ground.

The car continued to hum, bullets whirring without end, and the doe's leaping grew less pronounced, her bright eyes grew cloudy, and gradually her pricked ears drooped. From inside the car could be heard voices: "We didn't get the wretched thing—hey there, but it's really shaken up. Go smash its head. Get a bullet! Have it there in front of you and pull the trigger. Dammit—I scratched my hand! I'll get you!"

Sitting motionless behind the driver, biting his lower lip, his slightly windworn face darkening, one man was saying nothing, a barely contained threat glinting in his eyes. Over and over he whispered to himself, "What's wrong if the hand that would smash its head gets grazed? But playing with the life of an innocent animal is going too far."

For those in pursuit, all this took a short time to play out, but for the saiga it was a bitter struggle between two lives.

The saiga fled toward a hill and was away from those detectives; she wandered toward her calf, which lay motionless, resting his stiff muscles. But the more the men chased the saiga, the more she struggled across the deep, broad steppe. None of them could tell how many kilometers they had chased her. None of them could count how many times she had been shot.

In the end, the saiga's two ears lay against her neck, her mouth fell open, her short tail flicked, and she stopped moving with any regularity, cantering sometimes, and then trotting. The bullets had cut her buttocks, which had begun to turn pale, and a pinkish blood had begun to trickle along the grooves. But the saiga summoned the last of her strength. In her life she had reared several calves, she had overcome ten thousand obstacles, and she didn't wonder how on many occasions, with the strength of her swift legs, she had escaped the enemies who were chasing her and returned to her sleeping calf. Although antelopes don't get hurt by animals, they have no lack of enemies!

"Are there any bullets?" She heard this yelled several times from inside the car, and then it fell quiet, and the guns sticking out of the windows fired, the bullets scattering around her legs.

"What now?" said the man sitting next to the driver, as he threw the empty casing away.

"Let's blast that beast away!" the driver quickly chimed in.

She had turned back to the calf, who had escaped with its life, and she suckled him with her tired udders. And although she had a great wish to smell her calf's little tail as it flopped back and forth, her legs were stiff and unmoving and her entire body trembled, the breath pulsed without force in her chest, and her two ears, which had recently been twitching prettily, had now flopped down, and finally she knelt, her strength all gone, and lay down.

The car stopped, and the contrary saiga, who had been flee-
ing in pain for a while, gave her life into their hands, and the
two of them got out laughing, and came to where the animals
lay.

If she had been barren, or a male antelope, she would not
have had the power to stretch her stiff wooden legs to stand and
flee. But because this saiga was not like that, she revived
and rose up, her misty blue eyes staring in surprise.

Though the men were on foot, they were unable to catch the
saiga. They grew angry and obstreperous when they couldn't
complete their task, and although they threw large stones at
her, they didn't hit her. They exchanged glances and returned
to their car and again set off after her.

The saiga again knelt and lay down. As the car sped past,
one of its wheels knocked against her.

The car turned and stopped, and the so-called hunters were
amused now by how the saiga, whom they had been unable to
finish off, was unable get up, and so in high spirits they came
to where she was.

As she lay there, her whole body convulsing before death,
the saiga summoned up her strength and looked at her hidden
calf, her eyes abandoned by life's spark.

"Shall we finish it off, then, shall we do it?" one of them
asked the others, as they stood next to the saiga, hands on his
hips. The saiga bent again and looked at her calf, who slept
there peacefully, and the heavy iron starting handle came down
on her head, and she let out her final breath. The driver prodded
her eyes with the point of the starter.

"She's gone," he said, and took a bite of some sausage he'd
pulled from his pocket.

The two teats of the saiga's tired udder rose, like her two ears
that had been alert and moving before she had fled, and the
creamy-yellow milk that flowed from them turned brownish as
it seeped into the sandy earth. The man who had been sitting

next to the driver kicked the saiga where she lay lifeless, turning her over.

"Right, let's go. What can you do with a scrawny suckling saiga? If she'd been fat, we could have boiled her and eaten her fat. Do you have any time left out here?"

"Half a year," replied the driver, and he looked down at the pinkish blood trickling from the saiga and smiled proudly. "Good shot."

As they went on in the car, the man sitting next to the driver said,

"It'll be interesting to tell people about this."

And the man sitting behind the driver thought, *I've got a lot to talk about with you, you've broken the law.*

The car sped away, throwing up dust, and so it disappeared. The light of the risen sun shone searingly over the saiga, and the broad steppe silently shimmered, and from the horizon came a large black vulture, slowly soaring . . .

Songino, 1954

10

A GREAT MYSTERY

O. TSEND

In the depths of winter, Jargal, senior physician at the New Life collective, had returned to her home region in Zavhan province to spend her vacation leave. The collective where this young woman worked was situated on the main road, halfway between two relay stations. For that reason, she returned by the Egiin pass, coming down through an area where there were cattle belonging to the collective next to the road along the Botgon River. From there, because there was only one way of getting to the center of the collective, she explained this route to her driver. Once the car carrying the young doctor had left Zavhan, it journeyed a whole day, and at midnight came to where the cattle belonging to the New Life collective were pastured. Lights shone from the herders' accommodations. The cozy cattle pens looked magnificent in the light from the harvesters.

"Which is your place?" the driver asked, and the doctor pointed at the wooden building closest to them. To tell the truth, she didn't know this was where the collective's cowherds lived, but while she certainly knew that this was not a place with which she was familiar, there was really nothing to do but get out here. The driver stopped the car next to the wooden building Jargal had indicated, but, thinking what a strange, cold place this seemed, he hurried needlessly, in case the motor should freeze after stopping for such a short time. He removed Jargal's cloak and suitcase and drove out onto the road. A man who could have been the director came out on hearing the sound of the car and walked over to Jargal.

"Oh, it's our senior doctor. Did you have a good journey?" He greeted her happily with a warm and robust handshake and led her inside. Tired from the road and chilled by the cold, she felt how lovely it was to enter the building, warmed by a fully lit stove.

As soon as Jargal entered the building, she sat on a chair adjacent to the stove, warming her hands by the fire, and while she was wondering *Who was it who recognized me so well on this dark night?*, not many came to mind. Because the door was closed, she was thinking of how there was no other sound but the ticking of the clock, the quietness of the radio, which was ill suited for the space, and the crackling of the dry branches in the warm stove, and that she might be the only person in the building. But then the door opened and the man came in. When he turned to look at Jargal, he was standing there with a smile, a strong, brawny man with a long awkward scar on his face. She had sometimes seen him at the collective center, but even though she had never had cause to quarrel with him, Jargal felt fearful and ready to get up. It was not due to the scar on his face that the man's laughter seemed like a grimace, Jargal thought, but because the sharpness with which he looked at her gave him the appearance of being ill at ease, and somehow dishonest.

The director's name was Bayar. He was interested in where the senior physician was headed, driving through this region. Was there a lot of snow where she had been? As they talked about how there had been heavy snowfalls that year, he stoked the fire in the stone stove, and he said, "Warm yourself here, Doctor, and I'll see to some food," and so the clanking of ladles and pots began. Jargal sat, surprised without reason, and looked around the room. But in her mind, there was a clear image of the brawny man's grim countenance. His was a deep scar, which began above his broad forehead, and as it wrapped around his nose, there were also a few scars alongside on his cheek, and as they too wrapped around his cheek, these few deep scars appeared like small depressions. She talked with Bayar about this and that, and the narrow eyes below his thick black eyebrows continued to gleam like a fire ablaze in the pitch darkness of night, and it seemed to Jargal that he was a rather frightening man.

After Jargal had graduated from the National University, it had been almost a year since she had come to the collective as the senior physician. Very soon after her arrival, Bayar had come to the clinic for the first time, leading a spare horse, and told her, "We need a doctor where the cattle are."

She was going to send her junior, but Bayar protested that he himself would take the senior doctor. Jargal and Bayar had had words, and Jargal was now thinking of the unpleasant language Bayar had used that day. She had said that there were some very sick people in the clinic, that the senior physician couldn't just go off, did he think that "senior physician" was a meaningless title, that she just sat around receiving the best food and drink, like the Buddha to whom the old people offered sacrifices? But he was cunning. "If a person sees you and doesn't give you something," he said, "there's no point in your having this grand title," and he went off accompanied by the junior doctor. From that time on, whenever the doctor saw Bayar, she wondered why that cunning, obstinate bastard hadn't come back. Had that fellow had a fight with an animal? She wondered if perhaps he'd robbed someone, and sustained this permanent scar on his face then?

She had asked the two people who knew what had happened to young Bayar's face, and each had answered her, "It's a great mystery." Bayar himself, when asked what had happened to his face, had said only, "It's a great mystery." So in the end, she had accepted Bayar's harsh words, and assumed that he might in fact have robbed someone and beaten them to death.

So when she ran into Bayar, she felt some trepidation. But today, she had goose bumps thinking about this meeting on his turf on so dark a night. But other people talked pretty highly of Bayar, and Jargal couldn't think of when she had heard anyone say anything bad about him, so perhaps she herself had no reason to think this way. What's more, throughout the collective, they were saying that a woman called Dejid, whom they described as very sweet, had been living with Bayar, but how could such a woman spend her entire life, the whole of her youth, with a man with so ripped and disfigured a face? Still, Jargal had been chatting with a young woman who had told her that, since even the local children cried from fear at Bayar's face, and notwithstanding that those two were living a good life together, Dejid had very soon gotten married to another man.

Bayar had been a little anxious when the senior physician had suddenly appeared at his building, and he'd thought to prepare some food and drink in a leisurely manner, and had busied himself in the kitchen. Jargal sat there thinking about Bayar; she changed from her traveling clothes and washed her face and hands, and went into the building's main room. The room was spacious, and had a large mirror and the alphabet in a frame; there was a radio and a closet for clothes. While it gave the impression of a comfortable home, Jargal's eyes alighted on a few dozen books packed tightly together in a glass-fronted cabinet. Before the car had arrived, Bayar had been sitting, reading some random book, and had not bothered to close the pages.

On the back wall of the room, Bayar had hung a framed photo of his face, taken a few years previously, before he had received that permanent scar. But Jargal looked at the picture, and she couldn't believe her eyes . . . no, had Bayar really been such a man? What a fine-looking young man. Thinking about how such a man could have changed so, Jargal gave an unhappy sigh. Between Bayar today and the Bayar in the photograph nailed upon the wall, she thought, it was like the difference between Heaven and Earth.

Bayar had been really good-looking. Jargal looked for a long time at this picture, in which Bayar was smiling inexplicably; she thought how now he still had those sharp eyes . . . no, it was all too unfortunate. She felt sorry for Bayar, that such a terrible thing should have befallen such a fine man. And even as Bayar and Jargal sat, watching each other, eating dinner across the large, stout table, she felt sorry for him.

After eating, Bayar went into the far room and prepared a bed for her. "You must be tired from your journey, it's already night. Have a good rest."

"Tomorrow, could you take me to the collective center?" she asked.

"Of course," he answered. "I've got work at the center anyway."

"I'm not good with horses. If you have a peaceful ride, could I take it?"

"Don't worry, Doctor! Early tomorrow, we'll hitch a horse to a sled and gallop away amid the swirling snow."

Jargal would be happy to glide along the snow on a sled. Bayar rummaged in his family chest and brought out some things in a bundle, and from these he took a black-speckled wrap, which could have been made from animal hair, and when he placed it across Jargal's legs, the young woman doctor stood up with a scream. Bayar was distressed to have so upset the doctor, and he took and folded away the snow leopard's pelt. Jargal herself was not a little distressed to have screamed and upset the director, and she thought to calm Bayar by talking about why she was fearful of the wrap.

So Dr. Jargal began to talk. She said six years had passed since then. "It was when I went into the human anatomy class at the National University. My mother was not well, and I would go back when I had time to my home region. Around sunset, the car I was in stopped on the far side of the Egiin pass. My driver was quite an old man.

"The driver got out, and once he had said a blessing over the stony road through the Egiin pass, he said, 'I'll tighten up the screws a little in the light. You get out and stretch your legs.' It was the final month of winter, yet although it was cold, the power of winter had softened a little. They were herding the sheep out in the country, and as I went down across the empty wild landscape, I can only say that it was lovely. I moved away from the road and crossed a few rocky hills.

"In the soft breath that heralded the coming months, the lighter my mind became, the more I wanted to go forward, so what could I do? I had left the car far behind, I knew that I had gone quite a long way, so I thought I would go up onto the small dark gravelly hill ahead of me and then go back. But the more I listened, the whiter the snow seemed on the southern hills this side of the pass, and I thought that it was my ears that were rumbling because there were no birds flying about. So as I walked ahead, up the dark, rocky spur, I briskly sang a song, and then there was the sound of a gun firing. 'Oh my!' I shouted, beside myself with fear, but I could see nothing.

"Then from directly in front of me some kind of spotted animal leaped up. It was exactly like that wrap. Again there were two gunshots. I thought I'd turn and run, but in my fear it was like my feet were nailed to the earth, and I couldn't move. The animal fell on the open ground about twenty paces in front of me, but then he leaped again, this time right at my face . . . for the third time, the sound of a gun came from behind my shoulder blade, and before that frightening creature reached me, from nearby a calm and stooped old man, not unlike my late father, appeared and pounced on the animal, and they fell to the ground. I suddenly revived and ran back to where the car was, and as soon as I arrived, the driver, who seemed to have been running out of patience waiting for me, began to grumble. I could barely talk about what had happened, but I asked the driver to go help the other man. The elderly driver was struck by my request, but our car had gotten cold and wouldn't start. It carried on like this for a while, as the evening gloom set in. In that moment of concern, perhaps I pointed in the wrong direction, but when we went the way I indicated, we stumbled about among the rocks and found nothing. It was finally night, and I was concerned that we had lost our way, and when we finally found the road, the driver grew angry and blurted out, "Frightened ears will always hear owls! Wipe your eyes! Get rid of whatever's in them." We traveled in silence for a while, but he knew I was very upset, and started to comfort me.

" 'If someone who's not hungry sees a wild animal, then that person will certainly pass the wild animal by. A hunter won't find himself in trouble before a wild animal. Humans are strong. So if there were three shots, how could the animal still be alive?

"They're not made of iron, right? That animal's certainly been flayed and stripped of its skin by now,' he explained, and we sped toward Ulaanbaatar, traveling both day and night. Yet I wasn't comforted; we talked about it again and again as we traveled, and I cried miserably that I had left that man there, my own victim. Every time he looked at me, the driver coaxed me more gently, and in order to strengthen my heart, he showed me the many medals pinned in ribboned lines on his chest. 'You should know we shot at each other quite a bit for me to get these. I fought twice against a Japanese samurai,' the driver told me, 'and I shot a general dead.' "

All this while, Bayar had uttered not a word. He sat there, simply nodding like a mute. Someone other than Bayar would have cut this young woman off early, he would have said, "That's not my concern." But Bayar would have said, "Look at me, I saved your golden life, I fell victim to the claws of that snow leopard that died without attacking you, the skin on my face was ripped away. I show my face, scarred like a mountain gully worn by the wind and rain. And you, madam, you who were not attacked, when you were put to flight, you cast aside that book you were carrying. Did you mention that? Or did you forget? From that time until now, you've not held on to the idea of meeting that man, yet I could take out the one thing I've held on to, a thick book called *Anatomy*. But then, maybe, there would be your name written on one of the first few pages. But I was confused, I tore out those first few pages and put them on my face to stanch the blood, and so some of them were destroyed, and your book ended up ripped, like my face." And yet Bayar said nothing. His heart was beating forcefully, and he seemed to turn his head.

The young doctor carried on with her story, but although she knew that she had thrown her book away as she went, she didn't mention that. "But now, I am wasting my human life. I have quite a few complaints about how my life is going. I would be ready to give my life for the man whom I left with that wild beast, though sadly he's completely disappeared now." When she spoke, she seemed utterly despondent; these were true words that she was carrying through her life.

Of all that Jargal had recounted, these words seemed to enter Bayar's veins and turn his heart. After Bayar had listened to the young doctor's story for quite a time, he didn't say anything about all this being "a great mystery." He said, "You should go to bed, Doctor. It'll soon be dawn," and left the room.

*　　*　　*

After noon on that brief winter's day, Bayar took the young doctor home, and then he went back, singing the song she had taught him on the way. A few white clouds were gathering in the clear sky, and a single floe of ice floated on the broad river.

He looked at the natural springs, which stood out among the hollows of the mountain landscape, pushing their water out through the ice; they glistened as though the snowy peaks had been brought down and placed there. Bayar was thinking all the while of so many things. Six years earlier, a trap he had set had lured some kind of wild animal; he had thought to follow its tracks; it seemed to have glimpsed the iron eyes of the trap he had set among the rocks. He had followed the tracks, but before he'd realized, he'd been up close with a snow leopard, and, as much in awe as he was full of fear, had hidden among the rocks. Suddenly a young woman had appeared, as though she had come out of the gully near to where Bayar was, and as she'd come close to the snow leopard, she'd been singing something. That she'd been singing right in front of that savage beast seemed to be saying, "I'm here!" Snow leopards are starving in the springtime, and when it saw that young woman, it had made ready to pounce and smash the life within her. . . .

Bayar was thinking how, a few hours before, he had been traveling along that swirling snowy road with that same young woman, and now he was unable to forget this young female doctor. He thought of how, in the morning chill, her cheeks had turned slightly red, how he had pulled the wrap from his pocket again and laughed and said, "You sounded so young when you screamed!"

After he had taken Jargal home, and while the young doctor had briefly slipped out, he had quietly placed that book on her pillow, together with the wrap made from the snow leopard's pelt, but he had not prepared all this. It was as though the book was inscribed with the words "A Great Mystery."

As Bayar rode back home, his mind was full of thoughts, and he urged his horse on, as though suddenly he felt he was going too slowly. He hurried along the snowy road, leaving behind him the twin tracks of the sled, the hills of the New Life collective center awaiting him.

> How fun it was in the sled,
> traveling the snowy road!
> How happy was I,
> to be there with you!

He was singing a verse of a popular song, which had caught in the deepest recesses of his heart, and the faster Bayar urged his mount forward, the more he was hoping that Dejid would be there when he got back home. He suddenly wondered why he was thinking this. It was absurd. "Dejid won't be looking after your place, will she, she'll be with some other man! You know that." The cold winter wind was telling him, "Stop this nonsense," as it whistled against his face.

1956

11

BUNIA TAKES WING

B. RINCHEN

I t was the tenth year of the Manchu Haan, the one Protected by Heaven. The Manchu governor, based in Uliastai, was interested in seeing the monastery at Erdene Zuu, which had been built by Avtai Haan, and during the broad summer season, when the monastery was holding the *tsam* celebrations, he came on a visit.

High-ranking Mongols and commoners came from the neighboring districts to watch the tsam, and the monastery was extremely busy. The Manchu governor saw the many tents pitched here and there; the finely dressed men from the steppes, their faces bronzed, their chests wide; the elegant women with their exquisite faces, how they rode in on horses with neatly trimmed manes, with smart saddles and cruppers; how they galloped together on the wide steppe. He saw that these Mongols, with their horsemanship, their physical prowess, and their strong wills, were a people who loved freedom, whose culture was more ancient than that of the Manchus. He thought that without a certain amount of skill, it was difficult to govern them, and he felt that the policies of the Lord Protected by Heaven, informed by the teachings of the yellow hat sect, exhibited great wisdom. He looked with wonder at the superb crafting of the tsam masks at Erdene Zuu and was delighted at the skill of its artisans.

The Manchu governor, who had participated in the war against the two *aimags* in the west and in the restructuring of their borders, was slight of body but a serious horseman. He slept little and rose early. He went out of the *ger*, which had been erected for him in accordance with an instruction from the abbot, and looked around in the sunshine, breathing air scented with the lovely flowers of the steppe. As he gazed at the roofs of Erdene Zuu's many temples, he saw what appeared to be something moving on the roof of the main temple. It was too big to be a bird, and he was amazed that someone would go out onto the temple roof at the crack of dawn, but indeed it was a man.

He stared, wondering what a man was doing up there; it appeared that he was jumping down from the top of the temple. On his back there looked to be something like a parasol; like a spider, he was flying in a web on this clear autumn day, his parasol carried on the gentle winds of dawn, his arms spread out across the parasol, as he slowly disappeared from sight.

A little while passed and again he saw the man very clearly in the morning air, on top of the monastery's main temple, and again the man jumped. The Manchu governor thought it very strange and waited for him to jump once more from the temple roof, but to no avail. His attendant officer came out and paid his respects. The governor nodded in reply and went into his own ger, thinking that he would come out at the same time the following day and see what there was to see.

And so the next morning, the man again leaped from the temple. Maybe he thought that everyone was asleep. Because there was nobody around for him to disturb, he jumped unseen for a fourth time, and the Manchu governor, who had watched him from a distance, was amazed. Because all the dancers had already returned home, the governor was also returning that

day to Uliastai, and at the farewell ceremony given in his honor
by the governors and the high-ranking monks of Erdene Zuu,
he spoke with wonder to the abbot of what he had seen those
past two days.

The abbot, a plump man given to beating his many students,
listened to what the old and imposing Manchu governor said to
him.

"I'd guess it's these rowdy monks misbehaving," he said.
"I'll look into it, and let you know how I punish whoever it is
who has so ignored his discipline."

Mom's stroking my back, her hands are so gentle, thought Bunia.
He opened his eyes to look, but his whole body was stiff and
there was an unbearable pain in his lower back. He was surprised to find that he was lying in the lonely mountains, laid out
"like a reclining lion," his right arm stretched out, his left arm
underneath him, as was the old custom with dead bodies. But it
wasn't his mother stroking his back with her gentle hands. A
shaggy dog was licking him. When the young monk had
moved, it had come up close to his face and licked him. It had sat
there and wagged its tail, and with blinking eyes it looked at
Bunia as though to say, *Try to get up!*

Bunia recognized the brown stray as a dog to whom every
day he would throw scraps of meat and bone. His whole body
ached as he moved to stand up, his mouth was dry, and he felt so
sick that it seemed his head would break apart. His whole body
felt smashed to bits, and when he opened his eyes again, his
eyelids were swollen like cowberries. He was surprised that the
earth looked as it had before, that it was the place where
the bones of the monks of Erdene Zuu were left. There were a
few clouds in the sky and a fresh breeze was blowing, soothing
the sick young man's body like a fan.

Bunia's mind was unraveling like a tangled mass of ribbon,
and he wondered how and why he had arrived at this graveyard.

Why did the earth and the sky, which he already knew, seem strangely yellow? *How long have I been lying here?* he wondered, and suddenly he recalled everything that had happened to him.

The morning following the governor from Uliastai's departure, the sky had been overcast. Bunia had gone out, carrying his glider up to the top of the main temple of Erdene Zuu, so that he could once again fly down. He fixed the lines under his arms and leaped down, each time steering himself in a different direction. As he landed, he would quickly roll up his glider and run barefoot back up into the temple. One morning, he had caught sight of a small statue of a monk, flying with his upper robe spread out toward the Buddha's abode. And so, following the example of his teacher's old glider, he had stealthily patched together some scraps of cloth that had been used to wrap religious books. At daybreak he leaped from the top of a fence. He made a hole in the center of the glider for the air to pass through, which increased its size. He trained and trained, jumping from ever higher buildings, and when everyone had gone to sleep, he secretly carried out repairs. At daybreak he jumped from the top of the temple as though it were merely a small building. Again and again, without ceasing, he jumped from the high temple; more and more he thought about flying higher and higher. He thought about how his eyes had been opened that morning after the official had left. He felt ever more encouraged to fly, but as he climbed the temple once more, he looked down and saw some of the brawny monastic caretakers lurking on the stairs at the entrance to the temple, looking up at him. *That's done it*, he thought, and extended his arms into the air, like a spider in a web, following the wind. He wished that the wind would cast him over the walls, and he heard the sound of footsteps behind him.

Now they'll get me—help me sky, help me wind, throw me over the walls! and he was grabbed at the legs; someone shouted, "Get him, get him," and he was dragged down, helpless.

"You scoundrel, what are you doing?" A heavily built, pock-marked caretaker had his arms tight around Bunia while some of the others were pulling his glider away, and so they took him before the discipline master.

This is bad, Bunia thought, and his heart raced as the care-takers held him on both sides and forced him toward the discipline master, a monk who went to sleep early and rose early, and who now sat turning a prayer wheel.

"What have you been doing, you wretch? You have made a lot of trouble for the monastery, and your lawless behavior has come to the attention of the governor. You'll be thrashed severely, as a deterrent to the other students." He viciously scolded him and sent his students to inform the abbot about this renegade monk and his lawless conduct. They returned and said that the abbot wanted to see for himself how it was that Bunia flew.

They brought Bunia to the temple from where he had flown, his glider fixed under his arms, and all the community had come together as one, and they had him kneel, fearful, before the abbot. And the abbot said to him,

"Try to fly for us, show us what sort of demon possesses you!"

Bunia's whole body felt terror at being so scolded, and again he climbed onto the temple and fixed the glider under his arms, and because he was so afraid, it seemed as though he was fading in and out of consciousness. As he looked down from the top of the temple, he looked down at the senior monks in their red and yellow robes; they looked to him as small as sparrows, and he nodded when the discipline master indicated to him to jump, and as he jumped he whispered to himself, *Mother, make my glider like the great Garuda's wings, let it carry me seven mountains away.* This Bunia remembered happening.

As the glider spread out, it lifted Bunia and bore him upward, demonstrating how he had flown so many times, and he guided the glider along the path of the gentle winds of dawn. And as he passed over the senior monks, sitting on the green lawns below, their heads were clear to him, brown and bald, like ladles of brass, and they were pointing at him in amazement, and there were vague sounds coming from them, and he came in to land at the base of a wall along which stood many stupas. He looked with fear at the many monks coming toward him. This Bunia remembered happening.

That day, the discipline master addressed the community, lashing out with his staff at a pillar. He spoke about those actions that were incompatible with monastic vows. He had the monk Bunia's glider burned and had him given a hundred lashes on the back, with the caretakers being the ones to begin the punishment. This Bunia remembered happening.

His friends watched, terrified, as he withstood the inevitable pain on his back. *Mother, Mother!* he cried, and as the voice of the caretaker counted the beatings, *ten, eleven . . . fifteen, sixteen . . .* he lost consciousness . . . and now he realized that he was lying in the resting place of the monks of Erdene Zuu. He thought, *They dumped me here because they imagined me dead*, and he raised his head, and it seemed that his back was cut, that the back of his neck was sliced. As he groaned, the shaggy dog stood there, wagging its tail, licking Bunia's chapped lips.

He got up, but the pain pounding in his body was unbearable. Bunia briefly lost consciousness, and again he came to, and it seemed to him that he was completely alone, that the shaggy dog was no longer there. He was crying, the tears coursing from his eyes, and he screamed until his throat was hoarse, until there was only the sound of wheezing. "Mother," he whispered, "Mother!" and he licked his dry lips, and in vain kept opening his dry mouth. His back was beaten and red, it looked as though it had been scorched with iron; the boy's entire body was feverish; his head felt as though it were tied up with iron, and his temples seemed to be beating *thump thump*

thump. It seemed to the child that he was lying in their old tattered ger, close by his mother. It seemed she was telling her son that that year he would become a monk, that she was sad; she was stroking his back, her gentle hands stroking upward from his feet, and his pain subsided, and it was as though his body had become quite light. Bunia imagined that he was floating in the air, suspended beneath his glider; *Mother*, he was whispering, and then, just before he lost consciousness for the final time, there was his dead mother's voice, *My son, come here, where are you?* calling him as though from far away, and he said, *I am here*, his throat wheezing, and he stretched out his legs, his whole body at rest.

In 1928, eighteen years after the establishment of the Mongolian state, I was traveling through the western areas of Mongolia with the German Mongolist Erik Haenisch. At the Geser temple in Uliastai there was a very interesting museum, run by a fellow named Tseren, also called "the Russian," and I presented a wooden seal given to me by the Sudar Library committee. In one of the rooms in Tseren's museum, I noticed with interest the old accounts written by the governors of Uliastai. In the account concerning the eleventh year of the one Protected by Heaven, I discovered information concerning a monk at Erdene Zuu named Bunia, who had flown using a glider. It was sad to read from the Uliastai governor's account how Bunia, this bright little monk at Erdene Zuu, who had through his own effort predated the German Otto Lilienthal's attempts at flying, had been mercilessly beaten to death, and it's a shame to think that talented men such as Bunia were not able in previous times to practice their skill.

It was twenty-nine years ago that I made some brief notes from the account written by the Uliastai governor, held at the museum at the Geser temple, of how Bunia had flown his glider in the eleventh year of the Protector of Heaven, and how he had been beaten to death. I wrote this story during the final month of this summer of 1957. Two years ago, I went with the Czechoslovak scholar Pouha to visit the museum built by the Russian Tseren in Uliastai, but it was no longer there, nor was the Geser temple. The original manuscript of the Uliastai governor's account was not available at the regional archive, which had been renovated during the preceding few years, and this account of the Mongolian aviator was unfortunately not part of the historical record, but I have written this story to remind future readers of this young monk's name. I wrote the basic narrative as though by a serious monastic official; the tone of Bunia's account is very much the language of a young man of about fifteen years; and I treated with gravity the details of his terrible punishment and death. I remember clearly even now what the Russian Tseren told me about the stories the elders had told during his own childhood, but I have long forgotten the fine language of the original account.

1957

12

WAITING FOR WHAT HE HAS LOST

D. NAMDAG

I n the autumn of 1939, one of the army chiefs came into the desert in a green open-topped car to find an old man called Nyamaa. Although he had come on the matter of a young chief who had fought heroically in the Battle of Halhin Gol, he could grant no happiness to the family.

In the place of honor in the *ger*, Jamyang, fifty years old, wide of face, broad-chested, the hair gray on his cheeks, gave a deep sigh. "So then, my mother had three sons," he said, and he clenched his teeth, not a single tear falling from his eyes. He went on, "That year, our middle brother . . . our little brother now . . . ! His country owed him so much, he fought so bravely, but now he has lost his life, what joy, what happiness will we get?" And he could not hold back his tears, and down they poured.

Sitting lower down, her face flushed, barely fitting into her simple blue *deel*, his wife said, "Oh dear. How harsh is this earth!" And she held her head in her hands, tanned by the Gobi's warm, dry air, softened by milk, and she howled.

Meanwhile there was a fleshy little boy dressed only in trousers made from scraps from his mother's deel, his eyes wide in sadness for his mother and father, staring at the brazier as it cast ashes around. Nyamaa, who had celebrated his eightieth birthday, was sitting beyond the child; the old man would surely be in mourning now that his hero had lost his life. But he was hard of hearing, and his eyesight was poor. When the army commander had first come, bringing the sad news, Nyamaa had looked at him as though thinking, *Is this about my youngest son?* But then, as usual, he sat with closed eyes, moving his lips. And so, when he eventually heard the woman's howling voice, he opened his eyes and looked at her.

But he could not tell whether his son's and daughter-in-law's faces were weeping or laughing.

"Oh, my children, what is it, what are you talking about, what's making you laugh so loud?" At this question, the voices were gathered in, and there was silence.

Not long before, while they were talking, the old man had come in from outside. The man and woman whispered together, "Did Dad hear what we were speaking about? Did he have some intuition?" But they were concerned that he might have heard the sad news. This was because, some months earlier, the old man had written, in a letter to his son, "The day of my death has already passed, it won't be today or tomorrow. The troubles of my own life are finished. I'm only waiting for you! The blood throbs in my veins and my soul is suffering in case I close my eyes without meeting you again. Put my mind at peace! There is no refuge for my soul!"

Jamyang spoke of this now, and his wife repeated it, and the army chief, sitting in the place of honor, grew distressed. But whatever piety had been born in the old man's mind, gripped by the fire, he was carefully observing everyone, blinking his red eyes, circled in blue.

"So what are you talking about? Why are you ignoring my question?"

Jamyang was resentful; he stood up weakly and walked about moodily. "Dad," he said, "your youngest son won't be coming back this year."

The old man was shocked. "Why not?" he said, looking up.

"He is a hero, he fought bravely in the Battle of Halhin Gol. He won promotion. So he has a lot of work, he cannot come back this year and has sent this army chief."

"I see," said the old man, and smiled with pride. "No," and his face changed. "So when is he coming?"

"This time next year, he says."

The old man narrowed his eyes as he thought. *One year is a very long time. Will I still be alive?* he wondered. "By the way, what month is it now?"

"It's the fifteenth day of the middle month of autumn," replied Jamyang. It just came to him; it was a lie.

The old man repeated, "The fifteenth day of the middle month of autumn." And then, "Never mind, I'll cope." It was as though his "I see" had been meant to suggest to those nearby that he was considering when to live and when to die. And then, "I'll definitely let you know when I'm going to go to my son."

From that day on, Nyamaa counted each day without fail, and as each day came, he would say proudly, "My youngest son's a hero! And he's been promoted, he became a great army chief. He has no time to come home this year, he's got so much work to do." And every time he said this, his eldest son was saddened and felt pity for him. But there was no chance to take the deception back. And the stronger the old man's faith became, the more his son tried to make it better.

And each time he said loudly into the old man's ears, "Yes, sure, he'll not come back this year, he'll come next year," he would also say, in a low voice, how he regretted what he was doing.

In this way, Nyamaa spread the news among the local people. At this time, while they remembered the fine qualities of this man who had passed away, they were sympathetic to the old man who waited for him, thinking him alive and healthy. But everything gets old and loses its power and vigor. In this way, not only did the people's kind sympathy disappear along the way, but they were talking about him as ridiculous and senile.

But the old man forcefully held on to this empty faith. The more he thought, *It is no simple man who becomes a hero in a great national war,* the more his mind became alert. But he was on his own, and there was nothing left to him but to talk.

And as he talked, he augmented his tale; he mixed it up with the amazing deeds of people in history, in which the heroes of the stories are truly revealed, and his discussions with those who were mocking him and leading him on became all the more bizarre.

The old man's health also did not get any worse. He was happy to rise early in the morning and to go to bed late at night, and to drive the animals to market with a whip and with his voice. And as his mind grew brighter, so his body also improved.

On the one hand, his son and daughter-in-law were pleased with this, but on the other hand, they were constantly concerned lest he found out how he had been tricked.

But in this world, just as there is nothing that does not wear thin, so their concern grew slack and weak.

Who is it who can hold up the constant flow of day and night? While humans and animals followed the same direction of life, the months flowed past and the seasons turned, and all of a sudden it was autumn, and the autumn mists were on their way. During this period, the old man, counting the days, one by one, was waiting for the one who would not come back. Sitting down, standing up, smoking frequently as he churned the *airag* with all his strength, he would act as though he was looking out for something, shading his eyes with his hand upon his forehead. And as he counted the days, he realized that the full moon day of the middle month of autumn was approaching.

At this time, his son and daughter-in-law were already thinking again about how to manage their deceit. One day, Jamyang went out to search for livestock. He said to the old man, "I'm going to town. I'll find out when my brother will be coming back." When he came back, he said, "Now my brother is far away, learning to fly a plane."

"Hey!" shouted the old man happily. He thought that flying a plane was by no means something that a regular person would do, and he was proud that his son was conducting himself so exceptionally.

Jamyang said to him, "Because of this work, my brother won't be able to come back."

"Good grief!" the old man shouted, and almost fainted. When his breathing had returned to normal again, he asked, "So when is he coming?"

Jamyang said, "Next year," and, taking out some scraps of an exercise book, he read from it, telling him, "This is a letter he sent." He read with cunning and skill, as though the old man were a child.

The old man was smiling at each word and when, at the conclusion, he heard, "My darling father, I shall come back on the first day of the first month of autumn. Try to stay fit and well until I come," the old man shouted happily, "Yes, dear!" In fact, this was not the middle month, but the first month, so it appeared that he had a year, not such a long time, to wait.

"Send him a letter back," he said, "saying, *Fine then, your father can wait alive and in good health until then!*"

Although Jamyang was not a thoughtless man, it was because he really could not mention to anyone that he had managed nonchalantly to deceive his own father that the locals began to chatter, both disparagingly and with affection, about the old man. Some of the more meddlesome among them, passing around the vodka and airag, probed inquisitively into the fine, pleasant time of autumn, and the old man was unable to resist revealing the working of his proud mind.

He began with, "My son, the hero, is learning to fly planes," and the more his story compared the mythical Garuda with today's airplanes, the more they mocked him. The old man lived another year in good health. As he counted away, it was straightaway the final month of summer, and just like the previous year, he watched the churning of the airag and the cream thickening in the pot. But there was nobody to whom he might pay special attention. The locals had many interesting things to talk about, and he paid no attention to his son and daughter-in-law, who, as before, were looking after him. Jamyang said something to his wife, and came then and said into the old man's ear,

"Try to keep calm, Father! You know it's not certain that my brother will come back this year."

"What do you mean?" said the old man, staring at his son.

Jamyang said, "Who knows what sort of obstacles a man will meet in his life?" and he wanted to add a few more words.

"Of course he'll come," said the old man, looking away angrily. But the old man could get Jamyang to say nothing more, and he himself uttered not a word. In his mind, he said, *My son will come back, of course he'll come*, but he could barely complain at what his elder son had said: *It's not certain.*

The old man said not one word that day; he gazed down at the earth and sighed. His son and daughter-in-law worried about what they should do. "In any case," they said, "this is one way for him to relax. Whatever we do, let us encourage him now."

The old man decided he would not sleep that night. Early in the morning, he rose and watched the horizon, sitting astride a dilapidated dung basket, inverted and placed to the east of the ger. According to his reckoning, it was the first day of the first month of autumn, and he was convinced that today his son would come, *of course he would come.* His daughter-in-law, who had finished milking the cows, brushed this aside, saying, "Won't you have some tea?" But he decided, *I will take nothing until my son comes.*

His daughter-in-law was upset and she went inside; she said to her husband, "In any case, this is one way for him to relax."

The old man was still sitting. *My son will come,* he thought. *Of course he will come. My son and I will meet very soon. My son and I will meet and embrace, and he will lift me from this dung basket and enter my ger.* Then he prepared what he would say to his son and daughter-in-law when they entered his ger, he would voice his complaints once and for all. The sun rose, its heat scorching, and he thought that his son would come back during the course of the day. The noon passed and the sun declined into the west, and he thought that he would come back during the evening. In his mind, though his son had not come during the morning or during the day, he would certainly come during the evening.

The evening twilight came. Because the old man's vigor was already sapped, instead of gazing out at the horizon, he was just bent with age. But while his son and daughter-in-law could see that he was sulking, *In any case,* they were thinking, *this is one way for him to relax*; they were reluctant to needle him.

Late at night, the old man went into the ger; he fumbled his way in the darkness, got into his bed, and lay down. His faith remained as before: *My son will come. Of course he will come.* He lay there, hard of hearing, listening to the sound of his son and daughter-in-law arguing.

"Dad's really senile. He's been getting senile, what can we do for someone like him now?" So saying, they fell silent and went to sleep.

Suddenly he heard a sound, droning in his ears, and he got up quickly, thinking, *My son has come back.* It was a dream. At daybreak he sat without food; his ears droned. The dream continued; the old man went out of the ger, it was day and not night, and as he watched the great bird whistling, descending through the flecked clouds, his natural state was as it had always been, but his face was clearer; the clothes he wore were shimmering, their colors glowed. At this, the old man was very happy, he had never seen such happiness in his life, and the dream was at an end. He had taken his final breath.

1962

13

THE GREEN-PAINTED CAR

TS. ULAMBAYAR

H and graduated that year from tenth grade with particularly good grades, and had been well prepared to head off
to college. Because she was the only girl in her family, her parents cared for her as if she were a most precious lady; they had
brought her up as the fiery apple of their sharp eyes, and now
she was eighteen. Her father was intent on sending forth a
beauty from his family, while her mother had done everything
she could to produce a well-educated person, lacking nothing
that other people's sons had.

Hand had grown up dressing in fine colors and savoring delicious tastes, and yet she was spoiled, and presented a poor attitude toward customary good behavior. In the evenings, she
wouldn't agree to go out with her parents. If there was a special
reason to go out, she would say she was busy with something
until a certain time. One day, though, she hadn't spoken to anyone, but she was constantly looking at her watch as though she
would in fact be going out; she had done her hair and tied her
ponytail, and dressed in her best clothes. Her parents saw how
she never left the mirror, but neither inquired as to where she

might be going. She tended to talk about this and that. But on this occasion, she had said nothing.

"I'll be back soon," she said quickly, but neither of her parents thought much about it as she hurried out. Now she was eighteen, and they could think of no reason to pester a young woman who could be someone's daughter-in-law and ask her what she was doing.

There was one other person in the world who knew the reason for Hand's speedy departure. He had been one of the neighborhood children and had been in the same class as she right up until the tenth grade. His name was Bold.

Since Bold had completed the tenth grade, he had uttered not one word about his love for Hand, and then, after he had decided to go to a foreign college, he had said to her,

"Hand! At four o'clock on the eighteenth of August, I'll be going to the train station. Would you come at three o'clock to the corner to the eastern side of Building 85? I'll be waiting for you there," and with that, his face had flushed red.

And this was why Hand was right now hurrying there. She had never before had such a meeting, and her soft and tender heart was pounding; she was thinking of what she would say when they met. She'd say, "Please write me lots of letters," but she couldn't think of what else she'd say. It was strange how short of breath she was. But what did that naïve young girl, who had never approached the shoreline of love's warm ocean, understand about the situation in which she found herself?

Hand looked at her watch. It was twenty minutes before their meeting, so she for sure wouldn't be late, and her mind relaxed. She crossed at the intersection on the eastern side of the tall and aging cooperative store, but a green-painted sedan came at high speed and, using the wide street as it wished, left Hand's clothes drenched with the dirty, muddy water from the potholes in the road. People looked at the car and said,

"What a wretch! It's like he's stolen someone's car and now he's on the run."

"Proud drivers are like wild animals when people are watching. Only a bad driver drives too fast."

"What a blind, dumb beast!"

"How can he think of driving a car like that?"

"A car painted green like that can only be a Pobeda or a Warszawa."

"You should really give such rowdy animals a piece of your mind!"

"Didn't you get the license plate?"

"We should stop such class traitors on our roads!"

"Oh no!" There were many who were upset that a woman might have been harmed in this way. And one, a somewhat strange, supercilious type, said, "But this cute little thing!?"

Hand heard his shameless words. She couldn't understand it, he was just standing there, staring like a hare chased by a fox, looking at her now dirtied clothes. *Am I going to go on my first date with the man I love looking like this? No way. That would be a bad omen, what with him going far away for the first time. The most important thing is that, if I go like this, it would seem really bad to him! So what to do? If I go home and change my clothes, I'll be an hour late!* She was so upset, and she ran back toward home, crying pointless tears.

And from behind Bold, who had stopped to watch for his date's arrival along the street, his mother said,

"Why are you waiting so long out in the wind, my boy? It's time for you to go, the car's come, it's waiting for you. Where's that damned driver, who couldn't bring these two loving hearts together? I should go find him."

1962

14

IMAGES FROM A SINGLE DAY

B. BAAST

Last year, as summer gave way to autumn, Sambaa, Mr. Dugar, and myself rode out to an encampment to the north of Delt, and from there to the southern side of Yolt, where we arrived at the milking division. The late morning sun was giving way to the burning heat of noon. The horses we rode were being pestered by flies in the unpleasant heat of the day, and were forever tossing their heads. They moved forward, bucking and snorting, and pretty soon they were drenched. When the heat is so intense, we Mongolians describe the blue sky not as that overly clear blue sky that foreigners are so desperate to write about, but as the dense heat haze of a deep glowing blue that smells of burning. What did we look like, then, as we rode along on our horses under such conditions?

Mr. Dugar was frowning and uneasy, as though he had no business gazing out at the distant horizon and whistling; he rolled up his sleeves, wrapped the skirts of his summer coat around his thick thighs, and went along with his lapels loose and his felt hat bouncing slantwise. When I looked at Mr. Dugar, he kept changing his position in the saddle, like a little ball slapping back and forth between a child's palms, and shifting between wailing and intoning, falling forward when the horse pulled on the reins or else slipping out behind when the horse started.

Mr. Dugar and I looked at Sambaa. He had a thin woven hat perched on his large head; he had pulled up his baggy old canvas trousers and tucked them over his thin groin, put his heels into his iron stirrups, tied up his outer shirt with the saddle tongs, and rolled his undershirt, which stuck to his chest, right up to his armpits, the sweat from his entire body trickling from somewhere like water among rocks. And apart from the fact that his horse was warm and getting tattooed by horseflies and bumblebees, the poor thing was also exhausted by his battle carrying this stout man, whose body was running with a dark and teary sweat. The horse seemed also to be weeping a pale grayish sweat, bitter and salty like urine.

We descended toward an escarpment and followed a ravine, where most of the flowers—peony, henbane, bellflower, delphinium, lily of the valley, globe thistle—were dark and light blue. In the heat of that ravine, where pairs of many-colored butterflies were enjoying themselves, what would be the fate of these many butterflies? And what would happen to the scent of these many-colored flowers close by, and their syrupy nectar? There had been no rain recently; it had begun to be very hot on the path, and when seen from afar, riders on horseback following that ravine must have looked like grain roasting in a heated pot.

Now, on the high point, what we might call a peak, there was a cow standing in the wind, looking toward the northwest, flicking her tail.

"It's not just our elders—the animals too have more experience," said Mr. Dugar. "There are cows out on that peak. Standing downhill from here there are some young ones, and standing opposite us are a miserable two-year-old calf, a three-year-old bull, and a four-year-old cow. They could hardly be suffering from a fever, so presumably the cows out here on this peak must be really happy."

And yet this wasn't the case. The calf and the cow now began to jump about. The horseflies and the bumblebees were having a joke. The cows were all running about, their tails raised, knocking against one another, and one of them headed at top speed up the escarpment, like a crazed beast.

"You see that?" said Mr. Dugar. "That one rushing about is being pushed around by the horseflies and the bumblebees, forced up onto the higher ground. They're most likely saying to him, 'Die! Just die!' "

As we watched, some of those poor cattle reached the high ground, while some of them remained below, confused. Then they trotted downhill, as though more peaceably, and there wandered about.

"Now those pests are dragging one of them away downhill," Mr. Dugar continued. "And they're telling those poor cows, 'We're going to die, so you all should die too!' So thanks to these masters of the mudbound ox, as they call 'em, the cow knows what they're doing. Beasts are really bestial in that sense."

I couldn't stop thinking about that old saw, *A demon's young are smart indeed*, but then one of the calves rushed upward, flashing its tail. It reached the cow up on the peak and circled it like a spindle, and then it trotted back down. Then it was the cow who was rushing around with her tail up.

"That poor cow—which one are those wretches pushing about now?"

"And she's headed this way!"

As we watched, she was coming toward us.

But we were fine. Or rather, we had also attracted lots of horseflies and bumblebees and other bugs to us, so we could barely move. . . .

The cows came together like a whirlwind of dust, and perhaps one had stumbled and fallen, for suddenly brown soil came shooting out. The cow wailed and appeared to fall even as she rose up. Again she wailed as she struggled to rise. A few paltry wails, and then she lay down.

Mr. Dugar said, "Has she broken a leg, or smashed it, or maybe there's some other reason? There's something like a blood clot . . . Something's come out on the ground. And in this heat—what now?"

"There's really something there."

"She's a milch cow . . . if we're not careful, there'll be another orphaned calf." Sambaa and I were talking through our tears.

Even as the young calves moved about the barren, but still lactating, cow like restless demons, she remained unmoving, and so we did what had to be done as best we could and killed her, bloodlessly on the waterless earth. As Mr. Dugar said, with what seemed a great sadness, "This was really a case of 'I'll die, so you die too!'"

We went over to the cow. She had found a mousehole and had gotten one of her hooves stuck.

Perhaps cows have been milked for many years on this lovely hillock. My eyes fell away from looking at this suffering. My heart trembled. A dark brown blood poured out onto the earth from her pierced nose. We might believe that a single milking would yield a hundred liters of milk, yet now the white milk of life trickled from her four pink and distended teats.

"What's going to happen to this poor creature now?" asked Mr. Dugar.

"She'll be poisonous for the horseflies and bumblebees and midges and insects, so they'll not eat her. We should make sure to take her away from the earth! In this heat, it's important to hurry. At the bottom of this gully to the south is where the owner of these cows lives. A single *ger* . . . an old man and woman. This is what we'll do. Go and let them know I sent you to get wood, salty water, and bandages, and bring those things quickly." Sambaa and I agreed, and set off. We had forgotten how hot it was. Who knows how we managed, but before long we had arrived at the encampment.

After the evening had set in, we rode back, carrying the pale red cow, and placed it outside the ger. Now that we were looking at the poor pale red cow, we were content to believe in what the collective leader Mr. Dugar had said.

"She's been poisoned, so she'll not be food for the horseflies and bumblebees and midges and insects. We should make sure to take her away from the earth!"

Oh, it is good to think how true is the wise saying that our laboring livestock herders are like the tent of the blue sky, like the sharp, clear, broad steppe.

When I saw solid dark rainclouds from the northeast covering the night sky above the broad steppe, with thousands of stars glittering like inlaid pearls, it looked as though not only had those wretched horseflies and bumblebees and insects smelled the scent of the wind, rain, flowers, and *airag*, but also they were gathering together, all a-tremble, ahead of the dark mass of clouds.

The following day we headed away, deeper out onto the steppe, toward more encampments and more livestock.

Sergelen, 1964

15

BLUE AS WATER

P. LUVSANTSEREN

O ne fresh morning in the final month of autumn, old Jantsan, wrapped in a thick *deel*, pushed noisily against the
felt door of a small gray *ger*. Blushing like a young man amid the
heat of the food and tea, he came bustling out in a swirl of vapor.
The brown camel, saddled and lying down beside the hitching
post, looked at him as if to say, "Did you trip over the rope?"

Behind Jantsan appeared a long-limbed long-haired hatless
young man, carrying a saddlebag of black leather, blinking and
sneezing against the sun.

"Father," he asked, "did you take the binoculars?"

"No, no I didn't," said Jantsan, irritated, fastening his hat.
He went over to the saddled camel.

The son went past his father and stood, waiting, holding the
camel's leading rein. Jantsan came up beside him.

"So, Chuluun, please don't go wandering about with a gun,
leaving that poor mother of yours all alone. Try to act like a
man! Get her to sew the skirts. . . ."

"So, try to come back quickly then," his son said, and,
intending to help him mount, took him from the left side and
guided him toward the reclining camel.

"No, I'm fine. I can ride by myself. You always think of me as a child. Hold the dogs." And as Jantsan got on and adjusted his saddlebag, the old camel started up.

Jantsan wiped his runny eyes and got the camel walking slowly toward the outline of the mountains, blue to the northeast. The very tips of his and the camel's noses grew cold in the autumn chill and began to run. Jantsan sat with his face turned away from the cold, and walking over the small rough hillocks, at some point in the late morning they came toward the Bosoo plain.

And here, on this plain, in the broad beauty of the summer, the horses and the camels clustered in the pastures alongside one another, the plants and the flowers turning and rolling, and the feathergrass that had faded and withered around the tethering lines swaying and swaying in the gentle wind. A single huge rock stood in the middle of the plain, as though waiting for the broad season of summer.

The camel was an experienced beast, not too young for its rider, who sat calmly upon its back as it stepped out briskly along the sandy track. The rider observed with his beady eyes how the camel's beard was tousled in the wind, and the thought that his breast was absorbing the cool, bright air pleased him.

Now that it was autumn, he was delighted to be on the road again, it was like old times. Having tethered the camels, which had grown fat, the caravaners had prepared their camels' saddle pads, tethers, and leading reins, the pegs, bells, and tents; they had gotten warm clothes together for the wives they so loved, for their younger and older brothers, and for their dear friends, and had given them gifts and letters. Now with the breath of winter's approach they were leaving behind the spacious relaxation of summer, and the livestock and the people were milling around, the young camels bellowing out into the world. The nights were covered in a clear dew, a light hoarfrost, and when the gentle wind of autumn, as though sighing across the yellow steppe, exhausted with all the summer craziness, fluttered calm into the mind at one moment and at another moment lifted the pennants aloft, that was the time that percolated through the minds of the caravaners more than those of other people and dwelled for days in their hearts.

Jantsan had started by following his father, who himself was a caravaner, and had gone on the road at twenty. At that time, the young men all sang the praises of Shuher's daughter, *hulan of the western desert* they called her, and because Jantsan had his heart set on this girl with her pink cheeks and high back, and as soon as he heard, during the final month of summer, that he was joining the caravan, he rode off with a night-black horse from among the herd. And he galloped the horse until, exhausted, they came to the southern branch of a river, and to his beloved. And he returned as the yellow rays of dawn cracked the rocky cliffs of the southern slopes of Bayantsagaan. He didn't go home, but persuaded one of his neighbors, an old woman called Nambaa, to take him in, and he slept until noon, half covered in a light summer robe.

But that morning, his father asked the animals, "Where did my bad little wolf cub go to?" Hearing the news, he took the halter to the old woman's home and, seeing his son lying peacefully in the place of honor, *pfft* he whispered into his mouth, and the young man started. His father threw back the covers, grabbed hold of him, and beat him out the door with the halter, his britches hanging off his buttocks. And when again he brandished the folded halter, beating him with a *thrap thrap* against his buttocks, he also beat Nambaa's rafters, stirring up the dry sooty dust.

"Hey, Mr. Lamjav, what's up?" Nambaa was running about, confused. "Please stop—what's with your poor son?" She managed to hold him back by the belt and angrily threw the ladle she held in her right hand down onto the bed. "For God's sake, why are you in such a foul temper?" And she ran outside, cursing him.

When some young men who enjoyed a scrap, hearing the fight, came inside, Jantsan, who had put on his shoes, could go nowhere and stood there like an accused man before his father. His father sat astride Nambaa's bed, rolled up his sleeves, and moved in to attack. He panted heavily as he berated his son, packing alternate nostrils as he did so with yellow snuff, which little by little dropped down onto his lapels. "Thought you'd get the better of me, did you? They tell me you galloped off by night, and galloped back again, and then went to sleep, hidden like a thief in someone's home. Where did you learn such behavior? Look at my face! It looks like it's been sucked dry! Go off and be a caravaner. Go off and be a burden on the road, you piece of garbage. Put your belt on." And, so saying, Lamjav turned toward the door. "Go away, you lot!" he yelled violently, "this has nothing to do with you." And he chased out all the people who had come inside. Then he said, "So I didn't get the better of you. If you have the chance to screw yourself senseless, then just take it." And he sat there for a while, silent, watching his son with a look of great disgust.

Meanwhile, as he had been told, Jantsan put his belt on quickly. "Get out!" his father yelled, and grasping the halter, he stood up. "Go to that woman today and say you're not coming back! But come back before noon the day after tomorrow. If you don't come back, you'll be sorry." Jantsan felt calm, he did not get out his pipe and tobacco; he watched his father go, and as he watched his father come back through the door, he could only laugh. "Go home, take your saddle and bridle, and be a man. Don't dress like a beggar, don't drag my name through the mud!" And then, reluctantly, his father left.

Roused then in the dawn, Jantsan rose and galloped away, and for two days of abandon, this curvy girl called Dagiimaa keenly pressed her sharp nose and her thick brown fingers against the chest of Jantsan, who was all to her that a man should be; she embraced him to her warm breast, weakened the reins of his loving mind, and in their simple apprehension of first love, they wished that this pleasure might have no end. This time of joy seemed to them like a lifetime, and until the gray night of their deep sleep pulled back the tent flap, she whispered with her warm breath behind the ear of her lover and for two days he experienced the pleasure of a loving woman. They spoke of their future, they were proud of their present, and in their eyes the ember of satisfaction remained ablaze, and their cheeks remained flushed and ruddy.

These two, then, passed the time, melded into a single day of happiness, thanks to his father's kindness. Over a day of shining white, Jantsan had been making love to this delicate girl and for the first time had grasped what people meant when they spoke of loving someone until your heart ached. He had held Dagiimaa in an awkward embrace, smelled her fresh perfume, and, as he looked into her open gaze and slowly kissed her, there was a white goat, its long forelock like a single horn, standing there, sticking out its chest, gazing upward with yellow eyes as though to say, "What are you doing?" "Lecherous old goat!" said Dagiimaa, and she hurled a stone at it, and went bright red.

Whenever Jantsan thought about this event from his youth, he couldn't help but laugh, and the tears covered his eyes. But his father knew his son's mind, and, dressed in goatskin against the winter's night, with the seam of heaven pale and glowing and the innumerable stars blinking, he led his son out onto the sheltered steppe and offered him a letter of advice, in the form of a melodious tune, to salve his mind.

"People, they say, are animals who first came from our ancestors; they struggled for life until the red river dried up. The best people are the caravaners. The caravaner puts up with the fresh winds. He puts up with thirst and hunger. As he moves, little by little, as one of the best people he becomes hardened like a bone; he must have the heart of a man. The stronger the cold wind, the greater the caravaner's warmth; his physical exhaustion is lost beneath his camel's steps, and this is because his mind is awakened by the sound of bells. A man crazy for a young girl cannot be a caravaner. Nor can someone be a caravaner if they can't get energy from the chill winds, or from simple food. Only a man free from chronic illness, with a good body, who is honest and upright, who is not a slacker, whose intention is to be helpful, who has sharp eyes like a fox, who has a keen nose like a wolf, whose ears are fine-tuned, only such a man can be a caravaner. In the end, the caravaner will become ill on the road and will recover by licking the earth in the place where he finds himself. The happiness of men is said to be the wilderness. Many years spent as part of a caravan, growing accustomed to the wild winds, stops the mind from messing around in the corner of a ger. Someone who is weak of will and incapable can never be a caravaner." And this was what the father taught his son.

But how could someone so easily forget the suffering of the mind? Jantsan listened to what his father said, and as he swayed back and forth as though hinged at the pacing of the camel, his heart, which felt that it had always known Dagiimaa, was distressed.

"Bring me silk, blue as water, and sesame candy," she had said, smiling, gently gazing up at him, as he left her there. He continued to think of Dagiimaa's bright eyes, and whenever he looked upon a river or the deep blue sky, it was as though he heard in his ears the voice of the woman he had left behind, speaking of silk, blue as water.

But these two were not destined to enjoy a life together under one roof. When Jantsan came back, bringing with him a piece of blue silk whose color did in fact look something like the color of water, having unfailingly kept it wrapped up in his belt and having daily wished for happiness, they had already dispatched Dagiimaa to adorn another family. Time and time again, this is how it was. The lamas had told her family that his family was not acceptable, so what could they do? Those who have experienced the pain of parting from their life's beloved companion are those driven apart by the storms of time, which have washed their wounded young hearts.

After Dagiimaa had gone, Jantsan was for many years a caravaner on his father's route; he established a new ger, he took a wife in the dawn light, had two sons and one short-lived daughter; he was successful at everything he did, and he ended up in padded drainpipe trousers, herding the sheep from the back of a gentle horse, and he grew to be a wrinkled old man. But his mind remained as sharp as ever and he wore away the land, thinking about the silk, blue as water. And he grew old, thinking about such things as he journeyed, about the fluttering wild winds, the lakes and waters of his people's homeland, the high skies dotted with stars, the powerful fire that builds up strength against the cold wind, the sweet songs that dwell in the ears for days, the coarse black tea, the skins, and the cloth tents; and as he thought about all of this, he grew sad. And when the autumn freshness fell and set the caravans in motion, everything seemed to be without meaning. No one knew that the little old man's strength was growing weaker every day, that he felt such distress in the corner of his ger.

Jantsan had decided, then, that before his strength was quite finished, he would at least see the caravan move off.

The camel, slow and serviceable, stepped out quickly and peacefully, lulling the familiar and skinny old man on his back. From time to time, he stretched his neck down to the side of the road and nibbled at the shrubs and so, in the white light of evening, the local town hove into view.

Jantsan went straight to the entrance of the caravaners' cloth tent, where there was a fire glowing. Inside the tent, he heard the sound of people talking and laughing.

Jantsan took off his saddle skirt; he rubbed his eyes, cleared his throat, and entered the tent. There were four men sitting there, their faces ruddy and warmed by the open fire.

Jantsan greeted them all and, going to the visitors' seat, sat down cross-legged and warmed himself as he listened with interest to what was being said.

"Are you on your own?" asked one of the caravaners.

"There's a couple of us," Jantsan replied. "Me and that poor brown camel of mine."

"Oh, so you still have your sense of humor."

"Well, I'm not dead yet," said Jantsan in reply. In his mind he was really quite content.

They passed the food around. Here and there, smoke plumed up, the perfume of fatty meat wafted about, and knives gleamed, with short blades and long. A white-chested black dog squatted, watching at the tent door, now and then opening its mouth wide. The caravaners sat eating and talking.

"When are you going back?" asked fat Lhagva, whom Jantsan knew well. And Jantsan asked in return,

"Did the eastern crew go already?"

"Not yet."

"I'll only go back when they've all gone."

"How so?"

"I might live to see the caravan next year, or I might not. I should keep my mind alert. Can't mess around at home."

"No reason to spend so many years as part of a caravan. You've been on the road for many years since you were a child, but our mind also moves when we go to the monastery at Zag and back; it's quite close from here."

"You say I've been on the road," Jantsan began, "but if you think about it, that's what a man does. It's tough work, but it's good. I was about twenty when I first joined a caravan. I wanted to try it. If I hadn't tried I could hardly have become an experienced caravaner. One night, they said to me, 'So, Jantsan, bite this.' I was amazed. 'What do you mean?' I said. 'Here,' they said, 'bite it,' and they had me bite down on a long white piece of feathergrass. Mr. Bayar explained about the long piece of feathergrass. 'Now you'll go up that mean old mountain pass. Everyone chews feathergrass as they go along, and recites the White Tara mantra.' I thought that I should do as he said and bite that piece of feathergrass. Then I thought the old sod was making fun of me. So as I bit down on the feathergrass—he didn't realize this—my lips froze. Then Mr. Bayar was really a sad clown."

The caravaners sat there, listening to Jantsan, getting to know him, stoking the fire. Sometimes Jantsan would speak as though he were making it all up. But it was undoubtedly even better than the truth, and they sat and listened, laughing until they were blue in the face.

"There was a miserable fellow called Naidan, he ended up in a really bad way, yet when he was young he was a real caravaner. He was a smart, lucky wolf, hardly felt the cold. When it was bitterly cold in the depths of winter, he would pull his hat down under his chin. His beard would be covered in frost, and his nose, hooked like an eagle, would rumble. He was known for his singing. He loved to sing. But he just rumbled away, wordlessly, tunelessly. He said that he loved his way of rumbling. One year, I went with this man Naidan, little-ears Natsag, who was in charge of guarding the salt, he died last year, and a relative of mine named Toiv. Oh my God! Little-ears Natsag had such bad luck! We didn't even start to prepare a decent meal on our journey. He started by putting some roasted flour in a bag. When he went to sleep at night, the flour trickled down from the bag into his nose, and he snored until he buzzed. Naidan, though, was an angry beast; he yelled, 'Take off his trousers and pour the hot water on him.' When Natsag went to sleep one night, we really did take off his trousers. But, oh dear, the poor guy had been bagged, but he didn't get it. He noticed someone standing there, holding a ladle of hot tea; he started up, grabbed a bowl, and held it out. He was perplexed that we were laughing. What was wrong with grabbing his bowl? He covered it with his hand. Why had he jumped up so quickly? We were joking, laughing a little, we pushed him, 'Lick your bowl,' we said, and he said, 'It's no problem—it's mine,' and he licked the bowl and slept. Now, that dog was also pretty damn crafty in his life. One day, the two of us were riding along, one behind the other. It was quite a warm day. Natsag was in front of me, leading the way. And as he went along, he fell from his camel. And as I went along, I couldn't see what had happened. I watched him, got off the camel, it was like he was hiding something. 'Are you messing around?' I asked, but he said nothing. He stood up, his eyes strangely wide. I was waiting for what he might say, but he looked at me and said, 'I just fell as I got off the camel,' and he shook the dust from his clothes. It's a pity, he had so much life experience. When he went to bed at night, he made a point of sleeping among us. If he got cold at night— not a good thing to do, this—he would take someone else's covers to cover himself. When he woke in the morning, he might put on someone else's shoes. There are many stories about Natsag's eccentricities. Whatever you say, though, he was never unpleasant to people. Now, caravaning is basically a mindful occupation. An optimistic man will never have trouble in a caravan. I was a man just like all of you." Jantsan spoke and ate until he was full, and then they sat around the fire and chatted until it was time to sleep.

Finally the caravaners said, "We should stop talking and sleep. We're moving off early in the morning." They arranged their beds a little and lay down. The night seemed to be getting very cold. Jantsan moved in among the covers, and with a groan and a cough, he began to snore.

Lying amid the folds, he looked as small as a child. During the night, with its dry, fine snow and overcast sky, a storm raged and fluttered the edges of the cloth tent until dawn. And when morning came, the storm had abated.

Jantsan woke up and, seeing the white light of dawn, he stoked the fire in the tent. In the heat of the fire, in the smoke from the dung, the caravaners were sleeping soundly. Jantsan went outside and waited for them to wake up, and sat for a while stoking the fire, and he boiled tea.

As he walked in the cool wind of the morning, he took a keen interest in the caravaners' camels. He looked closely at some of their eyes. He checked down between their back legs. And then when the caravaners woke up, Jantsan went among the loads that had been prepared. He looked through all the packs and tried to lift one of the bundles. He walked around energetically and came back to the tent. The sun had risen, and the caravaners were finishing their breakfast and packing up.

"So, Dügersüren," said Jantsan, "look smart, come and get the documents. I'll load up with Lhagva."

"What do you think you're doing, lifting a heavy pack?" said Dügersüren, but Jantsan ignored him and walked away. He brought the lead camel and got it to lie down.

Lhagva went to one side of the camel and loaded the pack. While he watched Jantsan, wondering what he was doing, he spent some time in the gentle wind securing the pack, pegging the camel's lower lip, while Jantsan loaded his half of the camel's pack. Lhagva quickly balanced the packs on either side and they moved on the next camel. And Jantsan did not get tired, but loaded up another camel. But as he loaded the third camel, he couldn't manage to lift the pack and kicked it with his pointed shoe. He couldn't move it with his foot. Several times he tried, but he couldn't do it; he was panting and his face grew red as a shamed child's. He put the pack where it had been, leaning one corner against the camel, and without looking at Lhagva, he replaced his hat and went off. Lhagva watched as he went and sat by the pitchers, looking out. His head hung down, he gazed at the earth and waited, unmoving. Meanwhile the caravaners were talking among themselves.

"Mr. Jantsan got really old."

"He should be lying down at home. He's like a child, doesn't know his limits."

"Is he okay now?"

"Sure he is. Right, let's load up."

When the caravaners had almost finished packing, Jantsan said, "Which camel should I put this on?" and he brought the tent.

The caravaners gently mocked him. "He's tired, but he still managed to bring the tent." They said, "Bring it here." Jantsan brought them the tent; he was thinking, *These men are better prepared than I*, and he hurried to bring the covers, mattresses, and cooking pots, before anyone else brought them. And finally he loaded his camel with a saddlebag that held his belongings and set off at the front. He appeared extremely keen to take the lead. He led them from the main encampment of the *sum* until they reached the mountain pass at Shar; he stepped out like a true caravaner.

They came out onto a mountain pass, and he got down from his camel and took the saddlebag that held his belongings. Inside the saddlebag, in the case for carrying a Buddha statue, he kept a single metal bell. With a blue offering scarf he tied this bell of his around the neck of the very last camel in the caravan. "Travel safely, now!" he prayed. "Be lucky on the golden road!"

The caravaners moved off, and he remained alone on the pass. The column of the caravan straightened out upon the distant road, and the large echoing bells beat back and forth in the pacing of the camels.

They looked around at Jantsan. He watched after them, and stayed on the mountain pass until the sound of the bells became disjointed. The column of the caravan grew ever smaller, the sound of the bells grew faint and died away, and all around was an awful silence.

Jantsan stayed behind; his big black eyes were watching the caravaners, his eyelashes were damp, and he looked into the eyes of his brown camel and then toward the horizon, blue as water, and he called to mind the ancient and the eternal, and he grew silent and sad.

With a long sigh he stood and looked back, watching with sharp eyes as though he expected to hear an answer from the infinite, deep blue skies. The mountains, which yesterday were brown, had emerged this evening wearing hats of snow.

1966

16

HE CAME WITH A SPARE HORSE

S. UDVAL

On the first morning of the lunar new year, I woke my mother and we went outside. The sun rose over Han Uul, offering it a crown of gold, glistening like a ruby through the weave of branches in the willow trees along the river, and a few small birds came to chatter away on the roof ring.

We washed our hands in the lake of melted snow in the livestock enclosure and went back inside. "Get dressed quick," said Mother. While I washed, I was thinking about Ariunaa, and I wondered whether or not my older sister's husband would be bringing the gray horse.

I grabbed the offering scarf, thinking to offer my mother new year's greetings, and brought out the candies she liked, hidden away in an attractive glass, and my mother kissed me and tears came to her eyes.

I wasn't one to give my mother much to be happy about. She was the peaceful world that propped up my life. Once a year I made her happy, by presenting her with an offering scarf. We drank our tea and put some before the picture of my father, and Mother threw some fat on the fire and brought milk for the ritual sprinkling. Then we went off around the encampment, bearing tea and food. All the while I was thinking about Ari-unaa; I barely registered what people were saying, but when I was coming in I heard what sounded like my brother-in-law arriving. The locals were also coming by with food and tea. Their pastries had a good color and shape. At our place, my slipshod ones were wrinkled and twisted. But they were not as limp as old Süh's. I had intended to take out the flour that morning and have them done by midday, but I kneaded the dough half-heartedly, and gave a few to Mother before heading out into the encampment. What was the point, though, since only I would be eating them? Two families will each do their own thing, that's what they say.

My elder sister's husband was called Bürengerel. I was Dogisüren, the head of this *ger* that had remained in the family, a man big of heart and small of stature. When my brother-in-law sat at the rear of the ger, he seemed to fill it. He was a dreadful man; he controlled the lives of several families. With so many brothers and sisters, though, perhaps their tribe needed someone to tell them what to do.

I took a pot and ladle to Mother and went outside, and I saw my brother-in-law had come with a spare horse. I kissed him in greeting. It felt insipid. I'm hot-tempered: I'll kiss someone, but I'll also land a punch on them if they give me cause. But I could barely throw up my hands in frustration at my brother-in-law. But enough of that . . . He got my guileless elder sister. She's a thick-set woman, with creased eyelids like she's constantly laughing. He takes care of her, says he's "fattening her up"; she's always sticking her fingers into the yogurt and clotted cream and butter and licking them. And these she adds to the pot, and takes a bite. The food still tastes the same. She strips the fat from a sheepskin. Even from a marmot, once she's skinned it.

There have been times when I've needed to speak boldly to my elder sister's husband. For instance:

"Could you bring me a gray horse from the collective's herd for the lunar new year? It would mean a lot."

"Of course!" He came over and lectured me. "But you should never ask anyone for something—it's like a beggar going through the bones. Before you ask someone, you should think wisely: 'I should stop relying on people. If I do ten *tögrögs*' worth of work, I should save two.' " I waited quietly, but inside I was fighting him. I threw up my hands when he pushed Ariunaa around too, but I never opened my mouth. *Fine, I won't walk away, I'll just sit quietly. If I save two* tögrögs, *how can I not spend them on seeds to plant? No, even if I buy potatoes and onions and plant them, I'll only be able to grow a couple.* I let it go.

I saddled up my own gray horse and went off, leading the other gray, and my friend Sharavhüü—I called him Blossom— came alongside on a motorcycle. "Where are you going?" I asked, and he said, "I went to see Amaa's family, and now I'm off to Buuraijaa's." And then, "I'll be seeing Ariunaa! She says she's going to the *aimag* center." Inside me, thoughts were swirling about, that I should say something to Ariunaa or extract a promise from her.

I didn't think it was a big deal to go see these two local old-timers. I'm a good sort.

I took some cardboard from around the ger, put it inside my coat, and quickly galloped off. I stopped at the signpost for the road leading to the Brigade HQ, wrote an announcement on the cardboard in old Mongolian script, and lodged it there with a broken branch. As I went quickly to the other side of the hill, I seemed to hear behind me the sound of a motorcycle, juddering to a halt beside the signpost. Soon it headed off toward the Brigade HQ. I went back and looked from the north, and saw the brigade chief's gray IZH motorcycle and green *deel* disappear around the skirt of the hill. Troublemaker. He had taken my announcement and thrown it away. Again there was the sound of a motorcycle. This time it was Sharavhüü, and I quickly hid.

He seemed to have stopped beside the signpost. I came out but didn't dismount. The other man had come out from behind the hill. If I hadn't come out ahead of Sharavhüü, I could have been riding pillion with him, off to greet Buuraijaa with Ariunaa. When Amaa came out, Sharavhüü had already arrived. It would definitely have been faster to come on the motorcycle. He and Ariunaa came outside. She pushed Sharavhüü so that he almost fell. Sharavhüü said,

"Did you see the announcement left on the road?

"You mean the cardboard on the signpost?" I said, nonchalantly.

"Yes, what did it say? 'They're selling blockades and yellow sick in the previous plaice at the Brigade HQ, and boobs and Tobago in the western plaice.' There's no way someone could be selling such things—who are they trying to fool?"

I looked at Ariunaa, and my face was saying, "Right, well . . ." because it should have said 'brocade and yellow silk in the previous place, and booze and tobacco in the western place,' and I looked at the dimples in her cheeks (I really liked looking at those dimples), and that sweet goddess of mine looked at us both and laughed.

"Thank you, Sharavhüü. You should go. I'm going to ride with Dogisüren." She went into the ger. I started to mouth "I won" to Sharavhüü, but stopped short. I wasn't a kid.

Today, with its clear light and its prayers for good meetings, was a really good day. I greeted Ariunaa's mother. When I greeted Ariunaa, she whispered, "You wouldn't take advantage of Sharavhüü just to stick your beak in, would you?" and I felt shamefaced when I said, and loudly, "Not at all!"

We said we'd go and greet Buuraijaa, and the old lady said, "Fine, fine, but come back early." When I had gone to Buuraijaa's place in autumn, she had looked at my trousers and said,

"Wow, is this blue-gray stuff some kind of tarpaulin? Where did you get them? This is what children wear."

"No, no. These are stylish trousers, they're called jeans, they cost the price of three horses. They're really a horseman's trousers. Horsemen in Mexico have begun to wear trousers like these, and I wanted to try them for myself. Now I'm thinking to get hold of a wide oval hat and wear it low down on my forehead."

Buuraijaa continued, "In the old days, the nobles used to have precious stones called *jins* on the top of their hats, and nowadays this is the name of the trousers with labels that you all are covering your behinds with. You children are certainly the nobles of today!" She was really a spiteful old hag!

Out on the road I helped Ariunaa from her horse and held her, and kissed the dimples on her cheeks. The horse didn't shy. I made to tie the reins back behind the saddlebow. That horse was a smart one. We looked good with these similar horses, gray like the color of birds. "If we gave a couple of horses to the collective," I said to Ariunaa with a chuckle, "we could take these ones."

"That would be a bad deal. But we know how good they are."

"Are they not as good as other horses like them?"

"They'd be horses of different colors."

"It's easy to adjust to a horse's color. But you should like its character. Now, why don't you talk with my brother-in-law?"

"Tell him everything?"

"Yes. Ask your mother as well as Mr. Bürengerel. He's forgotten that you're home from the army."

As we went along, talking about things, and sizzling with the electricity of love, a dark shape rose up at the side of the road. That damned Sharavhüü stopped his juddering machine, set it on the center stand, and stood in front of it. He got my girlfriend riding pillion. "Six thousand," he said. "That's the price of how many horses? And it's fast. To feed a fine horse, it's about the same as spare parts and benzine. It doesn't get stuck in the mud. It doesn't stumble in the snow."

But no way was it better than my gray, who was the color of birds. In any case, when we came that night to Ariunaa's, we didn't wake her mother up.

Late 1960s

17

SUNCRANES

S. ERDENE

I am sitting beside a dried-up well, near the ruins of a monastery, and I am bidding farewell to the sun on this summer evening. In the fifteen or so years of my life some amazing things have taken place. There was a monastery. And then the monastery no longer existed. Although I don't precisely understand the situation, I don't let it bother me. When I was young, I would climb the blue steps, hanging on to my mother's hand. When the monastery appeared, many monks came together; there were the sounds of flutes and trumpets, the scent of incense and camphor; the buddhas glimmered in the candlelight, the wrathful deities with their protruding fangs and the peaceful deities free from wickedness. I would bow to the buddhas when I was told to. All these places are gone, as though fallen away, and only the stone ruins of the temple remain. Goosefoot grows amid this rectangle of stone. I don't let it bother me. Extinction is a part of life, and thus there is extinction. Even the well is dry. I think how they said that my father was the one who dug this well. Even my father is gone. The temple is no more; neither is my father, nor many other things, and all that was before is now made new. There was a war then, years when able-bodied and reliable men from my homeland were called up to the army. My brother went too. Nobody knew whether he would return. They said that men were being killed on the battlefield.

I am also going tomorrow. Going to the provincial school is not like going to war, of course, but who knows what will happen in this world where everything from the past, even humans, vanishes?

I was thinking about this, throwing gravel into the well; it fell to the bottom with a crash. I sat there until the sun set, as a farewell to the sun of my homeland. It was the evening milking time. The smoke that warmed the families' cattle enclosures lay leisurely upon the green, green steppes of August. Close by the spring, by that tree from my life before, there was a scattering of magnificent red cranes. They seemed to have been turned red by the evening sun; the chicks were running around, extending their wings as though trying them out. Although I realized that these cranes had come in from far away, in my heart I was happy with what I imagined to be the cranes of my own homeland. The fresh green trees before me turned roseate in the light of the setting sun. I knew these young trees, which had grown up with me, I knew them utterly. That solitary old larch at the source of the spring had grown old and bent. It was natural that the old trees died and the new trees grew.

When I was young, after the rains, I would run to the edge of the woods to catch hold of the rainbow, and these young trees were not then blocking the path. So these infant trees had grown up with me.

The cattle were hanging around the monastery, tossing their heads in the smoke; through many summers they had been filing out into the pastures. From time to time, a large red bull from Baruun Hot would send the cows scattering, bellowing as if to say, *Is there any bull to challenge me?* The terrace of summer pastures, covered with wormwood and violet, seemed fresh with grasses. The children were making a commotion as they separated the sheep, and out to the east of the encampment, a drunken man on a white horse was yelling and waving his red woolen mantle. It was the monk Tehiin Palhai. What sort of man got called Teh, like a wild goat? And what was with Palhai, or Smasher, the name we called him? It was as though he had gotten the name in his youth to show what a beast he was. Palhai was one of the few men who had remained in our area; he drank *arhi* all the time, to the annoyance of wives and children. One of his hands was crippled, which was apparently why the army had rejected him. These red cranes had flown as though carried by Palhai's yelling, and after wheeling around above the mists, they dropped down again by the spring around the solitary tree.

The sun was setting. Tomorrow I would be far away; I would not be sitting at the edge of this spring or on the railings of the cattle pen, nor watching the sunset over my homeland. This red bull would keep scattering the earth, and I would be far away from the cattle as they bellowed in their youthful silver voices to prevent the daredevils from butting one another. I smiled to think of Palhai locking horns with this bull, smashing his skull open.

Outside the house of our neighbor Mr. Sangid, they had finished milking the cows and had come together to talk in sweet and ringing tones. Their voices fell gently amid the evening's freshness; it was as though the meadows were traversed by a thousand gleaming rays of the setting sun.

As I look out, the sky seems oh, so far away,
and the rains are coming fast.
As I think about it, the world seems oh, so far away,
and life is coming fast . . .

They think about their husbands, gone off to the army; their song is sad and full of melancholy. Now I am old enough to understand that people love and miss each other. Thinking of these things, I almost cried.

The nightingale on the River Ganges
comes out and sings . . .

Where is this river, the Ganges, which my mother says is in the Buddha's land? Do these cranes come from there? How broad is this world, with its birth and death! The time is coming when I will reach this river called the Ganges. "People are born upon this earth, which is not eternal," my father told me. "May they have direction and wisdom." If we have direction and wisdom, then may we reach the River Ganges, not just the regional school.

The sun set as the women's voices sounded, and the red cranes became regular blue cranes. Farewell, sun of my homeland! As though the cranes had been waiting for the sun to set, they flew now toward the distance, into the low-lying bank of blue mist. Farewell, my cranes! Tomorrow I will be far away from you. . . .

The night was warm with stars. My mother sent me away with some offering scarves in my pocket. She said, "Go and visit the elders, tell them to take care while you are away." I believe that people far away hear the prayers of the elders, and so they are fortunate on their journey. One thing was better for me than hearing a prayer. You could say she was my girlfriend. While I waited for her under the solitary tree at the spring, my heart throbbed, *toktoktok*. Why did my heart pound so for this girl alone? It seemed that perhaps in this world there were animals listening for a sound under such a warm starry sky as this. On the wild steppe, the horses neighed, the frogs croaked, and the dogs barked and barked. And it was as if the horses wanted to call out to other horses, the frogs to other frogs, and the dogs to other dogs. The one for whom I waited seemed to be moving barefoot through the air, soundlessly stepping, taking vague shape in the starlight.

She sat close by and said, "I had to wait for the yogurt to finish boiling. Have you been waiting long?" Until recently, while we were playing secretly in the eaves of the building or among the goosefoot and wormwood on the lonely summer pasture, let alone in our playing now, we had not been fearful of coming close to each other. We had desired each other in secret. We heard each other breathing, we sat silently. There was no noise except that of a horse, hobbled nearby, chewing at the grass. The girl gave off the scent of boiled *airag*; she wore a short gown, made from material in which curds had dried. But I wore a new cotton *deel* from the store, and leather shoes, and in the darkness I was eager to show her the new clothes I was wearing. The leather shoes had been something I especially wanted. My mother had gotten these oversize leather boots in exchange for a single head of livestock.

"Sampil's father, Baatar's mom, and everybody gave me money. My mother said she would give me half the money she makes from her wool. I'll send you leather from the *aimag*."

"The local shop has some really great stuff," the girl said hopefully.

Our voices have changed too. Mother said that I should have a voice as deep as a man's. The girl produced a sharp, loud sound over her normal voice, and now there was a sweet voice in her chest. In the darkness, I felt the sad and gentle glance of her eyes. I would go away to the provincial school while she would stay behind boiling yogurt. I grew lovesick for her. She walked barefoot, her feet dirty from cow dung, in her short gown of material in which curds had dried and, kneeling down, I turned to her with staring, tearful eyes.

A child's relationship shatters simple purity, and inevitably this one time shows life's experience of sadness in the world, but I never thought that the day of such a parting would arrive. Love, though, is not only in thoughts, it is corporeal too. A line of silver dust traced the seam of the sky and a thousand thousand stars glimmered in the summer night. Such is the sadness and joy of life. I swallowed my bitter, silent tears, my distress at the sudden flight of childhood, and inside I felt a little more at ease.

"I'll finish at the local school and I'll go to the military academy," I said. "I'll become head of the regiment and go off with you. By that point, I'll only have known the pleasures of summer."

"I will be waiting for you. My brother has become a caravaner. If he goes to the local town, maybe I'll go with him. Please write me really long letters."

"Sure."

"Your mother must be getting worried now."

"My mom says I am becoming a man, as my voice has gotten deeper."

She sighed and gently took my hand.

"A lock of my hair," she said. "Remember, you cut my hair to make me a *komsomol?*" Indeed I had cut her hair when I was a naughty little boy to make her a *komsomol*, like the women at the time with trimmed hair. Who would think that this bunch of hair, smelling of childhood, was so precious, like a wish-fulfilling jewel?

The girl knew it in herself. Life is like a story, and it is not like a story. It is an absolute truth that the story is as it always was. A lifetime passes through the story of life. We were both feeling it; we lay down and gazed up at the sky. If only this story, with its simple wisdom, would come again! In this sad moment of separation, I asked Heaven to whisper me a story. And Heaven told me its story. A flock of cranes were flying along the line of silver dust tracing the seam of the sky. It was like I was saying to myself, *May these suncranes fly far away, with the light of the sun of my homeland.*

"Suncranes! Look at the suncranes!"

Life is not a story. What I have inherited from my dear young friend are baby curls scented with childhood. To what land have those suncranes gone, taking with them the light of the sun of my homeland, and the final simple story? I shall think to myself, *I shall fly far, far away.*

1971

18

THE CRICKET

S. DASHDOOROV

H e was so very happy. Yes, he was happy, and in his happiness, he was so happy that his feet could barely touch the
ground. He'd gone straight to the ministry. This capable fellow,
Jamiyanbuu, from the factory under the auspices of the ministry, was attempting to find out whether they did in fact need an
accounting strategist. Should the opportunity arise, he had it in
mind to meet with the director of the finance division and have
a brief talk with him. But he didn't get the chance, because on
the stairs he came face to face with the minister, and the minister came forward, thrusting his hand forward.

"How is work going?" he asked. "And is your family well?"
Jamiyanbuu had never dreamed that such a thing might happen. His agitated state had made him flustered, like an oversized lamb, and he grasped the minister's hand and shook it,
declaring,

"It's good, minister, my family's good." As he watched Jamiyanbuu chatting away intimately with the minister, an adviser
from the technical division, a sallow young man with an idle
gaze, came to a sudden conclusion. He figured that one of the
accountants in the finance division had produced some figures, 153

and so wasn't Jamiyanbuu then coming to see him, and with this in mind, and feeling that he had to greet him warmly, the young man waited until the two men separated, and stood about in the corridor.

When the minister and Jamiyanbuu parted, each had confidence in his own perspective on the appearance of their strange bowing ritual. The adviser rushed over to where Jamiyanbuu was standing, preoccupied and happy, oblivious to the minister's having disappeared into his office. The adviser's false smile, always prepared for action, spread across his face, and the dry glint in his green eyes glimmered beneath swollen lids.

"Well then . . . Mr. Jamiyanbuu, how are you?" and with his sweaty hand he grasped the other man's hand hard, and with an intensity that amazed Jamiyanbuu, who gazed at his puffy eyelids.

"Ah, you're the journalist!" he went on. "I read a piece of yours . . . you write well. You observe carefully, and you're revealing some significant problems too . . . your ideas are clear. You keep to a high standard, right?" Jamiyanbuu's little heart was beating hard; he wondered if something similar might have happened many times previously. He said, with an air of self-satisfaction,

"I have . . . sufficient time for leisure. . . . I have much to do. Book-keeping, inspection . . . this and that," and he was thinking, *You know, of course, I'm being promoted.*

And then, ingratiatingly, explaining the need to absent himself, "But yes . . . sure, all of us have a lot of work." It wasn't that Jamiyanbuu had ignored what the other fellow had been saying, rather that he had plunged into the waves of his own happiness. The adviser, his words utterly forgotten by Jamiyanbuu, headed to his work like a man happy to have a special task to accomplish. In addition to imagining that his coming to the ministry had been noted by many people,

Jamiyanbuu had criticized the lack of care shown by the workers of one particular district in tending the lawns and trees that had been sown and planted by the springtime Saturday workers in the city's newspaper, and he felt the minister and those responsible in the ministry must have seen his piece that had been published about how it was every citizen's duty to care for the lawns and vegetation. That young advisor's words— "you're raising some important issues"—rang in his ears, the minister's kindly face appeared over and over in his mind; he was so excited, he couldn't sit comfortably. He was showing off to his co-workers. He grabbed the phone and called his wife.

"Ah, is that you? Oh, nothing in particular. I went to the ministry, met with the minister . . . he asked after you. You know, he even asked about the kids' schoolwork. That's how he is. He asks something every time we meet. Sometimes it's *Can he help?*, sometimes it's *What do I need?* But today that's what he asked."

As he talked, he was thinking whether the people he was working with had taken note of his mentioning the children, he was thinking, *Please look at them, not at that little fellow Jamiyanbuu, who's been checking up on everything.* And then he called one of his close friends.

"That fellow's a strange one . . . I met with him today . . . we chatted a while. I told him my complaints, about all the work I've got. When we met he told me everything all at once, dammit! You should have seen it. My piece in the newspaper . . . there's a lot of commotion about it at the ministry. He says some people are saying I've brought up a lot of important problems. Still others are saying that I'm keeping up the standards. That fellow? He's got some ideas . . . This work . . . well, I don't have enough time. There's a lot I'd like to get involved in. . . ."

And with the self-satisfaction of a man who had completed his task, he took a break from turning the pages of documentation and accounts in the small ledger.

"Perhaps the head accountant's in? Let me see . . ." and again he grabbed the telephone. As soon as the head accountant picked up the receiver, he said,

"Hello. I'm working for the ministry. Were you not asking about me? I met with the minister. . . . He was asking after you. . . . I was saying how I had a lot of work, and some complaints too. . . . Yes . . . my mother-in-law was saying her younger sister wasn't doing so well, the boss was worried about her. What? Where d'you say . . . ? That's right . . . Yes, Chief, I know people at several newspapers. And he was asking me to write something for these newspapers. . . . They've been talking about something that I wrote at the ministry. I'm always thinking of publishing something about what I'm working on in the financial division. We manage the figures well, the property . . . and socialist property is good for the economic figures, many people struggling together free from debt . . . I've written a lot about this. Not only this, but I'm bringing up some important problems based on practical considerations. . . . Not only that, but now there are accountancy strategists who seem to have been degraded in the theater . . . but there are no such people in our division, nor in the ministry. . . . I'm thinking I should mention something about how our actors slander those official financial workers who are standing on lookout among the haze of socialist property in our country, how they diminish our reputation before the people. I'm always thinking to talk about this to the workers' committee or to the council of deputies," and he was excited now, the people five rooms away could hear everything he said in just a single breath. He didn't realize that the head accountant had already grown annoyed, nor that he had put the phone down at the other end.

"Criticism too, my own criticism." And then, "Hello . . . hello . . . why's the line dead?" He dialed the number again.

"Ah, is that the head accountant? The line got cut off . . . What? No, I. . . ."

Disconsolately, Jamiyanbuu replaced the receiver, and from somewhere behind him a churning brightness came flying into his face. Jamiyanbuu turned pale, and his thin eyelids reddened again, and his gaze became foggy, as though he had been upset by something. His co-workers had a good idea of his excitable character when he had met with some high-up official, so they let him float away on his ocean of distress, and each carried out their work without attracting his attention, each clicking their own abacus, each peering at their own columns of figures. They understood that the angry voice of the head accountant should not be rumbling away in Jamiyanbuu's eardrums, filling his chest and rising and falling with his breath. And to calm himself, Jamiyanbuu sat singing a song of national honor in a choked voice, and rustling the documentation spread out before him.

1979

19

THE WOLF'S LAIR

D. GARMAA

O ver the past few days, sleep had fled from old Baldan; he would lie there, watching the starlit night. Sometimes he would kick and kick the blankets about; there was no place where his feet could get warm, and, falling into a fitful sleep, he would dream about various things. In the morning, he couldn't tell whether he had been dreaming or if it had all been his imagination. His son and daughter-in-law slept soundly with their children in the bed to his right. The felt *ger* was dark, a single ember ceaselessly aglow in the mouth of the stove.

"No, no . . . you're not dying, Baldan. You're not going downhill. And sixty-seven is not the end of the line. My father, poor old fellow, he was pushing eighty when he died."

He thought about this, and about how Jamsran, who had been close enough to quarrel with Baldan all their lives, had recently visited him.

"My dear Baldan," he had said, "you're wearing that nun's hat pretty early. You're such an old woman! Ride off to a mountain peak far away and take a look at the distant shapes. You've gotten old, but you're not dead yet."

In fact, Jamsran didn't irritate Baldan; he never used harsh words, and he helped him. He had been in the army, where he had been in charge of a unit; he was known for his book-learning and had worked as a secretary. And although Baldan kept his distance from Jamsran, when they were together there was one important thing he tended to ignore. But thinking about it now, the only fights they ever had revolved around Baldan's son.

"You're making an animal of your son, he's inhuman. . . ." Jamsran had said that when the child was young.

"Away with you! A father thinks that his son will be a man just like him. And nobody thinks that the child born to them will grow up to be a thief and a liar. Do I stay aware of things just for my own sake? Someone who has become a man has his own destiny. The fates know!" Baldan argued.

Why had they fallen out like this in the first place? Baldan drew up the blankets as though to find the point of his thought, and he ignored the fact that his feet were cold. The embers in the stove had gone out.

Baldan thought about when his son was young. *My son lacked for nothing; the neighborhood girls made a big fuss of him. While life kept the home going, my son was just as shrewd as his father, he was a man who took with him the earth where he had been sitting. Life was all about the leather strap wound around your thumb, about your possessions and livestock. Nobody gave them to you. . . .*

The dwarfish Baldan was a clever man. That year he had climbed up into a vulture's nest. Because his body was agile and small, he had reached the vulture's nest by heading up the scree. The people from his area said that he had taken something from the vulture's nest. They said that he scrambled up to the nest, up a steep and precipitous peak, and that he had found a golden ax there and a rope ten fathoms in length, and had grown rich by making off with the golden ax and the rope. Baldan had actually taken a few scraps, some wood and stones, and the animal bones lying around from the nest, but he'd found neither a ten-fathom rope nor a golden ax. But he had also found, among these various things, a severed finger with a golden ring, and that was something about which he had told nobody.

My God, thinking about it now, it seemed distasteful. When Baldan had been particularly broke, it happened that he had sold this ring of refined gold and so acquired his first head of livestock. After that, Baldan thought himself happy with his profit. In winter and spring, he followed the wolves and took a good bag. He said the wolves held a good profit in their lair. You shouldn't attack an animal in his lair. That was Baldan's approach. Baldan had understood this when he was a child. And for this reason, when it was well into springtime, he had taken his five-year-old son out to follow the wolves. On the path into the mountains, they had talked about the conduct of life; he kept encouraging his son and told him that there was nothing to be afraid of. His son was frightened of going straight into the lair; his face turned pale and white, he screamed and ran away. This made Baldan angry. With all his might he dragged the young creature, braced in his resistance, to the entrance of the wolf's lair, tied the rope to him, and pushed him into the cave. There was no way the boy could get past his father. His gaze pleaded a thousand times, *Please don't make me go into the beast's den;* his face was blanched; anyone other than his father would have been swayed by pity for the little boy. But Baldan was greedy and would not forego his profit, and he pushed his son into the wolf's lair. The child disappeared into the dark rocky cave, wriggling like a worm, and right then Baldan's mind grew uneasy. But a few moments later, Baldan saw that the prey he had pursued was yelping at the bottom of the bag and struggling at the end of the rope. After that, Baldan decided that by his own hand, he would raise his son to manhood.

When Galsan was at school, Baldan made him join up with some other children and take part in fine art and pioneer work. And then, some years, Baldan did not send his son to school. He begrudged any involvement of the child with his mother, with other people, or even with other objects.

In middle school his son had invested a lot of energy in developing his physical strength, and tried to outdo his father. Baldan was unable to draw his son away from the games he enjoyed. In fact, the more the child grew, the more he was absorbed by his schoolwork, and Baldan's every cell strove to beat down all that his son loved and found interesting. One autumn, Baldan did not move to the local town. And his son did not go to school. Jamsran came to visit.

"What sort of idiot are you? You'll make the child lose his way. Send him to school right now!"

Baldan did not hold back. "Dammit," he said, "do you know my son's mind? Only I know my son."

"You think that through your own wisdom you can school this child of yours in life. But what is this wisdom? Cunning and greed . . . you have cut your son's childhood away from him. In the town I once came across a puppy beaten to death; its eyes had not even opened. This is what comes of getting these wolf cubs to mix together. The teachers are saying that your son does not make childish mistakes, that if he finds something that's been mislaid, he doesn't give it back."

These words from Jamsran seemed to Baldan like an insult. *A man*, thought Baldan, *is not required to be wise. It would be wise for me to educate my son with my own understanding. I guess he will make his own destiny. . . .*

Such was Baldan's thinking as he kicked and kicked and found no sleep in his dark ger.

When he woke in the morning, the sky was clear, but the wild steppe lay under a thin snow, like hoarfrost. Galsan was saddling his horse, drinking his tea.

"I'm heading out. It's going to be a fine day, what with the new snow. When the sun comes out, it'll get hot. The time is coming to move to the spring quarters. Dad, could you think about giving Tsetsegmaa a hand drying off what's in the shed?" And so saying, he rode away, carrying his gun.

As his son left, it struck Baldan as strange how, set apart, he had grown to manhood. *Look at him go. He's a mountain. . . . But I was his father . . . such a puny little creature, I could have fit inside a dung basket . . . damned wretches, we didn't fight too much.* He proudly thought that if he fought every year, he would win the local competition and win a colt. *My son is a man like the mountains, but he has grown up and has not turned away from his father's words. He is a man just like me, cunning and shrewd in everything. Where is there a father richer than me?*

His daughter-in-law went out to pasture the sheep and later, when she came back, she embraced her son, wrapping him in her skirt, and went to the shed.

Baldan entered the ger and rushed out, gulping down the lukewarm tea he had made amid his paradise of wood. To the rear of the shed, behind a stack of filled bags, there were some sections from the felt roof of the old man's own ger. It was time to bring out the sheepskins that last year he had been unable to make ready by drying in the air. Remembering that his son had asked him to find the time to tidy the shed, he went inside. The spring sun was like a mother, melting the snow in the winter quarters, and water dripped yellow from the felt roof of the enclosure.

The things in the shed all declared that his son had truly become a shrewd man. What did they not have here? Bags of rice flour, a lovely saddle of wood and new gray felt, and leather for the saddlecloth and saddle flaps, which seemed rare in the countryside. Although Galsan was known in the cooperative as a shepherd, it was really only Baldan's daughter-in-law who did this work, and she gave her husband the reputation for being a good, hardworking man who raised the cooperative's herds. Baldan's daughter-in-law was loyal. When Galsan said to her,

"We should treat our increasing livestock and wisdom like twin lambs," she said,

"Don't do so much dirty work just for riches, Galsan. It makes no sense to me. . . ."

Galsan could say nothing in response. In fact, Galsan seemed to be grave and taciturn, a sober and honest man. He went every winter to get medical treatment in the local town or else in the city, and he took with him something that city people needed and came back having found something for someone in the countryside to feast their eyes on.

Profit was Galsan's one skill. Only his father's childhood friend, who was now Jamsran the brigade chief, realized that every man grew up without giving up anything for the sake of profit.

Jamsran came to talk with Baldan. "You need to say something to your son. Really, it is not because Tsetsegmaa alone has been looking after these sheep that Galsan has done nothing. I know everything that's happening, but the information hasn't yet reached you."

"Wait a moment! How has my son been causing trouble? He's a creature who barely thinks of living. Does he drink, is he a thief? He only takes part in the work around the cooperative. Why do you view my poor son like chewed-up flesh, like garbage? What trouble has Galsan done to you?"

"He makes no effort nowadays. Poor herders at least discuss buying something, but he says nothing at all. They say the man has the mind of an animal. There's a problem in that he gives no thought to working for the people. He acts only for his own personal benefit. You know what this means. Envy is like a demon . . . and envious is what you're making him. He was such a lovely child. Look at his classmates in school . . . Bazar's son's a scholar. Nyam's daughter has done really well as a doctor. How did the herders Dalai and Gombo become famous as People's Heroes? You ruined your son by removing him from school. Yes, you're right. Nobody thinks that your son is a thief or a liar. But, by teaching him to put aside what he finds has slipped from someone's belt, you've made him just copy your character. . . ."

Baldan could not say anything to Jamsran. He didn't like to think that his own dear son, whom he so defended, was a bad person.

Just before noon, the snow that had fallen during the night had all but melted and a warmth had spread from the winter quarters. As he placed the narrow cushions and felt roof patches around the enclosure to dry off, Baldan found, in a sheltered spot beneath his feet, some plants just barely managing to grow. These plants were the first signs of a warmer season. From under the manure, the green shoots stretched tenderly up toward the sky.

"Hey, Tsetsegmaa, look here!" shouted Baldan. "The plants are growing. . . ."

Tsetsegmaa came running. "Where are they?"

As they both eagerly looked at the plants, there was a clanking of stirrups from the hitching post.

Galsan galloped up and dismounted. He seemed in a great hurry.

"What is it?" asked Tsetsegmaa, seeing from his face that there was some urgency.

"Not now . . . is there any cold tea?"

"Inside, in the teapot."

"Dad, come here!" said Galsan, putting his gun inside the ger. Baldan looked at Tsetsegmaa, as though asking her what was happening, and went into the ger.

"Tsetsegmaa, saddle up the quiet black horse!" shouted Galsan from inside the ger. "Won't you come with me?" he said to his father. "You don't get out around here much, let alone on a horse."

And while this was happening, Baldan was thinking about what Jamsran had said to him. "I want to go and see the distant mountains. I have gotten so old and I've still not died."

"Yes, okay . . ." Baldan said, "I'd really like to go out into the wind." He happily loosened his belt to change his *deel*. *My son is so smart*, thought Baldan, *he knows his old father could become a demon at home*. And while Baldan changed his clothes, Galsan went outside and in a high, quiet voice, seemed to be arguing about something with Tsetsegmaa, and then all was silent.

Happy and excited, the old man went out, light on his feet like a child. The calm black horse was already saddled. His daughter-in-law came up to where he was; she gently asked him,

"Dad, do you really need to go?"

"I am going, my girl. I have to go. I can't become like some old nun. I'll go out in the wind. I'll go up to the top of a mountain far away and take a look at the distant shapes." And Baldan embraced his daughter-in-law, and, as though in pursuit of something, he rode quickly away.

It was a gentle spring day; smoke swirled from the black earth, shimmering in mirages, and streams of yellow snow melted into melody. Baldan was slowly crossing the hills, moving farther away from home, his old man's mind truly awake; he sensed the stiffness in his back relaxing, and his feet relieved of the pain that had warmed him throughout the night.

The old man rode along happily with his fine and virtuous son. Last year, age had shown him that the world was not eternal. In the last month of spring, he had driven his few animals, and had brought them all to his son's place. Baldan had done as he wished, he put on his nun's hat, boiled up the tea of a calm mind, and sat there and watched his grandson.

In his youth he had galloped along, had followed the path of life; he had prayed to the gods of profit; his homeland had appeared beautiful under the spring sun. The more crags there were, the more the wolf cubs loved it; the more the mountains sloped white under the blue haze, the more corsac they provided; and the mountainous northern taiga with its ragged trees was never stingy to Baldan with its sable. However much he hunted, whether overtly or covertly, he traded and passed it all on to the city; Heaven knows with how much he padded his dwarfish body and filled his purse. He wouldn't say he got nothing but profit through hunting, it was not so . . . in autumn he traveled by caravan, in spring he tended the trees, in the summer he sailed a raft. . . . And it had all made Baldan truly happy. Baldan thought about this, oblivious to all the craggy slopes they had crossed. At the bottom of one huge crag, his son dismounted. Baldan also dismounted.

His son put down the bag and rope and went up the crag. Baldan followed him like a child. His breathing was not strained. The cubs had come out and were running around and now, at the top of the crag, two or three of them were playing around dwarfish Baldan. Galsan sat down and, with a smile, started to smoke. His father sat down next to him and caught his breath. The craggy southern slope offered them warm shelter.

"This is the wolf's lair. The wolf cubs are whining. If we can get them we'll get a good price. A big profit. Dad, take a listen!" He spoke quietly, sucking at his pipe. Baldan listened as he stooped forward toward the hole. It was true. He gauged their number from the yelping. "Seven or eight pups," he said, "no real profit. We really shouldn't kill them."

"Sure we should!"

"No. There's no more than eight. . . ."

"One will get fifty *tögrög*, they say. That's four hundred, dad!"

"Of course, my son."

"Is that all?" Galsan said, knocking his pipe against a stone.

"What do you want me to say?" shouted his father. "If we lose such a profit, we'll be miserable."

"True enough."

Baldan suddenly understood that his son, big as a mountain, would not fit into the wolf's narrow lair, that it was pointless for his father to do anything but bag the profit with his own underdeveloped body.

"There's nothing for it. I'll go in!"

"What?" said his son. "Such a mean thing?"

"No matter. You went when you were a child. Right then. . . ."

"It's dangerous . . . shall I help you get inside? It doesn't look good. . . ."

This is what his son shouted, but his father paid no notice; it was clear that he was really saying, "You should go in."

"Let's go, son," the old man said and went to the mouth of the cave.

"Think about yourself. Do you have to do it?" said Galsan, taking the rope.

"Yes, I do. I'll try to get inside," said Baldan. His son double-tied the rope around his father's belt, and Baldan entered the cave, breathing heavily.

"It's dangerous, Dad. I've got a good hold on you. But please be careful. I knocked myself on the edge of the rock."

The old man was a little scared by this, his heart pounded and his breathing grew heavier, but he knew that his son was concerned and so he didn't let on, and he entered the cave. Now the old man knew this cave. This deep cave was like a well, with passages branching off inside. In one of these passages the wolves had made their lair. As he went on, the old man thought how he had gone so many times into this cave as a child. His son had gone inside just once.

The old man went farther and farther into the cave. His fine son held tight on the rope, in case his father hurt himself on the rocks. But these two men did not realize how, one day, they would lose out to nature. In the morning, the female wolf, whom Galsan had shot and wounded, having ripped something or someone to pieces, lay down in her lair, snarling.

1982

20

THE BALLAD OF THE UNWEANED CAMEL

G. MEND-OOYO

I

There fell from the sky into the narrow sandy gorge of a mountain pass a single huge blue stone. But if you were to look at it, you would see not a stone, but only a camel lying down. His two humps stood out against the sky, their skin sagging, weak and emaciated. He stood with his legs apart and slapped at the swarms of black flies with his tail, and even the grasses irritated him. Tears flowed from his eyes like pearls of spring water, and in those watery eyes, the sky stretched a deep blue to its farthest edges, and there rose a pale blue mountain, which seemed to him to be in the way. Behind this mountain ran a great red pass, where soil tumbled down and where the water was sucked dry. In the skirts of the fine sand, he practiced walking ten paces at a time, and with the sun's help he crept forward, meter after meter. And the farther he moved, the more the place lost its sting and grew attractive to him.

On the silken sands, fine as hot ashes, his intestines became strained and perforated and his two hocks ached with stress, so much so that he could barely move a few centimeters at a time.

There was a well behind him, full of cool, clear water. His rider had taken a bucket and filled three wooden troughs to the brim, each one to the depth of a meter, and the camel gulped the water down nonchalantly. The water dribbled down and splashed the flies on his humps, terrifying them. He twisted his long neck around and looked behind him at what was happening. He gazed in thought toward the edges of the sky and remained happily where he stood.

The midday heat gave way to coolness, and he took pleasure in gobbling down the red calidum flowers, which sucked the liquid at the edge of the salt marshes. The time sped by like wind; the darkness fell in a haze of ancient dreams. His body became tired and the colors of the world gradually faded. The quick-witted camel's final desire, his breath continually rising and falling, was to have the red calidum of the Gobi in his mouth, in his warm body, as he took his last breath. And with the passing of every second, his entire body withered, he felt his desire for the river dry up like the padding in his hooves, and he saw the light-blue mountain as a cloth tent at the edge of the sky. His body longed for dampness, he wondered from where it might come, and tears dropped from his black eyes in watery cascades.

2

In this sandy pass, the unweaned camel developed at a great pace. The late spring arrived with damp snow. Taking no notice of the undulating landscape, the camel ran over two valleys toward a bright, shining star in the south. The wind howled, the feathergrass and the flowers caressed the soles of his feet, and his speed gradually rendered his body light as a feather. Though the weight on his back was not distributed particularly evenly, it didn't trouble him. His rider would occasionally lash out at his rump, and he would hurry forward. Since there was no moon, it was pitch black. From time to time, the drowsy birds beneath the caragana and on the branches of the elms and poplars flew upward with a start while the rider, though quaking inside, remained calm in his body and kept himself focused on the path ahead. The sweat dripped from the camel's body; he rested while dawn lightened the morning gloom. He ran and ran. The land went up and down, the land rose and fell, he was almost flying, he was almost in flight. Such was the power granted to his four sinewy legs. In fact, only the heavenly Buddha knew why he was in such a hurry. In the bright light, a film had descended upon the arid Gobi; it was as if the desert had no limits. And as the camel pushed on, he paid no attention to his body as he crossed the desert, all he could feel was his own sinewy power.

At midday, during the middle month of autumn, the body of the unweaned camel was bright yellow, like hills of rippling feathergrass; his loose beard fluttered like tassels on a standard. The more he galloped, imposing and majestic, the more he was like a mighty dragon, twisting among clouds.

3

Time passed. The unweaned camel felt all his energy drain away. Somehow, in the eye of the shining sun, he crossed the narrow sandy pass. Like hemp wilting amid stubby feathergrass, he briefly rested his fine neck. The scent of wormwood melded into the rafters of feathergrass, but he felt no desire to bite it. If he only had his legs, he would stir himself. If he only had hooves, he would gallop away. Black clouds moved across the setting sun, casting shadows over the cloth tents of blue and red, and the birds of night took wing. The last of the day's strength snapped, and finally it was night. Not a breath of wind.

The movement of birds stirred a gentle breeze, and those dark-ling birds who were not acquainted with the melody of the wind flew in upward circles, coming to rest in the branches of a nearby elm. But they had no strength left to observe him; they moved only as much as he did. The curvature of the full moon, like a new three-ply bowstring, cast light upon the gloomy path, and a deep darkness descended.

4

The gorge was covered in pebbles of various sizes, smooth and round like animal droppings. Wild cotoneaster grew on the honeycomb of land beyond, and a warm wind had permanently settled upon the hollow to the rear of the blue mountain.

The camel was barely able to balance himself on his four legs, which were like twigs of cotoneaster. Barely able also to raise his spindly neck, he managed for the first time to see, in the rays of the full white sphere of the moon, the ghostly form of the four-sided blue mountain, rising up like a cotton tent. Soon he was tethered outside a gray *ger*, from which smoke rose in plumes. He kept his eye upon where he had come from, fol-lowing the mountain as he circled the peg that held him fast. He missed the Gobi, missed heading into the wind with the herd. He was desperate to reach the eternal mountain; everything else had fallen away. As he trotted out, the eternal mountain bounced up and down, and when he lay down in the hot sand, it seemed peaceful and dignified. The days and months passed and he grew used to this mountain, this celestial tethering post. The four seasons came and went, his fluffy beard floated like the rays of the sun and moon, his two humps stood erect like bridle studs. As the herd traveled beyond the mountain, he was in the vanguard, his lovely long neck an ornament, and his rider named him Nosepeg, for the peg in his nose that had prevented him from being weaned. He crossed five narrow passes, looking down as his hooves, with their velvety black hair, stepped on wild leeks. In his bouncing gait he was like a celestial mount; his fluffy beard fluttered, and riding him was like riding upon an utterly unruffled flying carpet.

When his rider rode out from a similar group nearby, quickly threading his way along the horizon of the blue sky, he felt his stretched sinews relaxing; his velvety hooves itched. His whole body had a lightness like warm feathers. But the fact that he would not be heading out on distant paths, that he would just be twisting and turning in this same pasture, saddened him to the core. There would be no one to ride Nosepeg over the winter and spring.

But his straight and elegant back and his long legs had nothing to do, and he thought of how he might occupy himself in such a miserable situation. One evening in the middle of spring, when the wet snows had fallen, and when the wind blew in squalls, a man came up from the pastures and, attaching a leading rein to the camel's nose ring, placed a load of weapons evenly on his back. How could he understand why he was being prepared so hurriedly like this, without being tethered and deprived of water for even one day?

5

Nosepeg wanted only to creep and crawl and steal away. In the middle of the night, he opened his mouth like a lion, a bird screeched from the darkness, and a cold shiver ran through his whole body. Off in the shadows, like an ancient evil, the old black bird turned on its perch. Nearby, the glorious moon seemed to come close, sitting there like a roseate guard, shifting its eyes from side to side. The bird's screeching song had been a bad omen.

The hills drew closer. He saw, indistinctly, how the tent of the blue mountain seemed to tower overhead.

The network of cattle paths gave him comfort. To have lost so much power was a miserable thing. After a short rest, he crept forward. . . .

6

The yellow Gobi, covered in tamarisk, was a perfect land of Shambhala to which the Yenshöö clan had become accustomed. They had been blessed by Heaven, with thrones of carved sandalwood placed atop their precious red camels. Others had been stirred by the voice of Heaven and had crawled, seemingly unthreatened, from their miserable lairs. And so it was that one night, robbers entered the Yenshöö encampment through a hole opened by the darkness of the clouds and, snatching their booty—along with girls and women, screaming alarm—they ran away. The Yenshöö's legendary men were sufficiently well armed to give chase, and for many days they pursued the robbers to exhaustion far away. The weapons were blunted, their bullets spent. They sent emissaries and an order was given, which meant that Nosepeg was loaded up with the weapons and bullets and ridden away. At first, Nosepeg went some way north, and he did not feel tired. He sailed past a couple of valleys, some brightly colored hillocks, the rubble of a steep cliff, saxaul and poplar trees, and from time to time he would pass by a herd of cattle who would take notice only of the weapons. As one half of his load slipped gradually from his back, down onto the road, he would come occasionally upon the stinking remains of a dead camel. And this was a bad omen.

The robbers turned their strength to fighting back and proceeded still deeper into the country. Another night passed, but their legs took no rest and they kept galloping on. The following evening, they came to where there seemed to be ravines at every step. Then, suddenly, at dusk, they saw what they thought was a familiar-looking camel loaded with weapons. The camel had reduced its speed and had no time to regain its energy to match the robbers' pace, and then they roared past.

His rider gave a sudden tug and, though the peg had almost split the camel's septum, he had nonetheless already left the ravine, where some of the robbers remained. Now, a quite different, quite dazzling country stood out amid the regular landscape, and a whistling sound cut the sky. The camel's right foreleg screamed with a burning heat. One bullet fell short, but another bullet whizzed through and Nosepeg felt his rider fall to the ground. As much as he tried, Nosepeg couldn't pull himself up. His left foreleg was also burning. He was moving under his own steam, he was steering his own way.

As he twisted and turned, gently and deliberately slowing, Nosepeg's misted eyes could vaguely make out, among the cliffs and ravines scattered all around, riding saddles on the backs of many camels just like him. As he hobbled along, a man flashed by and grasped his leading rein, which was brushing the ground. As he was slowly pulled to a stop his energy grew slack, and his four feet came up short as though he had been pegged to the ground. He only had just enough strength to keep himself from falling over. Although the man pulled down on his wounded nose and shouted at him to lie down, however much Nosepeg tried, his four stiff legs wouldn't bend. The warm blood flowing in his two front legs stopped him moving forward; how could he even know his own name right now? The universal river had brought him among those similar to him and he found himself in very pleasant surroundings. *Oh, who is the soldier who has peace of mind?* Though his back sagged and his body, forever shouldering weight, had grown light, his two front legs had grown heavier. And just then, there was a loud commotion, fire glowed in the twilight, bullets shot through the air, and uproar reigned.

The fighting had started again. In the darkness, members of the Yenshöö clan, bearing arms, came riding into battle on their camels. Nosepeg alone remained in the ravine. The sound of the fighting moved farther and farther away, and he was immediately overwhelmed by a terrifying silence. But of course, all silences that come after a great commotion are terrifying.

After fifteen minutes, his two front legs could not bear the weight of his body and this ship of heaven collapsed, lying down with his two humps like a pair of stupas. The sound of battle was far off and his ears, stuck as they were to the ground, heard it only vaguely.

7

Who knows how many days or nights had passed? Drifting in and out of consciousness, he had stayed there, lying low among shrubby bushes, away from the noise of the fighting and with only a few gray birds for company. Poor Nosepeg remained all alone in the world of humans. He lay, barely able to raise himself to his knees; he turned his black eyes, bulging with tears, and looked for a while toward his own world. And then, without a moment's delay, he crept forward. How could the cameleers who devoted themselves to great battles know what he was doing? One man, exhausted by many days' fighting, came to the ravine where Nosepeg had been left behind but found nothing. The poor suffering camel didn't even know that he had left the field of this wonderful battle. Autumn came, and it seemed that the summer months had drifted to a close.

8

Nosepeg the camel rested a while and then crept forward. His poor belly had been cut by shards of stone and by rubbing up against caragana plants along the path. The journey home had been nothing special. To look at the sky, it would seem that dawn was breaking, that light was appearing in the east. The earth was a rich place. Now, though, how could his feet take even a step? If only his legs would work! He stood up. If only his hooves would work! He wanted to gallop. In the dawn light, he could just make out that same ill-starred black bird sitting on a rock near his head. How long had this bird been following him? This shouldn't be happening.

You were given eyes only to see the salt marsh where you were born. His poor neck had grown thin as string, and it pained him to lift his head, which was the color of sandalwood. Only his black eyes remained as they were before. But still he crawled forward. And so he came to the edge of the salt marshes of the Gobi, all covered in tamarisk, and his entire body felt shattered. Who knows how long it had taken? As he lifted his neck for a final time, his black eyes looked upon the place of his birth and there he saw the light-blue mountain, like a cloth tent.

He perceived the universe as more clearly blue than it had been before. Over the hundred hollows of the light-blue mountain, over the whole world, he saw the sun rise, shimmering. And toward the west, inexplicably, he saw a curtain of red dust. A few men of the Yenshöö clan were returning from war; they had chased the robbers and had retrieved the stolen booty, their women and their girls. Nosepeg looked in their direction. A man on a camel emerged from the middle of the dust and as this one approached, it seemed to him to be another dragon. The sun grew brighter, filled his eyes with the new morning. The bird of eternal misfortune flew up from his perch on the camel's rear hump and alighted on his fore hump. *And now he is sitting on my head.* Trying not to look, he closes his eyes to the incomparable clarity, to the deep blue of the sky, to the gilded yellow of the sun, to a herd of camels and to the absolute power of the light-blue, tentlike mountain.

But there is no darkness. He sees the great iridescence of the world sink into his body. The muffled sound of people talking sinks into his ears. And at this very moment, Nosepeg the camel, as though greedily gulping down the blue atmosphere of the Gobi, covered in red tamarisk, with its light-blue, tentlike mountain, in the breadth and serenity of springtime, takes his final breath.

1989

21

HULAN

S. ERDENE

Hulan and Me

I was seventeen. A poor thing I was. I reckoned myself a man.
But that summer, I realized that I was truly a timid fellow. One
day in July I went with Genghis Khan, who was from my area,
and his wife to the *sum naadam*, and we started out early. Genghis Khan's real name was actually Tsamba. It was I who had
given him this somewhat alarming nickname, although I
had never told him. I helped him train his racehorses. After the
evening moisture had settled, I brought these animals back;
they were naïve as I was, and had storybook names like Chestnut of the Wind and Lightning Wild. I fed them, and in the
morning at dawn I exercised away their stiffness, and I watered
them during the day. I helped Genghis Khan in other ways too,
aside from these menial jobs.

Yellow Tsamba was about thirty; he had yellow slit eyes like
a snow leopard's, curly brown hair, and a long chin with a
groove down the middle, and his short bowed legs paced forcefully; he was a man who constantly held his fists tight. I never
saw a gentle look in his yellow eyes. Snot-nosed kids were

afraid of his glance, they trembled and held their shoulders tight, and they didn't move, as though they were wearing wooden trousers. Tsamba was rich, with livestock and gold and silver, and he was extremely keen on dealing in horses. In spring, as soon as the grasses began to sprout, he strung a few horses together and saddled them up, dressed in some good clothes, and set about dealing like a whirlwind. He hung around Herlen, Bayan-Ulaan, Galshar, and even out in Dariganga, and after midsummer he sent some fine horses jogging out; he kept records of their color and their paces, and they came back in the melody of the long song, throwing up dust across the lower slopes of the hills. Such was Yellow Tsamba's ability. Some of our fellow countrymen said that he was of a noble family, that he was a lucky man, yet the majority found him a boastful good-for-nothing.

But I thought he was a man like Genghis Khan.

Come dawn, we were galloping southward. There were two relay stations on the way to the *sum* center, the road was rough, and there was a pass named Jirem Pass. Around sunrise, Genghis Khan left us, saying he would go visit Tsagaan Tohoi. Immediately I felt happy inside. At seventeen, I at least had a sense of being a man. Yellow Tsamba's wife was called Hulan. Really, a wild ass, that was her name. Hulan had come from a distant region to be married; she was lovely like the moon, a creature restless as the wind.

That spring I had returned to my region, having spent a couple of years following my elder brother around the *aimag*, to find that Genghis Khan had taken this lovely young wife. I heard from acquaintances that he beat her constantly, that she screamed day and night. But I had not seen him behave in such a way.

Genghis Khan disappeared from sight. I brought together four horses that had been hardened in preparation for racing in the naadam and rode together with Hulan. The horses strode out well in the freshness of morning; the Khan had told us to ride them over the Jirem Pass.

I looked with fascination at Hulan, with the eyes of a thief; I felt an unusual sense of elation. When we galloped, it was as though we could go anywhere we wished.

The sun rose in the cloudless sky, the wind came rustling from the south, and shadows touched the near side of the eastern mountains, a rosy hue on the slopes of the mountains to the west. The dewy grass in the meadow soughed against the horses' legs, and larks came flying, flying up from the southern road.

Hulan was wearing small boots of red leather; she pressed the balls of her feet down onto the stirrups, the skirts of her blue silken gown bunching a little over her knees, her fine waist tied with a belt of yellow crêpe; she sat elegantly in her Borjgin-style saddle, her strong muscles stretching above her silken stockings, and swayed a little as her brown mount ambled on.

The brown horse with a white crescent on its forehead took the bit of the silver-studded bridle in its jaw and pulled, and to see its loins twitching a little, the hair all cunningly flat, was most pleasing, as though a cup of water placed there wouldn't spill, as though the horse and its rider were together like a work of music.

As for the clothes I was wearing, I had on a green twill tunic with frayed edges, army trousers with oval patches on the knees, and an old hat with a ripped peak. My horse was the worst of Genghis Khan's herd, a motley and bad-tempered thing.

Hulan looked toward the top of the hill, and she hummed a melody and looked at me from the corner of her eye, smiling a little scornfully.

"Won't you sing, Sampil?" and all my face could do was blush. I'm an orphan, and as the saying goes, an orphan has a pretty good voice. I sang when I went out to the horses, and I was obsessed with listening to how the sound echoed off the rocks. I licked my lips like a calf sated on milk and began timidly to sing "Going Out to Watch from the Northern Hyangan Hills." Hulan hadn't thought I would sing like this; she drew her horse in, and her bright eyes smiled. So my courage increased, and I spent all my wit and my voice singing about a mother yearning for her beloved only daughter who has gone to a distant place. Hulan took a kerchief from her sleeve and dried her tears. I was open-mouthed, dumbstruck. I hadn't realized it had moved her so.

"Sampil, you're a singer," she said, sobbing. But I couldn't sing anymore. Hulan slowly stopped weeping, and she looked gently at me.

"Sampil, how beautifully you sing," and I went a little red. . . .

It was late morning when we came out at the top of the pass. By that time, Hulan and I had gotten to know each other fairly well. Like me, Hulan was an orphan. We dismounted beside an *ovoo*. It was really hot, but the wind was fresh high up on the mountain and the conifers gave off a pungent scent, while the undulating Onon glittered and shimmered down in the copse below.

Hulan took in her plump white hands the red gauze scarf that passed over her crown and was knotted at her ears; she wiped her brow with it and gazed at me, smiling with an unknowable beauty. At that moment, I thought, *Genghis Khan, please don't come back soon*, and looked in the direction of the road over and over.

"What are you looking at?" the girl suddenly asked me.

"Genghis"—it just slipped out, carelessly.

"W-what?" She looked surprised, and I was floored.

"Oh, y-yes . . . Genghis . . . no, well . . . well," I muttered, grinning like a half-wit, and Hulan was even more amazed,

"What about Genghis?" and her eyes grew bigger. Only then did I find my tongue.

"No—isn't Mr. Tsamba coming?" Hulan was as surprised as before.

I said, "Yes, Genghis, it's Genghis," and now I felt completely done for.

"Mr. Tsamba's like Genghis Khan," I said.

"W-what did you say?" She fell backward, laughing. And then,

"Genghis Khan was only Genghis Khan after death. Heroes like Genghis end up wanting not to have beaten their wives. He'll be completely drunk by now. He'll be very lucky to get to the *sum* tonight, he'll be passed out lying on the grass with his knees showing from his skirts, a broken strand of feathergrass hanging from his mouth, and his eyes closed as though he were earnestly thinking about something," and she giggled mischievously.

"Pull me up," she said, giving me her hand. It was soft and warm.

Hulan immediately mounted her horse, and said cheerfully,

"Sampil! Let's gallop down to the river as fast as we can! It'll be lovely on the banks. Tsamba's not coming anytime soon. Let's go!" She gave her horse the whip and headed out toward the pass. I hurriedly mounted and galloped after her. "Sing something, Sampil," she said. The skirts of my tattered gown flew, and I managed to drone away as we went down the Jirem Pass,

A brave gray hawk
with power in his wings, my dear.

We came to the river, our horses in a sweat.

Hulan led me, and I was no longer *almost* a man, to an old ford. We dismounted in a thick copse of willow, poplars, cherry trees, and hawthorn, tied up our horses, and sat there, chatting easily. . . .

I knew what was happening.

"Hulan, there's nobody as beautiful as you in our region."

"I have other beautiful things."

"Like what?"

"Well, there's my heart."

"So you're happy with your life?"

"You think so? I'm under a man's control. I try to hide my pain. A man who thinks I'm an animal to be beaten for his own pleasure."

"Hulan, you mustn't live like that, get away! Does he threaten you? You have to go somewhere."

"Sampil, if only I were with a man like you . . . you are too modest. Kiss me. . . ."

A little bird who had come to sit on a branch of a willow tree nearby bent its head as though to say, "What is this?" and shifted its little eyes, which were like glass beads.

Hulan lay her head on her hands and closed her eyes.

"After you've gone to the aimag center in autumn, I'll leave Tsamba and come there. If I have work, I can live. I can sew, and if there's no work sewing then I can be a janitor. What about it, Sampil?"

"Yes, I could be a tractor driver, or just a driver! Oh, Hulan! What sweet little eyes that bird has . . . !"

When we came out onto the newly paved road, it was evening. But we had no doubt that our Genghis Khan was off in Tsagaan Tohoi, drunk. We thought about this with all the more happiness. Hulan rested on my shoulder, smiling, and I smiled and sang about the gray hawk, and the evening sun smiled over the hilltops.

How shall I exhaust the waters of the spring?
Why have I come to know a fine man's son in vain . . . ?

Someone was galloping toward us, throwing up red dust. Hulan suddenly grabbed her horse, looking at the man with alarm.

"Tsamba's coming," she whispered. I felt suddenly very unsteady; my heart was in my mouth.

"Where? Is he coming from the *sum*?"

"Yes, yes, that's him for sure. He's been to the *sum* while we've been here."

"What'll we do now?"

"Well . . . let's say we came down to the river to rest the horses."

"It's been a while. . . ."

"Well . . ."

We still had nothing to say when the fierce Khan arrived. He stopped his horse in front of us, glaring with his yellow leopard eyes. His collar was loosened, his face was swollen, and he removed the whip with its thick shaft and laid it across his horse's mane.

"Are you coming from the *sum*?" Hulan asked anxiously, and Tsamba ground his teeth together and twisted his mouth.

"Yes, from the *sum*. So you were lying in this copse with this little fetus?"

"Don't talk nonsense. . . ."

And then, with a vicious scream, and before I could do anything, Tsamba attacked me, pulling me from my horse.

"You piece of trash, riding my horse and . . . my wife. . . ."

Hulan was flustered. "Tsamba!" she shouted. "You're an animal!"

Tsamba rolled his yellow eyes like a madman, his teeth protruding.

He screamed again, howled "I'll kill you!" and grabbed at the tether and beat the horse.

"I'm leaving." Hulan wept bitterly. "I'll die before I live with you."

"Fine, then, but I'm going to get this snot-nosed kid you've been playing with," and Tsamba brandishing his thick whip like a club and rushed at me.

"Tsamba, stop!" Hulan grasped his arm. I almost lost my mind; I stood there motionless, like a nail driven into the earth. Tsamba jumped down and joined Hulan's horse with his own and quickly remounted; he grabbed Hulan's tether and galloped off, beating his horse mercilessly. Before me a red dust arose, and the sound of Hulan's agonized weeping faded to nothing.

Left on the road without a horse, I came to and waved my fist after Tsamba.

"I'll get you for this! I'll get you! Hulan'll be rid of you. See, you dog! Hulan's well rid of you!" and I was left to wipe away my snot and tears.

1960

Hulan and Tsamba

With the first snows I went back to my homeland. A lot of snow had fallen throughout that warm autumn, turning it chill in the wake of a monkey year notorious for its weather. The leaves in the copses along the Onon fell, and in the unrelenting snow, I became flushed with the cold. I took a vacation, a man without work and in no hurry. I traveled quite some way out of the sum center, through the relay stations, following the hunters who wandered with their families, and as I traipsed across mountain ranges, I reached "the waters that washed the fallen earth," and the snow fell even on the road home, when I saw the place where my umbilicus was buried. I came down the Jirem Pass slowly, and I was surprised to see the people and animals in such heavy snow and shocked by how scrawny they had become in the extreme weather, and I was thinking how strange were the changes in nature and in the weather. Time had made it easier for me to think about how, twenty or so years before, I had crossed this pass with a girl named Hulan and had inspired jealousy in Yellow Tsamba, who had pulled me from my horse. I had heard about Tsamba and Hulan's life together, but had not seen them yet. Apparently he had become rich and fat. From a young age, Hulan had labored hard at home, and it would be difficult to know what would remain for her after she had faded, after the beauty of her youth. Now I was thinking to see Hulan just the one time. Some twenty years before I had thought Yellow Tsamba looked like Genghis Khan, and although what Hulan and I had spoken of together, the desire we had felt, had not been realized, the poison had stirred in Tsamba, and like a real man I had grown determined. Now, though, I could look him straight in the eye and have it out with him. I could only guess at how Hulan was now; she would have lost her will in Tsamba's bondage. As I thought about such things, I didn't think that I might meet Hulan on the Jirem Pass. But it happens that, as though aided by some secret power, suddenly things thought about come into being. I hadn't thought about it before, but I would try to find the liverish red stone that some forty years before had been pressed down to bury my umbilicus.

As I came out onto the top of the first pass, I saw someone with a horse and cart riding downhill, followed by a white dog. When I caught up with her, it was Hulan. She might or might not have recognized me. She had her scarf tied down and her forehead downcast. She was surprised to see me.

"Hey Sampil!' she said, shocked and happy at the same time. "Where did such a curious fellow come from?" Her forehead glistered and swayed, it didn't seem wrinkled; a few gold teeth had replaced the flash of white. It was clear that she was trying not to let her eyes gleam, not to be the beautiful person she had been before. Nonetheless, to me Hulan seemed to have an inner beauty. I thought about how lovely she had been as a young woman. The girl from a poor family had become the daughter-in-law of a rich family; I didn't know the pain and the happiness she had experienced. To ride an ambler to the naadam, dressing in silken *deels*—these were what captivated the mind in the period of youthful beauty. Hulan was a sweet and gentle person, she had had no strength to escape from life's bondage. And I had been too young, too naïve. What was it to be seventeen? Hulan had been led along another path.

Hulan told me of her life as we went on. The sky grew gray as though presaging another snowfall; the Onon flowed blankly, cold and stiff like iron.

"Tsamba's gone hunting with a few men. We've a bunch of white dogs and a few fat oxen, but no children. I've talked about adopting children, but Tsamba doesn't want to. It doesn't matter. I've become useless."

"Don't you go to the cooperative?"

"No. Tsamba's the bursar of a carpenters' cooperative."

"An official. So he's a busy man, what with all the dogs and the oxen?"

"He is. And he puts it all on me. He distributes the oxen among families who only have a few head of livestock. I go along to divvy up the wages. He hides his property. He hides the money from me in the bank."

What Hulan said surprised me. It was as though she was talking about a nearby acquaintance, not about the man with whom she'd been living for so many years. She spoke without complaint, and not as a man's wife but as a kind of vagabond. I was overcome by sadness and cut in,

"Hulan!" I turned away; in my consternation I felt like crying. I had become a man, I was doing pretty well, I felt I could be a generation older than she. It pained me a little to call out her name. But I couldn't stop myself.

"Hulan! What we spoke about that time beside the Onon, how we would live. Do you think about it?"

"Yes. I am no longer that young girl. And don't you have lots of children?" she said, laughing a little.

"What a man I was, pulled by Genghis Khan from my horse, and weeping."

She laughed. "But you were a skilled rider." When she laughed, she had the same silvery sound, no different from her youth; it seemed to echo against the trees in the wood, weighed down by the snow. But this was a day when the trees in the wood would not echo to the firing of rifles, let alone to laughter. Hulan's laughter opened me up; it opened the eyes of my horse, exhausted by the damp cold, he pricked his ears. Even the animals knew that this was not the galloping of sad people, but of people who were happy and laughing.

So we talked together like this and so reached her home.

The enclosure with a building and a large white *ger* in the sum center was warm. In the place of honor were some colorful chests, two iron beds so that you might think that the people there liked a lot of time to sleep, and a carpet of thick quilted felt. It appeared that Hulan's mind, struggling for beauty and youth and fine objects, was tightly squeezed into these colorful chests.

Hulan made food for me, and gave me *shimiin arhi*. I downed two or three shots of warm *arhi* and was wondering whether I would meet Yellow Tsamba, otherwise known as Genghis Khan, when he came back from hunting. If he was as commanding as he had been previously, he'd probably insist, "Stay behind! Eat the meat from the oxen I've been hiding away, and keep quiet!"

"Does Mr. Tsamba still train horses for the naadam?"

"He used to," said Hulan. "His shameful boasting's gone now." Things change. Soft and fierce, good and bad, they fight against each other and finally all the strength to fight is lost. This is how life ends. I was thinking, *Hiding away gold and silver in a chest, gathering valuable livestock outside, you hold the earth. When it's gone, it's gone!* I gave a sigh.

"Sampil, you sang well when you were young. Sing something." I sang the one I'd liked as a child, "The Gray Hawk."

A brave gray hawk with power in his wings
acts in his youth without care.

While I sang, Hulan sat there, looking down, wiping away her tears. And outside the dogs were making a racket. Hulan filled my cup.

"Tsamba's coming," she said casually. When I was young, I wouldn't have sat there if she had said, "Tsamba's coming." Was I comfortable that the wife of a proud braggart was frightened of a beating? If I didn't give him a beating, I wouldn't rest. If I didn't beat him, I'd not relax, and girls like a violent brute . . . *Steel yourself! I'm ready for a fight.* The door was opened, and three white dogs came in, licking their lips. After them came Tsamba, chasing them in with a greeting. He clearly didn't recognize me. Whatever it was that had reminded me of Genghis Khan had now gone. He was a fat old man. He hung up his bow and arrow as he said, "That's quite a bit of snow. There's no way you'll get onto the mountain ridges. It's a whiteout. We only just managed to kill a single sow. . . ." In the end there was no need to fight with him.

Hulan saw me on my way. By the tethering line I took her hand.

"Good-bye then."

"When you come back, please visit us," she said. I said neither yes nor no, and galloped away.

Thirty Years Later

I woke from sleep in the hotel in the sum center with the rising of the sun. Through the open window fluttered a gentle breeze scented with the fresh water of the Onon; in the street a crowd of children were playing. The white linen on the brown wooden bed in the hotel's "luxury" room smelled of washing powder, but the pillows smelled of grass. On the low table next to the bed a warm flask of tea had been placed, with wild cherries, sour cheese, and clotted cream, which showed that the people in the hotel had noticed me. In fact, people around here paid quite a bit of attention to journalists, they tended to ingratiate themselves. What could be wrong with that? And I hadn't been back to my birthplace in so many years, what did it matter if I felt at home? Having been here about ten years ago, I felt I should go traveling now out on the steppe. It was true indeed, my homeland seemed to be aging with me. And over the last three or four years I had been dreaming about the landscape of the place where I was born, and making myself unhappy remembering what I'd done as a young man. It might have been Dostoyevsky who said that a man's greatest happiness lies in the impressions of his youth. I was bored of battling against the city crowds, but it wasn't that so much as the fact that the sun of my life was now beginning its descent that made me think about my homeland. So I had come for a vacation. Another reason was someone who had been tethered to my heart for thirty years. That person was Hulan. Ten years had passed since I had last seen Hulan. Yellow Tsamba had died some years ago. I had heard that Hulan had been widowed, and from time to time I thought about how my poor friend was faring. Thinking about how Hulan had been the love of my youth covered my heart in a sweet and gentle mist. When you talk about the love of your youth, it is as though in the sweet and yet truly faraway distance there are images and subtle echoes. When I saw her face and called to mind the events of my vigorous youth, even though it was so long ago that the possibility of her being with me had presented itself, the fact that Hulan was a widow seemed to seduce me from my melancholy loneliness. So, in those first impressions of love were preserved the origin of the errors and hindrances and good fortune of later life.

I was lying there, looking at the shell-white ceiling, puffing on my cigarette, and thinking about these things, when someone knocked gently at the door.

"Come in," I said, and the door opened slowly, and a tall young girl wearing a shabby green silk deel bashfully entered.

"Your horse is ready, sir," she said. I was amazed.

"My horse?" I said. "I had a motorcycle . . ." and the girl smiled.

"My mother sent a horse for you."

"Who's your mother?"

"Hulan."

At the mention of Hulan's name, I leaped up, and the girl passed me a slip of paper and swiftly exited, as though embarrassed. On a page from an exercise book an attentive hand had written, "How are you, Sampil? I was told you arrived yesterday. I'm sending my daughter with a horse. Come to the river around noon. You haven't forgotten the place, I guess. I'll be waiting for you there."

"My God!" I shouted. Hulan hadn't forgotten me. She hadn't forgotten how, thirty years before, we had spent a day by the ford over the Onon, exchanging words of love and yearning for something far away, and now she was recalling our youthful encounter in that place, it was like she was asking me to come to her home. I dressed quickly, and leaving the hotel, I took the gray-and-white horse, untying the tether from the post of the enclosure. The horse was old, but it carried a good saddle. It was Hulan's saddle. The saddle, with its short Borjgin-style saddle bow, its broad seat, its yellowed bone pommel, and its quilted saddlecloth bearing a faded design, was very familiar. It was strange. Thirty years before, this ornamented saddle of Hulan's had been brand new. A person uses a saddle for thirty years. But it didn't seem that the object and its owner had worn away at all. Such a long time had passed, and it was as though everything was still as it had always been, still stable. The obstacles that had turned me away when I was young were no longer there, they no longer applied, and as the time had meanwhile worn away and disappeared, still I recognized that old saddle. So I galloped off, my mind and body relaxing, and came to the ford over the Onon. My Onon! So beautiful, like young love. It was as though the Onon could at any time be a trysting place. It overflowed in the heart, not only with beauty but also with a kind of breathing, whispering, "It is the landscape that widens your thoughts, my son," a gentle melody to ease the mind in times of melancholy solitude. It seemed gentle as it flowed through the bright green copse of August, mixing with the clear sky and the sun. In our youth, an unbroken line of travelers had crossed the ford, but now it was desolate, with just a very few head of livestock, and with tractors plowing on both banks. The track at this time went straight down to the river, but thirty years ago, Hulan and I had led Yellow Tsamba's racehorses and spent the day by the ford, searching for a land far away from the track along which an unbroken weaving of naadam participants passed. Today I didn't mistake the place. I took a guess and came out where the cherry trees plaited with the willows. Hulan had arrived first; she was shy like a young girl.

"You didn't get lost," she said, holding out a few large cherries she'd picked. "Eat," and for some reason she looked away. I put the cherries in my mouth and took her hand.

"How are you?" I said.

"Good," and she looked back. A slight tear came to her clear brown eyes. Hulan had a green belt of fine crêpe around her creased deel of blue silk, the ends tied off at the side, and she wore a thin hat in the old style; she seemed the same as when she was young. I noticed her red boots and silken stockings, just like she had worn to the naadam that year. Had thirty years not passed? Was it so easy to go back to our youth? The lovely sour scent of the cherries, the birdsong, the rushing sound of the Onon were all the same. Hulan's hair was jet black, reflecting the light. She had combed it across her forehead, tied it in a scarf. I thought clearly how she had tied it in a red crêpe scarf for the naadam that year. But now it was even more fitting that she wore an old-style hat. No matter that she had wrinkles at the corners of her eyes. The hair at her temples was not gray, but yellowish. Ten years ago, when we had last met, her face had not looked like this. Perhaps she had gotten better after Tsamba. Yellow Tsamba had been dead five years. Hulan was almost fifty, and her body was soft and robust. Truly we had returned to our youth. We were wringing some kind of regret from our hearts. Hulan was now someone who had consigned my desires, my birthplace, and my youth to the mists. Yes . . . a long time ago . . .

Hulan and I took our saddles and went to sit on the fresh grass, wet still with dew. Hulan took off her hat and stroked her yellowish hair with her fair hands, softened by summer's milk.

"I sent my daughter because I was afraid you wouldn't come. Did you think I wouldn't be here?"

"I didn't think about it. I was thinking of visiting you," I said truthfully.

"She's my only daughter, she's adopted. She came a long time ago. She's got a son."

"She's a good daughter. She's given you a grandchild?"

"Yes, a sweet little boy. He's the apple of my eye."

"You're doing well as you get older?"

"I'm all right. After Tsamba, the time alone was pretty good. It's hard without a man's hands. Tsamba had his own way, he was a man with tough hands, he got things done. I passed my life beneath those hands, and now I miss them. Never mind, such is a woman's lot," and Hulan's voice trembled; she looked down and plucked a blade of grass. We sat for a while in silence. The large wasps droned around the copse by the Onon, our horses lurked among the willows, ripe cherries fell here and there with a thud, and through the trees came a gentle breeze, scented with flowers and fruit, and I felt at ease. Hulan let out a long sigh, stretched out her hand, and stroked my gray hair.

"Oh, Sampil," she said.

"The naadam that year . . . you and I tied up our horses and yearned for something far away. I was seventeen, such a naïve boy. Until today . . . the kind of person you were . . . I . . ."

Suddenly my heart softened, I couldn't keep the tears back. Hulan took the ends of her belt and dried my eyes, and her eyes, copper like ripened cherries, looked at me with love. Our gaze met for a long time; it was like the light from our eyes was being absorbed into eternity. From Hulan's soft neck, with its fine wrinkles, came a gentle warmth, as though scented with flowers and fruit. She blushed, the veins rose on her neck, the lines of aging stretched out, her eyes shone, and she was changed to the Hulan of thirty years before, and she was smiling. I embraced her neck and closed my eyes, I listened to the beating of her heart. All the while, we could hear a throng of children crossing the water by the ford, and a man admonishing them,

"Take care of one another. If you fall in the water, you'll be in trouble."

The desolate copse beside the Onon bent and swayed to the children's clamoring voices, the birds sang out their songs; it seemed impossible for Hulan and me to get away from animals and other people. Hulan got up hurriedly.

"Old Dash said he'd bring the children to gather cherries. The apple of my eye's with them. Look at Sampil!" she said. I was amazed. Sampil. "Yes, I gave my grandson your name." A dark lump stuck in my throat. *How strange this world is*, I thought. *Is it not a rare reward for love, that the love of my youth should give my name to her grandson? Is it not a reward for that love, with which we're forever thinking about home, with which we love someone?* Hulan and I quickly mounted our horses; we came to the path the children were on and followed it for a long way. We were anxious not to come straight out of the copse, and we went by the two paths that came together at the riverbend, silly things that we were!

Hulan bit her lip and narrowed her eyes, as though thinking of something.

"Sampil, what should we do with this world that is passing us by?"

The children were thronging down at the ford across the Onon like ducks and geese, their clear voices echoing back and forth across the landscape, and the earth that swam amid the August sun whispered a future, and faraway experiences, in the river's gentle run.

1990

22

HEAVEN'S DAUGHTER

CH. GALSAN

One day, there was this girl, she was standing in the camp attached to the milking section. I don't know who saw her first or what she was doing, but as we raced around, she was gaping at all the animals around her like a rabbit trapped in a net. Apart from a rather old *deel* of animal skin and a fine belt of leather, her clothes were unlaundered; her tangled, knotted brownish hair covered her shoulders; but her face, legs, and arms were not scratched or scarred or chapped like ours, she was soft and clear as though she had been in clotted cream all summer long and had just that moment emerged. She appeared majestic, with her intense face and strong forehead, her wide and deep-set eyes, her thick eyebrows and her broad nose. Maybe she knew how to speak, but she said nothing, she merely nodded and shook her head in response to questions. We did know one thing, however, that her name was Hasaa. No one imagined that that would be all she would let people know about her. To hear the adults talking, there were feral children who had been secreted away in the mountains during the counterrevolutionary period; they had either died or were living as regular people among others, but in any case they had sent this one back.

Everyone tried to take Hasaa in, to have her at home and raise her. My parents tried to make her a companion for their only daughter, letting her sleep over at our home and letting her do anything she wanted. It didn't work. She wasn't interested in people. It was amazing how clumsy she was around the animals, how she was completely uninterested in work. She would find nothing to do unless someone called her, she would stand around outside as though she was waiting for someone. And whenever someone somewhere called out, she would start and look around as though she had done something wrong; you had the impression that she was not of this world. What else could we do for this creature who would not get used to human life?

She moved from family to family, until she seemed to be comfortable staying with a man and a woman, a childless couple, who were most happy to have a daughter. Come autumn, they dressed her to send to school, but some people warned them, saying "You could lose the child sent to you by Heaven if you send her away," while others praised the idea, saying, "Thinking not of yourselves but of her future, you are absolutely right to send her to pursue scholarship."

So she went to school, and when it came time for registration, even though she had to say but one thing, when they pestered her to give her father's or her mother's name, they could not get her to speak. "If nothing else, she could have my name," said the man who had brought her, riding pillion, down from the summer pasture of the Altai, after taking her into his home. But the girl was downcast and seemed to dislike his proposal. Seeing such a reaction from her, that good-hearted man who had been so hopeful to have a daughter, and everybody else who was present, were rather hurt, thinking, *It is true what they say—"A child born to other parents is cold."* A hot-tempered teacher came by and scolded her; he said, "What sort of wretch are you? You don't know your family name and you don't want to take your father's name, who took you in! Or were you not born from a human but from Heaven?" And one mischievous fellow said to her, "It sure suits you that you fell from Heaven, right?" And she gave an inscrutable smile and nodded in agreement. And as they looked at her, the angrier the teacher became, and the more mischievous the other man, and they said, "So, anyhow, since everyone knows about you and since your master himself wants it, let us simply call you Heaven, your father's name." And they really did register her as Hasaa Heaven. From that time onward, they loved this orphaned child, and she remained shy and silent. They all called her Heaven's Daughter, and this was the name that, over time, they accepted as her real name.

The girl showed no real ability in her studies. While she was awkward and careless in her immediate surroundings, she would gaze into the distance as though desperately expecting something. But as we watched her, she grew up; she was a lovely and solitary creature; it seemed either that she was constantly happy with everything, always dressed in fresh-laundered clothes, or else that her intrinsic neatness emphasized her majesty, and she was the cream of her class and of her school. During the summer vacations, she usually went to a summer camp for orphans, but later, maybe her heart had warmed up a little; she started to spend summer with the old couple, who really wished to adopt her. But then suddenly she went missing. Later they heard that she had gone off to her in-laws. So who were they? They were up in the northern part of the unit. He was from new money, the only son of a leading family. He had considerable skills, a clever young man who seemed to possess much glamour. So the story went that at first she lived the life of an orphaned girl, and later she was badly behaved, like a rich daughter-in-law. And later still they said she'd gone missing again. So, just as she had all of a sudden arrived, so all of a sudden she was gone. Word reached the local administrative unit, and they sent investigators, but they did not find her. Yet the rumors persisted. Some talked meanly about how these people had needed a rich child, while some ignored this and said that he had been a peddler who had set himself up with an income from some of the unit's camels and with the blood of some Altai marmots. They said, "How could so lovely a woman stay with him? It's understandable that she ran away."

I have no idea how long this type of talk went on. I left my homeland to study elsewhere. Heaven's Daughter is one of the principal memories of my young life. The year Heaven's Daughter arrived, we passed the summer at Blackwater Lake. The following year, there was a sickness transmitted by our livestock, and when we left, there remained but a single *ger* at Black Mountain. The autumn Heaven's Daughter went away, we were staying with my mother's relatives. My father and my mother's people went out searching for her, and then in winter, a rabid wolf attacked our sheep. . . .

Many years later, I was journeying through my homeland. I asked people throughout the area whether or not Heaven's Daughter had been seen again, but nobody knew about her. This left me rather unhappy, so I asked them, "So, have people around here forgotten about her, or does no one have anything more to say?" In my disgust I let the truth slip out, but I never thought that so terrible a thing might be held in these words. People used their age as an excuse, they quickly said that the elders had forgotten and that the younger people had not heard about her. At first I complained. In the end I doubted. Maybe Heaven's Daughter had never existed, maybe she was something I had dreamed up!

Finally, I remembered that she'd had a husband and decided to go meet him to clear the matter up.

It was a far distant encampment. A very young girl came out, holding the dogs at bay; it was as though an image, a delicate, tapering memory, had come to mind. I thought at first that the girl had been left behind, and that she had grown up. In the end, I realized that she was the lady of the house, that some years before, she had been a wife coming down through the Dörvöd homeland, driving the livestock forward.

Her husband was tidying the winter quarters, she said, and would most likely be back the following day.

The woman served me *arhi* and tea and prepared some food for me. I noticed her prominent forehead and sunken eyes, and my heart leaped into my mouth. We chatted warmly about livestock and money, of course, about how the grazing land was doing, and it seemed to me that she would have me stay the night. She wanted to hear news from the city. She was bored where they lived, in this corner of the mountains.

Had she heard anything about Heaven's Daughter?

She had not.

I took the path she showed me, leading toward the winter quarters. The sun had almost set, and I was drunk, and I was determined to meet the husband, thinking, *If he says he has not heard about Heaven's Daughter, I will relieve my anger and frustration by having a drunken brawl with him.*

I don't know how I got there or what happened, but at one point I came to; I had been scrapping with someone beneath the sky upon the dung-scented rocky slopes, the night lined with stars. He whined as though he were whispering an oath, "Yes, yes, yes . . . Heaven's Daughter, she was from heaven, she was my dream . . . she was your dream too. . . ."

1991

23

RAUL AND RAUL

L. ÖLZIITÖGS

for my dear brother L. Bilguuntögs,
and for my friend L. Tögöldör

Raul was born. Such a sunny and warm, a warm, but really warm, a strangely warm, haiku indescribable, place . . . Such a place, yes, such a place that he never would have himself chosen, there was Raul born.

And from such a beginning he would have to live, according to not his own choices but those of others.

From Raul's Life: Day 1

Raul: Mom, I want another egg!
Mother: Eat, eat. So long as they're not raw, it doesn't matter how many you eat.
Raul: I want to eat a raw one.
Mother: Well, you can't.
Raul: Why not?

Mother: My son, what would I do if you died from food poisoning?

Raul: I want to die, I'm going to eat a raw egg!

Mother: You ill-starred creature! Always contradicting . . .

Having wailed for an hour, this ill-starred creature swallowed a raw egg. Raul was six years old. Every day, this ill-starred six-year-old creature ate an egg. Every day, his mother, who was not ill-starred, gave her son a chicken's child to eat. And it was fine. The eggs were tasty fare.

From Raul's Life: Day 2

Raul: Dad, I want a dog.

Father: Dogs? No! You could have . . . some fish.

Raul: Fish don't bark.

Father: Correct. So you can have some fish!

Raul: A fish couldn't play with me.

Father: If you had dogs to play with, you'd get tapeworm!

Raul: I don't want fish.

Father: You'll have fish!

Raul cried. Loudly. The child pushed his right cheek and tumbled to the ground.

What's this?

Pressure.

No matter, Raul could wait.

The child speaks daily with his fish. Each is given a name. But because the child can't remember the names he has given to the fish, it is difficult to tell them apart. Raul is seven. Raul loves his fish. But . . .

One day. Life is but a single day. One day . . . to begin with, one red fish died. And then another red fish died. And another red fish . . . the mother fish, a big red one . . . Then alone there remained, finless and eyeless, a small shell. Raul lay down and gazed at the shell. It didn't move much, unlike the other fish, and so he took hold of the aquarium, went outside, and threw it from the eighth-story balcony.

Raul stood and watched how the expensive glass coffin smashed and crumbled; the shards glistened in the sun just like a fish's eyes. That evening, the child was all *Nobody broke it*; he stuck his face into his pillow and, unheard by his mother, his father, and his elder sister, he gently, and for a long while, wept.

Raul's mother, father, and sister did not forgive him. "You threw your fish out with the aquarium," they said with one voice. "You vicious creature!"

And for the next three years, this vicious creature dreamed about his fish.

From Raul's Life: Day 3

Raul is thirteen. There was a woman, wearing stilettos, in love with a man. Stiletto Girl first met him as "that man Raul." He saw his elder sister's small feet every day, and he opened his journal afterward and wrote on the first page:

> It is like everyone else's journal. I do not want to write entries like everyone else. So I will write, "Rather than saying 'I read a book,' Raul read a book." Raul it is who takes pleasure in the women who wear stilettos. When Raul is bigger he will like only girls who wear stilettos.

*　　*　　*

Raul: Mom, why aren't you wearing stilettos today?
Mother: My feet hurt.
Raul: Put your stilettos on anyway!
Mother: Why?
Raul: Because your toes look hideous.

Father: Quite right! My son is a man. You're a man, just like me!

Mother: So what if my toes look hideous?

Raul's mother and father argued. He watched his parents with interest. *So*, thought Raul, *why would a man and a woman live together?* And he spent the entire four months following thinking about this. Why? What excited Raul, for no reason, was not the word "couple" but the words "solitary" and "alone."

From Raul's Life: Day 4

Raul's mother was cooking food. *Huurga* with eggs. The smell made him drool. Yummmmm.

His hard-working mother placed the piping hot food before her son. Raul took a fork and put his head down . . .

Suddenly . . . again, life was nothing but *suddenly*. Suddenly, a live fledgling fell from Raul's mouth; it limped about, dragging its leg, which Raul had bitten, and ran and bobbed about on the dining table. It forgot right then that it was human food and headed toward the crumbs of bread.

Raul closed his eyes and erased the acrid taste of this little creature's blood from his lips. Although he had been chewing the bread, fried potatoes, jam, and lettuce he loved, the taste of the fledgling was not obvious. Raul cried. He understood himself as the place of the bird's burial.

The place of Raul's burial. He wiped away his tears and fell to thinking. His first vow: *I will never eat another egg.*

From Raul's Life: Day 5

Raul's daydreaming.

He's dreaming of nothing but colors. And the dreams come true. Once Raul had given up on eggs, his dreams were about strawberries. Sometimes the strawberries in his dreams seemed to be similar to the fish that had died "some ten years before," but he did not rush to hurry from his tasty pinkish sleep. One day . . . didn't we say one day of life alone?

One day, Raul read in a book, "the gods are partial to strawberries." Thus he came to believe that he was a god. Raul gave himself the name DEVA, and day and night he dwelled among strawberries. However . . .

However, DEVA did not grow wings. And things that are wingless are flightless. And angels did not appear overhead. Raul waited. He waited. He waited. When he was done waiting, he looked at himself in a mirror. And some strands of yellow hair seemed to come away in his fingers. Raul started.

"What's this?"

As he spoke these words, he heard a voice, very different, just like his father's.

For God's sake, stop it! Raul was waiting to grow wings, not a beard. He ran out onto the balcony and screamed.

That day, Raul knew that he wasn't really partial to strawberries. The strawberries in his dreams were too big, big as a fist, and they seemed even bigger, like big red eggs. Raul was conflicted. And Raul spent some years in such a state.

From Raul's Life: Day 6

Masturbation had not quite yet entered his life. But Raul was in pain. He wrote in his journal:

In Raul's dreams, for some unknown reason, he spent the time until nightfall with a woman; her legs were beautiful, she was wearing stilettos. And this Naomi, she was nicknamed Monkey. She had tried to kiss him. She knew that Raul was a man with Big Ideas. Big Ideas Raul—no, really, she meant Big Raul.

He wrote that when he was fifteen.

When he got to fifteen, he knew he was something special. He had a really good sense of smell. He understood that someone who smelled good was a good person. Raul hoarded the underwear of cute young girls, which he had stolen. The scent of otherness, of not-male, that hung in the girls' underwear pained him. One day . . . fortunately, this day did come . . . he found out about masturbation. Potentiality, utter potentiality. In this world, in fact, nothing is without potentiality. Raul counted himself saved from the commission of certain wickednesses. Now he was interested in the scent of women. Farewell stilettos.

From Raul's Life: Day 7

Raul walks the streets. They are packed. He doesn't like people. A young woman, a young man, a young . . . he treats them as himself. But taken all together, there is no humanity. . . . Raul doesn't like the word "community." Raul considers himself fortunate to have had no nursery schooling. But he lost his good fortune, he was abandoned at school. He was inducted. Raul is involved in not reducing his credit, as they say nowadays, in a lot of general work. That's because, for his parents, credit is really important. So Raul involves himself in it. Is it better to get tangled up together? This tangling upsets Raul. It hassles him.

*   *   *

Raul walks the streets. A young man comes toward him, long hair and a cold face.
Young man: Hey, are you Raul?
Raul: How do you know my name?
Young man: Your leather jacket's really cool.
Raul: Take it if you want. Here!

Young man: You're cool. How about coming back to my place?

Raul: What might there be at your place that would interest me?

Young man: Come and see!

Raul knew about many other types of music from listening to it at his sister's. The sky cleared suddenly. The young man with long hair and the leather jacket didn't begrudge this dude his cassettes. They became friends. They would meet every day, but only once a month did they talk. Raul was happy. But . . .

From where in life, like Mr. Suddenly, does this Mr. But emerge?

But there were a few problems at Raul's home. A few protests. A few struggles. A few irritations.

"Please turn that racket down!"

"He's hanging out with scum!"

"I'll find out who he's spending time with . . ."

"Rock music! Bang bang bang bang . . . !"

Raul listened to the bang bang bang bang rock music. For the first time, Raul felt that he was happy; he wrote in his journal: "I understand exactly how come my parents have never tasted fledgling!"

From Raul's Life: Day 8

Raul writes:

Nietzsche failed to express the crisis that occurred around his thirtieth year. How can people manage to forget themselves?! My own crisis began in my eighth year. Not mine, Raul's. It's not "I," in fact. From now on, in fact, I'll put an end to this "I" and learn, like my mom and dad, to talk of WE.

WE have graduated from middle school. WE are going to high school. The mind, unfortunately, has been taking notice of none of this. What WE learned is meaningless to US. With difficulty, WE passed the exams and went to a high school that Dad had heard about. It was like a high school. There was nothing there to engage the mind. Screwing around, just screwing around . . . With every step, these people became stuck to one another. WE hated sticking together with other people. WE stood it for three months and then left them behind. Couldn't deal with them. Many people, many smells. The combination of many smells is the most horrible smell in the world. No, by combining many smells you get a special smell of the world. . . . WE want to hold OUR nose and run away.

From Raul's Life: Day 9

Raul: I don't want to go to high school!
Father: You want to be scum then, is that what you're saying?
Raul: I just want to work.
Father: Don't talk nonsense. We'll not speak about this again!
  Get out!
Raul: In that case, I want to go to another school.
Father: What?
Raul: I want to go to a school focused on philosophy.
Father: Philosophy . . . couldn't you just think about life a bit?
Raul: I want to focus on philosophy.
Father: No!
Raul: I'm a philosopher!
Father: What about money?
Raul: I'm not going to be an economist!

Father: Imbecile!

Raul: I've decided, I'm going to focus on philosophy.

Father: Then clear off, I'm not giving you any money!

Raul put two pairs of underpants under his arm and left home by night. He furrowed his brows and vowed to himself: *I shall study philosophy if it kills me!*

That was his second vow.

Raul went through the door of the country's biggest university, four years had passed, he had combed and combed his hair. Nailed onto the door of every room was the sign NATIONAL UNIVERSITY. Suddenly Raul was frightened. For behind each iteration of the word NATIONAL was a second word—NOBODY'S.

He greeted his cold, scowling classmates. Raul entered into a group of glasses. Raul was in trouble among these philosophers.

"Professor, I have been assigned to your class."

"What subject?"

"Philosophical Approaches to Rock Music."

Suddenly . . .

An explosion like on a battlefield. With a suspicious glance, the professor looked straight through Raul's thin shirt and his heart, through to his lungs (the professor couldn't help himself).

"I can't teach something different to just one person!" he said, through clenched teeth.

Raul didn't understand why his teeth were clenched. If he thought about it, perhaps the professor was really not partial to the words "just one." He must have been a nonspecialist. Raul understood.

This teacher in the capital city, in the university, had a very loud voice. His voice was harsh, it hurt Raul's ears. Raul quickly shut his eyes and asked,

"Do you understand? This is my subject. . . ."

"No."

"Only this subject. . . ."

Another explosion.

"If you want to study education or ethics, then so be it. But if not, get out!"

"Education or ethics?"

Raul gave up with a laugh. The frost on all the glasses in the room melted. Raul's entire body bristled.

"Once I have paid my money and am studying, I can choose whatever subject I like. . . ." But before he could say this, Raul bit his tongue. He hadn't yet paid any money. Money, money, money. What should he do about the money? Though our friend, the one with the cold face and leather jacket, was in on Raul's plan to study philosophy, he was unable to sell his cassettes to help. Thus it was that they spent that year "resting." Raul sighed, he figured this period of "resting" could be understood as a period of gestation.

From Raul's Life: Day 10

Raul is sitting, in contemplation, in a hut of blankets. He is thinking about the lack of justice in the world.

Thinking. To pass time is the best method. How might you get done with this world in any other way? We are talking about getting done with school. Is that not also to say that getting done with life, getting done with the world, is the same thing?

To pass time is a bad thing. *Matar el tiempo. Ubit' vremya.* It's the same in Spanish, Russian, English. Literally, to kill time . . .

And sitting there, imagining everything that's gone, even the slaughter is pleasant.

Eggs, fish, strawberries, more eggs, fish . . . People flash before our eyes, Mr. This, Mrs. That, Ms. So-and-So . . .

Eggs, fish, strawberries . . . Enough!

Suddenly, Raul saw standing before him a live strawberry.

Girl: What are you doing?

Raul: I'm thinking.

Girl: What about?

Raul: None of your business.

The girl didn't get angry. Rather, she came and sat down next to Raul. They sat together, silent, past present future.

Girl: How about coming to my place?

Raul: What might there be at your place that would interest me?

Girl: I'll make you some toast.

Raul: Don't you have any sausage?

Girl: Toast tastes better than sausage.

She had a short skirt, this Strawberry, and a short chemise that showed her navel, and blue nail polish. She took big steps, like a man, and with every step her pale pink lingerie stuck out, and they moved toward her home. Her lingerie made Raul suddenly recall his youthful collection, and he wanted to try to smell this short young woman from very close by. They ate white bread, and as soon as they were sated, they got into bed. The girl decided to take the initiative and took off her clothes.

From Raul's Life: Day 11

Raul sat in the dock, his head bent. His father had not come to the trial. But his mother, wearing stilettos, sat in the courtroom, her long legs crossed, watching the judge, wiping and wiping her tears, stroking and stroking her hair until the trial was finished. The rapist's mother. Raul's mother. Nobody knew that this woman was a good mother, poor thing, that she was trained

RAUL AND RAUL

in collecting eggs, that she made such delicious food. The people would judge all of it today. And today she was a guilty mother. The guilty man's mother is guilty.

One of the judges wanted him to tell the jury what he remembered about how he had committed the act. Raul had acted in accordance with his desire. "My tongue acts, sucks a tongue . . ."

The presiding judge listened, open-mouthed, and Raul was amazed to watch how his appearance had softened.

No, no, it was not that he had a gentle face, but when Raul had met with this judge, who appeared to have softened, he had been happy. And precisely the same kind of voice cum glasses as the professor's grated on his ears. . . . From behind him, bang bang. One year's hard labor, in the name of the State . . . cracking, splitting.

Raul heard "in the name of the State" corrected to "in the name of Nobody."

Raul was punished.

Who?

God knows. That judge was really a fine man.

From Raul's Life: Day 12

Raul left the prison. His sister had paid 15 million *tögrög*, and after three months, he saw once more the faces of his family. Strawberry had some money, the Philosopher had some free time. He moved everything into her apartment.

When he came home from prison, he completely drooped. Basically, after he had sat around with prisoners for the first time, however much he tried, he was unable to look up. It was interesting how, the more he tried, the more his head bowed.

Young women passed him by. A strong smell, delicious, like fried meat, spread from far away, and the women wafted past him. And the more they wafted past, the more, the more Raul drooped.

Raul went to take a look at that place, but fortunately the car did not run him over. An official spoke to him through the window of the large, squat, matronly jeep:

"Are you blind? What are you doing, Crazyhorse?" he shouted, with a voice angry enough to smash the wheels of the other cars.

Raul the horse. The contemplative horse. The horse only wanted to be a philosopher.

Should he go home quietly then?

His mother and sister gazed cautiously. They were both dressed in long skirts. The criminal Raul. The demon Raul.

The man who for three months had not eaten a thing gulped down a plateful of eggs and was called away for just a moment. He went and rummaged in his library.

The guard, powerful like a jeep, who had insulted him and laid him low, told him that the red book had come. That troublesome Schopenhauer. Raul felt he needed to keep it out of the way.

What Schopenhauer had written from his own selfish perspective attracted Raul's interest. He took his journal and wrote:

Truly, this person sacrificed himself completely; perhaps he could have pulled someone from the black claws of death? My sister might have. Others . . . have their doubts. Others will have their doubts. . . . But I do not blame them. There is nothing to despise. Some people, it seems, know that it is not right to save a person when they are dying, if it's for the sake of research. Someone might save his son who is drowning. But as soon as his son had grown up he becomes an executioner, a thief. . . . Whose mistake? A person like my sister would have pulled him right out before he drowned. But what about me? No, the point is this I, what would WE have done? Are WE not good in the sense of being human, as OUR sister is? In fact, to talk about being good in the sense of being human lacks concreteness. It is meaningless to speak of a person with a good heart like MY sister in terms of "being human." So what does it mean to say that human waters are good or fresh? He's crazy, this Raul. No, it is WE who are fundamentally crazy. WE are guilty. WE are tired. WE do not want to struggle. When WE were born, WE were not happy. WE are useless, WE would feel pity. . . .

Raul closed his notebook.

From Raul's Life: Day 13

Raul: Sister, could you give me another egg?

Sister: Are you never, ever satisfied? How do you manage to eat so much? Shall I cook some more then?

Raul: Sure, so long as they're not raw.

Sister: Why don't you eat them raw? It's fine to eat them uncooked. Though you should eat them cooked! If you cannot do that, you can eat them raw! I'll be quick. You'll have a night of joy, and you'll pay for it! Do you know I work double shift? I'm tired. Exhausted.

Raul: If I eat them raw, will I get poisoned and die?

Sister: You're going to die. In fact, you'll be happy when you die.

Raul: I don't want to die.

Really, Raul didn't want to die. He left his sister's house, slamming the door, and there he sat and silently watched. He quickly stood up and ate the eggs until he was stuffed. But . . .

But Raul was in the hospital by evening, with a diagnosis of food poisoning, brought on by bad eggs.

RAUL AND RAUL

Sister: Raul, forgive me. Forgive your sister!

Raul: I didn't die, why are you crying?

Sister: Forgive me for saying that you would die!

Raul: You said that?

Sister You didn't eat yourself sick . . .

Raul: I stuffed myself!

Sister: Lying bastard! You poisoned yourself, did you? Did you eat raw eggs?

2002

24

EVERYTHING

S. ANUDAR

It is all nothing.
Everything lacks existence.

As for the policeman, he was on the lookout for Davaa. Davaa was the guilty one. The policeman was helping Ider get him. Ider was Davaa's friend.

Policeman:. . . you know?

Ider: I know. Davaa's at their place.

The policeman, the state, power, authority. A huge iron, pressing against the sky, with Ider below. From when they were children. Brothers, sisters, mother, father—he'd managed them. It wasn't a large black iron.

Summer. Green lawns. Yellow sun. Flies. A child playing with a ball. A three-year-old child, all alone, playing with a ball. On a green lawn. People walking nearby. The child kicks the ball. An unknown child. Ider feels sorry for this child. He does not know why he feels sorry for him. Ider loves his daughter. He loves children. His daughter loves her father. When he comes in from work, he's brought sugar. She's happy. A four-year-old girl, his child, in a yellow *deel*, sitting on his shoulders. With her small hands she embraces his neck. Her father says, "Okay, get down now," and she says, "Oh . . . what?" pretending she hasn't heard. Her mother comes out of the kitchen. "Okay, my girl, come here now."

"Oh . . . what?"

The three of them laugh. Ider looks at the photo. Seems there's something there. The phone rings.

Ider: Yes.

Davaa: Ider?

Ider: Yes.

Davaa: I'm at their place. Didn't you give them the money? I've got to get out of here.

Ider: Okay . . . when?

Davaa: Now.

Ider: Okay.

His sweaty hand replaces the receiver. As soon as he heard Davaa's voice, he got frightened. From the time they were children, the police would smash them with clubs. In school they had stolen, had always protected each other. Their hearts beat together. Suppose he's listening in on the call. If he spoke with Davaa on the phone, they'd be on to him—*Who's he speaking to?!* When he comes to hand over the money, the cops'll be lying in wait. A terrible fear. He's shaking. They know he'll be bringing the money. My one and only close friend. Ider's younger brother (Jargal) is on his way. Don't worry so. Don't worry, he's got to take the money. His heart's beating. The iron is coming to grab his beating heart.

Ider: You know their place?

Jargal: I know it.

Ider: So . . . nobody knows you . . . you go hand it over. They know I'm Davaa's friend.

Jargal: Fine, okay.

Ider gives him the money. Jargal takes it and leaves. Their hearts are beating together. Why do this? They'll get Davaa.

He knows everything. I'll be in prison. A black iron. The state. Terror. Why do this? Will Jargal get back? I'll be fine now. I'm worried about Jargal. Why worry? I'm going to prison. I'm worried about him getting back. I'm frightened. Terror. His wife and child returned from work and kindergarten. He watched them happily. They both go and change. Mother helps her daughter. On the large plain yellow wall, to the left, shines a light, the light of joy. Later they eat dinner together and talk. "That's him. A boy in my class . . . yes." Lovely. Ider listens, adds comments, inside he feels better. Ider likes being with his family like this, he's happy. He has a good face, a spot above his lip. His daughter asks something. He answers. *My girl's growing up. I love them.*

Jargal comes back. The wooden floor echoes loudly. They go into another room.

Ider: So?

Jargal: I gave it to them.

Ider: What happened?

Jargal: We didn't say much. I told them you were leaving.

Ider: When?

Jargal: Tomorrow.

Ider let him go. As Jargal left, the phone rang. The heart that had died a few days ago would die later.

Ider: Yes?

Policeman: Is that Ider's home?

Ider: Yes.

The policeman gave his name and rank: I'm calling about Davaa. Do you know where Davaa is?

Ider: . . . I don't know, no.

Policeman: Come at five o'clock to the sixth district. Suburban department.

Ider: Okay. Tomorrow at five.

Tomorrow then. Tomorrow at five. Davaa and I became friends when we were ten. He was never quite right. Fear. What am I saying? They'll get Davaa. Prison. What am I saying? A thick iron column up into the sky. Everything is close, is far away. It gushed out money for the guilty. What's friendship got to do with it? The child's ball. I love my wife. Evening. Dancing. With my friends. A change of role. A monk. The first meeting. I'm in love.

A person looks after their friends. He'll give a statement to the policeman. He'll look after his friend by sacrificing himself. He takes a yellow Ikarus bus. "Wow, it's really packed." His stop. A two-minute walk to the policeman's place. The policeman's place. A building, the sky overhead. A uniformed guard. Fear. A statement. Uniform. He goes into his kiosk and brings two notebooks. Paperwork. Nearby he hails a taxi. He takes the taxi home.

Fear. From when they were children. Iron rule. I love my wife. Evening. Dancing. With my friends. A change of role. A monk. The first meeting. I'm in love. Four seasons. Davaa. Great fear, the great state. Doubt. Doubt furthermore that he knows that I told everything. I know I'll tell him and he'll go and get Davaa. Doubt all the while. Jargal came.

Ider: After you went, I got a call from the policeman. He said to come today at five.

Jargal: And?

Ider: Well . . . should I go or not? He'll find me. He'll find Davaa.

Jargal: Davaa'll be fine.

Ider: Well . . .

They were silent. Lawns. Children. A child playing with a ball. People walking nearby. Flies. Ider's fear seems obvious. Jargal looks at him sadly. Doubt. My friend Davaa. A huge column nearby. No. I'll say nothing.

Ider: I'll say nothing. Say I don't know. You too, if he asks.

Jargal: Yes.

Ider: I'm going. Say nothing, right?

They understood each other. Respect. A lively march tune blared out. Comradely. Heroism shone forth. Determined Ider. Determined Jargal.

It was over.

Everything. When they looked, everything. When they closed their eyes, everything. Always. Everything.

Delger.

Snow, salt, a white color stretches over the ground. Two lights. A pair of electric lights. And in the sky, snow, a little snow shines in the light. Night. Broad in one direction, broad in the other direction. Inside, ashes. I have nothing, nobody then. And I have everything, and everyone. Always. I'll not be downcast because of this. I'm not sad. I want to be here. This is how I live. I'll tell myself *I'm happy*, and it's a lie; I'll tell myself *I'm sad*, and it's a lie. Everything is a lie. Here is true, it's not a lie. Nothing. Here everything is one thing. I don't trust anything I say, or think, or think to say, and I don't trust that I don't trust it. No need to think, it's not true, not about faith, about Stavrogin, about anything. No reason. Yes.

Everything.

Always.

There was someone sitting in the room. Ider. A gentle fear overflowed within him. The room was light. A wooden ruler breaks silently. Smashed gently like a fly. Slowly he presses the ruler. He breaks it gently, no splintering. His hand hurts. Everything is pretty good. Pretty good. Everything. It was time to go to the policeman. He's on his way. The closer he gets, his fear is as it was before, it seeps and drips as it did before. He says where Davaa is. He's come to the city. He was interrogated in the room. It made him want to watch the policeman carefully. "I don't know. I don't know anything." After a few words, the policeman said, "So you know then."

Ider: I know . . .

Policeman: So think then . . .

Ider: The district, the building, the floor, the apartment, the phone where they are . . .

And after three months, Davaa's case was decided. Davaa went to prison. They were far from finished with Ider. The witness, fear. The iron column.

Policeman: You know?

Ider: He's at their place . . . the address . . .

. . . Ider's house. The picture on the wall, the sun and the moon. Nearby, a mirror, clean of fly shit. A TV. His wife and child, sitting on the sofa. Ider enjoys watching them. It's right for me. If I went to prison, what would my family do? I'm unable to be brave, to manage things for my wife and child. And if I were all alone, without a family, what would be the difference? Davaa doesn't matter. I can't stop fear. From when I was a child. The flesh and blood of frightened people. On the screen. On the road. People looking behind, their outlook is white. He walks quickly. He needs to cut himself. He moves abruptly, to cut a vein. A blade against his right arm. He moves his left arm abruptly away, the right arm gets a bit stuck. Again. He moves it away again. Sweat on his arm. He puts the knife on his right arm and cuts, gently cuts. Too gently. Again. Too gently.

. . . a few years. Ider has a good life. A wife, a child, a job. The curtains pulled apart, happiness increasing. Everything happy. One single resentment. My one and only close friend. My one and only friend in prison. I snitched on my one and only friend. One resentment colors everything. When he meets with Jargal, there's an edge. For both of them. The man came and went. Papers in his hand. A light behind him. Many chairs. A high ceiling. People there. One single resentment. I was afraid; I snitched on my one and only friend. I was so afraid. When I did this, I was in the light. I had hope. It's right for me. It's right not to reveal the guilty, not to think of my wife and child, not to be selfish. This is hope, is light. The light is right for me. But how can the light of goodness shine if I am worried?

The window sill. White frames. Between the frames, the carcasses of many flies. Their remains upon the black earth. Legs, heads, thoraces, everything preserved in a gray dust.

A person looks after their friends. He'll give a statement to the policeman. He'll look after his friend by sacrificing himself. He takes a yellow Ikarus bus. "Wow, it's really packed." His stop. A two-minute walk to the policeman's place. The policeman's place. A building, the sky overhead. A uniformed guard. Fear. A statement. Uniform. He goes into his kiosk and brings two notebooks. Paperwork. Nearby he hails a taxi. He takes the taxi home.

Fear. When I did this, I had hope. He gently kicks the ball. The child runs in from behind. A three-year-old child. Why does Ider feel sorry for him?

They give Davaa an amnesty; his sentence won't be over when he's let out. Ider and Jargal are happy, but also disturbed, to hear of Davaa's imminent release.

Ider: What's going to happen to us?

Jargal: So you couldn't write Davaa when he was in prison?

Ider: I'll meet him now. I have to go meet him.

Jargal: Yes. You go meet Davaa when he gets out.

Ider: Let's both of us go. It'll be hard on my own.

Jargal: Yes.

The day of Davaa's release.

They smashed the bottle they'd found to celebrate with. Jargal had dropped it. Too uptight and nervous. They'd found another.

Davaa gets out. Spring. It's bright, and yellow pollen. Ider and Jargal wave at Davaa. They hardly find any words to speak, or any way to be. They're sorry. Look him in the eye. Nothing's different.

Davaa tells Ider: I understand. You're not to blame. It was right for you. I wasn't happy that you'd given me in. When you did that, it was right for you. I would have done exactly the same in your position. You're not to blame. Nobody would be. . . .

Jargal: Yes.

Davaa: What's the point of worrying now about what's happened. I have nothing to be upset with either of you for. I'm beginning a new life now . . .

And when Ider heard such wise words, a light shone in his heart. Hope forms. Everything's good. Bright. Happy. The two friends laugh. Ider cracks a joke; now all three of them are laughing. The sun is shining. The yellow sun of happiness. The sun of today's happiness, the sun of happiness for every day to come. *Calamity flees from the one who has loyal friends.*

It's over.

Everything. While they watched.

Always.

Delger.

Gerel: No, I'm not interested. (I'm interested in Gerel.)

I ask outright: Do you want to meet up? Answer: No, I'm not interested.

The one I'm interested in's not interested in me. She's not interested. No matter. The most important thing is that everything's good. Whatever happens, everything has to be good. It's as if you're watching yourself, imagining yourself from far away.

I'm like that. That's how I am. Everything's good. You have two "I"s, one is not a name, has no qualities or ideas, just "I," happy to be an oscillation of white. You're nothing, you need nothing. This other one is Delger, twenty-one, sensitive, well behaved. Delger is happy, unhappy, he fails. Whatever happens to Delger, everything is good for this nameless "I." Whatever I do to become Delger, to destroy Delger, from moment to moment I am failing. Now everything's good. If I squeeze my senses between the door, if I put a flame twenty centimeters from my armpit, if I use tools and instruments, then the two "I"s disappear and a new "I" appears—it's pain, only pain. This new "I" comes from the two old ones, everything else becomes just one thing, it's pain. Nothing else remains, it's just painful.

For now everything's good. For now—that is, this moment of life. Where? Who cares. At home with Mom and Dad. Here everything's good. A stop. A bus stop. People I know—what is it?—what is it? The bus comes. A few people run to get on. They all get on. Nobody at home. The kitchen. The kitchen floor. Everything on the kitchen floor. Today is an unhappy day: no, I'm not interested. Unhappy means unhappy. Unhappy is a concept, it envelops the concept, it goes inside, enormous. Yes—everything's good. Can't do anything. A tape, music. Mom and Dad are coming. They are good people. When they ask me something, I tell them. They're not irrelevant to me. I'm happy that they created me and raised me. Completely. Relevant things—me, my work, what I have to do, some people who are connected with what I have to do. My work— being, living, the ability to be alive. I am able. And if I am, I am not unhappy with what I have, it's good. Everything's good. Every morning, every day. The clouds thin out a little and the moon grows thirty watts brighter.

Everything at school too. I like coming here. Not that I like studying; it's my friends, people who know what to do. "A person needs somewhere to be." (F. M.) Many places are better than just one place. I have a stipend for studying. Teachers come and go. They give classes. I chat aimlessly with Baatar. Baatar's outlook is white, white plaster walls. "No matter. Everything's good." He looks through the window. The buildings of Ulaanbaatar, the sky overhead. Ulaanbaatar's inhabitants, vehicles transporting them. Private and public. Everything else. On our floor, there's a man who looks intriguing; he comes over. He's got to give me a fair bit of money. "What is it? What is it?"

"Hi." He handed over the money. We'll get rich sitting on the window frame. Baatar and Ime, we'll go do something. Baatar speaks with Ariunaa, and we arrange to meet the next day. We go to class. Lessons. Study. Everything's good. From when we were children. I thought about nothing until I was fourteen; everything was good. In the eighth grade I started to understand. Being here, sitting in this class, I was just happy to be here. So I said to myself, *Now you're happy, think about it, there's nothing better than this, you'll get nothing better.* Always, from now on. Every morning, every day. I don't think about how it began. I sat in class and understood that what was lovely was good. I hurried to my classroom. No matter when it would come to an end. Here and there. No difference. Sitting there, thinking about playing with children nearby, everything's good. Just the same, from now on. The lesson begins, ends, I come, I go, I live, I don't live, the important thing is that everything's good. Here and there.

Home, Mom and Dad. They say: Give it to Zolbayar. Okay. Far from their place. On foot. Spring. Nobody at home. I stand there smoking, and watch the light meter. For now no flies. Zolbayar comes. Hi—Hi—Yes—Thanks—Thanks. It's hot outside, windy. I stay at home that evening. Night, dreams, spring, nightmares now and then—I switch the light on. Another way—I'm not afraid. I'm interested in bad dreams; if I wait for them to come, they don't. Really I'm not afraid. If I pay them no attention, they don't overwhelm me.

Afterward it's morning, afterward it's daytime.

Classes at school come to an end. Baatar and Ariunaa are standing waiting at the bus stop. *When were we meeting? Sunday at six, at Saraa's.* Saraa is a relative of Baatar's. A pretty girl.

Unfortunately, her husband died. I didn't particularly like the dead man. My bus comes. Baatar and Ariunaa are waiting. Baatar's not married, he's a good guy. After he started going out with Ariunaa, they hardly ever met me outside of school. It's not comfortable, they're not behaving; we exchange a few bits of trashy gossip. The bus—the street. The broad sky, our city and our home beneath it. The lift's not working today. Home, a room. Watercolors. Globs of paint mixed with water. I paint a little, day after day. Four things in one thing. Sun, moon, earth, sky. Material colors and shapes, nothing more. Everything. Always the broad sky, always the empty earth, the red sun, the white moon. What I like the most—to paint a picture. Sublimation. I'll add a little red, the ground's a bit bigger, cut a little away. Make two circles with compasses. Measuring out the sun and moon, nothing else. I realize that everything's good, I feel the floor where I'm sitting, the wall against which I'm leaning; my eyes are open; I sit and feel the one thing that's inside me, everything. Everything's good. Happiness.

It's not that it's good, I'm not expecting something good, I'm not going to reject something bad, but everything's good. I don't fear anything. Two obstacles—the pain that comes when death and bad things happen. I don't know death. I don't regret death. But when bad things happen, I become somebody else. I have other interests, everything else, and it's the sadness that comes from everything else. Another life. Life doesn't matter to me now. That man's irrelevant to me. Now everything's good for Delger. I don't know what has happened to me, what to do, it doesn't matter, it would make no difference if I did know. What is it? That's what it is. Just exist, don't think about everything. The happiness that comes from happiness, there's nothing more. I experience this happiness despite myself. I am happy despite what's bad. I am not more happy because of what is good. I'm up against it. This everything.

This good everything. So there's a little suffering nearby. In the beginning, I thought about the reasons for this. Fear, desire for something, lack of something, improvement. Now there's no fear, there's nothing improved, nothing lacking. It is everything I desired at that time. Ashes. Something drawn in the ashes. A way out of the suffering that is everything I want to do. So everything must be good. I can say, I want to say, "Everything's good," and when I can, then everything's good. Sleep now. Shit in a bag is good when it's in a bag, and when a man's asleep, it's good.

I leave home early in the morning. The bus is empty. I like the bus better when it's empty. There's hardly anyone at school. Thinking of the money I've got, it'll cover four bottles of booze. Class, and class again. During the break I meet Zaya. A good friend. Don't you want to borrow some money? How much? Five hundred. Delger counts out five hundred. A man carrying a sheet of white paper passes close by. I don't go to the next class. I'll go to the store and get a half-bottle. The store. Two of wine, one of *arhi*. Yes. I come back and go to school. School. Who knows if I'll go to the fourth period? I have a smoke in the corridor. I have to meet someone. There's nothing to see. I have to meet Baatar. There's nothing to see. Tomorrow I'll find Baatar and talk to him about something, about today or the day after tomorrow, every day we speak about something. Well? I'm waiting for the teacher. There's a window nearby. For now there are no flies. I stop smoking, I like to come up to the window and breathe deeply. I inhale smoke from a burning filter. Notice how the clothes aren't burning with the trash. Quite good. Everything's good. You're all trouble. Trouble. I go home. I'll go home and drink a bottle. Everything's good. You're all trouble. It's hot outside, windy. At home, no wind, it's hot. One bottle, one glass, one person. Everything has to be alone. Everything is alone. It's good to drink wine and think that everything's good. The best. I feel something, it's not peaceful. I'm painting, something seems troubling, not peaceful. The trouble is too much, happiness has fled, has gone away. Too much: things that are too much bear a particular debt. I'll pay it. So what to do? Trouble. I'll get a bottle of arhi tomorrow, I'll drink these two now. Everything's good for me. I don't need everything, the main thing is something else, is tobacco, is wine. I'll die, you'll die, we'll all die—do what you enjoy. The red light of the curtain. I finish the two bottles. I paint a picture, drunk. I cry onto the picture, I paint with my tongue, I lick red color and swallow it. I paint my face. Up. Up. Down! Everything's good, I'll make it good. I'll push it beyond, that I can, I'll pay the debt in reply. I'll make it even better, more and more, I'll sink down into one thing, into everything, without closing my eyes. I think of nothing, I have a single desire, to paint myself. Happiness. So I'll go further and further, into something else. There is nothing else. Everything has no existence. Everything is always as it was, I am as I always was, the debt is as it always was. Everything is as it always was, is vomit. This payment. A curse. So I'll come back, into the selfsame happiness. So I am, I am living, every day every night.

The next day's meeting. Six o'clock on Sunday. I leave home and, as I put into my jacket pocket the arhi that had been in the pocket of my pants, I drop it and it smashes. I should have kept it out of my pockets. It echoes against the stone floor, a stink of alcohol. Half done is half done. I go to Saraa's and we're all gathered there, everything's provided, I enjoy drinking with my friends. Everything's provided. Our conversation goes as follows:

Baatar: Everything's good for me now. Ariunaa, money, work—everything's good. So I should give something in return for all this, I should give more than money. I'll pay money. I'm not afraid of paying. I can. Everything's a pile of stinking garbage.

Saraa: Life always takes too much payment from me. I was happy with Nergüi. Everyone around me dies, I lose them, they die, I feel anxious. "The ground where people are broken grows hard." I'm grown hard. Because everyone around me dies. If they had lived, I would not have grown hard. I'm hardened, happy.

Delger: I don't tell anyone what's inside of me. I don't tell anyone exactly what I think and believe. Only myself. Now there's nothing at all. It comes of being a person. I tell everything. So once I became silent, I learned to be silent. I don't say what I don't say. If I say it, I'll say it; if I won't, I won't. I spoke it. Everything's good. I know nothing.

It was good for us. Everyone's happy. Everything. Drink, drink. Everything's good. Later, it was tomorrow. I'm sitting in class, drawing a picture. Such a picture was me. It's hard to say that about myself, it couldn't be other than hard. It's possible. I don't know. And I still know what I knew. It has clarity. What is this clarity? An explanation. An explanation of clarity. An explanation of many words. To explain the words . . . further. Trouble. I exist as myself. I do. I would appear as I appear. I would. Possibly different. No connection. So I do what I think to do. Sometimes more, sometimes less.

I raise shellfish. The water stinks, it's slimy, they had food. Because of the seashells, I put salt into the water. A lot. So they died. Everything's garbage. Whatever people do is garbage. Whoever it is who does whatever, it's garbage. The smell is odd. Everything. Another person might see something quite other, but it seems like garbage to me. Garbage with an odd smell. I make garbage with an odd smell. Like something else. Thinking how they make something of themselves, when I look at myself there's a bad smell. It's all irrelevant. What does anyone think? Who cares? The important thing is desire. I have no control over my head. I make pointless garbage, it's as though I had done nothing, this is how it is. I want to do it.

Everything's garbage. I want to live. The bell doesn't ring in our classroom. The lesson ends. I go outside and head home. Outside it's a spring day, many spring days, the third month of spring, the third month of summer. . . . Every day. No wind, hot. Everything's good. A yellow Ikarus, just cleaned, a tidy Ikarus. Later, a little yellow earth stuck on. The sun strikes the yellow paint. Nearby everything is bright. I go inside and sleep, wake up, paint. Everything.

Morning. A morning drink. I don't want to go. I want to stay here. My home, I'm inside. I've got guests coming. Guests—my mind's hotel. Sadness, Happiness, their friends, everything. They knock at the door and come in. My door has a string lock, can't break it. I don't dislike that someone's come. Like them. Everything. I don't need to invite anyone. They don't have an invitation, not even them. Let them come. I'll be waiting. Tea? After they've come, I don't like to clean the cups. Let them have a place to sit. Everything has to be where I am. Tea? I like it when they come in. If they don't like something, they don't go there. Though I go, they stay. I'm living with them. With all of them. Everything. Though from time to time they stop appearing, I always feel them there, and their coming. They go nowhere. They cover, kill one another; afterward they revive, sometimes themselves. No connection. I don't know. I want to stay on my own. If everything is locked and the house burns, smoke gets in my lungs. I like cigarette smoke in my lungs. One cigarette. Another. I got left in the first class, I managed to get to the next, I had another, everything.

I haven't found Baatar in school, he didn't come. I'll expect to go down. He's got to come. I approach the wall and stop. He's talking with someone. Everything. He's come. We go into an empty classroom and talk there, smoking. Everything's good. Baatar: I had a dream, a fly's dried and frayed wing. I always forget. I know I'll stop now. I'll not move away, I don't want to move away. We two are one thing, everything. I know he'll do it, I'm not sad that I know he'll not manage it, be as you are, go as you go: we're always going. *We know absolutely nothing.* Yes. *So it seems that there's always one thing.* Always one thing. So everything's good.

In the classroom I look at a book. If you're good, everything's good; if you're bad, everything's bad. If you're good, it's good for you. I don't know such things. What more is there but "good" and "bad"? I don't know, there's nothing. Such a thing doesn't exist. Strange-smelling shit is neither good nor bad. No reason. Everything is fine. No reason. *Okay, I'll go home.*

The air is extremely cold. Windless. A warm bus. Warm people. Just a few. The driver sticks a picture to the windshield. A picture from a film. Shimmering. I never understand anything. My stop, my things, my everything. Every day.

One day. Another day. Everything.

The next day. Baatar and I stand around and smoke, passing it back and forth, passing everything back and forth. We laugh. We like to ridicule things. Baatar's waiting for Ariunaa. It's good to laugh. I had an image at first of Baatar's wife, and when I saw her I didn't like her much. She wasn't particularly nice to her husband's friend. On the other hand, we're quite similar. Now I've gotten to know her, she's all right. So I don't understand the life of people who are not me, the way they are. Different lives are pretty interesting to me. They're all rather similar. Another life—I don't trust it. It's interesting to think that a person feels nothing, has nothing, after they've died. They're all similar.

Ariunaa comes down. They go home together.

There's earth on the window frame. Someone pulls up near to Baatar.

They get into the car and drive off.

Zaya's also going. Zaya's talking with Tseren.

Zaya: You know Delger?

Tseren: Yes.

Zaya: The old woman's gone. Give the money to Delger.

Tseren finds the money and gives it to me. We go outside today and buy cigarettes, we buy cigarettes for the days to come. The days to come. Day after day.

Football comes on the TV. I'm interested in football. The strongest team definitely wins. Strongest? An explanation. The referee's got it wrong; the best attacker, luckily or not so luckily, gets his leg broken; it's raining.

They're watching football at home too. I go out—the corridor, the clean mirror, the floor, the room. Fate, destiny—what do they say? A plague of flies. A policeman on a bike. For some time the shellfish can hardly move, though then they do. It's a warm wind that brings torrential rain. Destiny, fate—with you, it happens, the very moment you sense they're there. A person sleeping is on the dead side. So I want to live.

We stand and talk. We like to talk, we like to stand. *We know absolutely nothing. So it seems there's always one thing.* Always one thing. Look over there. I never make promises to anyone. I was born like that. I don't owe anything to anyone. So everything's nearby. Everything's good. Baatar went, he'll not come back. They always come back. I'm not sure I'd come back. What you know is yourself. Everything is yourself. There's nothing other than yourself. So then. Let's go back. Everything's good at first; later it's not like that, and we go back.

One earth, one sky, one sun, one moon. They don't rise, they set; the new moon is not the old moon—I wonder. We are what we are. Everything's good now. I forget what was, I don't think about what exists. There's no time other than now. Just now. I include you in this, you never go anywhere. I never went anywhere—quick as a flash—here I was! Always. I've always been what I am, been what I'm not. I never have been. It's not that I exist. I don't know, I don't know that I don't know.

Here it's not good, it's not bad, it's not pleasant, it's not unpleasant. It's okay—one thing—everything. Leave what's here alone; there's no point otherwise, no other desires. If it seems like you have to do something, then do it, do what you do, everyone is what they are. Be what you are. For now you are here. Not these four walls. This one wall, upright. No point in breaking the wall, or beating it. This wall is everything. You shouldn't break everything, shouldn't beat everything. The situation you've broken, beaten, and ended up in, that's every-thing. Everything is in every situation. But I'll move a little away from here. *A little away from here.* Yes. I'll watch myself from a distance. I'm like this, I'm like that. I look from here and everything's good. I'll move a little away then, I have to be able to move away. When I can, everything's good. When you're far away you'll be pushed back, pushed back into yourself. Always pushed back. Knowing this, I'm not sad. Until the time when I'm not sad comes to an end, until this comes, then don't be sad. Later there's no point. What's important is now. Everything's good.

Today everything exists. I am alive.
Degii, someone on the phone for you.
Who?
Baatar.
The phone. Now there are some people coming for Baatar. So I have to be with Baatar, I'm not interested in dying alone. Baatar's calling me. We'll die together. I'm not going. No need to go. I'm afraid. It's easy to overcome fear. I'm not afraid. Other people's affairs are other people's affairs, they're irrele-vant to me. I don't cry when children fall over. I make children fall over. I make children cry.

I want to die when I die. Now I'm alive. This one here, he's not mine. Mine has never existed now. A person has to under-stand their own death. He's not mine now. So it's a regular day.

Everything. I haven't forgotten Baatar. No point in forgetting everything. Everything that I have exists always and constantly. Everything is with me, whatever happens, the words I have spoken—I think constantly about everything. If I exist, then everything exists. Whatever I have done—standing talking with someone, jumping from a cliff, whatever I do outside and inside, everything is constant. The nature of everything is in everything. Gray dust on yellowish earth. I always know. Suddenly, when something is or is not done, I know directly that it has or has not been done. I always know what can or cannot be done. I think for three days, and a new thought does not appear. Always. Every morning. Every day. Everything's good.

He said to me that he would have Baatar killed. I knew, I wasn't grieving or sad. Everything is grief here; if there are no cells, everything's good. If I grieve about everything, I'll grieve about everything. If something's good, then everything's good . . . Grief is better. If I am not feeling grief, then a little further and everything's good. I have no friends to meet at school. So in fact I didn't meet with Baatar. Neither Baatar nor I was born here. Why am I grieving that nonexistence has no existence? But why grieve that there is no need for what does exist, or has existed? If I do or do not grieve for everything, it's one thing, it's everything.

Home—school—me—two days. Just two days. I know how it is with me. Always ready for everything. When I'm at home, I know that I could be without a home, I'm ready. I know how I would be if I were armless and legless and blind, I'm ready. Nothing happened these past two days. Later Gerel came by to ask me something, I answered, and we went off together. Gerel's a sweet girl. Everything's good with us. We're in love. Our conversation goes like this:

Delger: I'm such and such a man, I do this, I do that. I like such and such things. Perhaps there's someone who doesn't like such and such things. That's what he said. How can I understand this? I speak about myself and you understand yourself. It doesn't matter. Most important is that something is said. Why and how.

Gerel: I'm always thinking about something.

Delger: Always about something.

Gerel: Talk about how you'll die.

Delger: I don't think at all about it.

We decide to get married. Not now, but in a while.

Oh Delger, you smoke too much.

I go to a resort with my class. Gerel doesn't go. Delger's sitting on the ground, smoking. The nature's beautiful there. Peaceful bare mountains. Bogd Uul, the holy mountain. The air's different from in the city. The nature's beautiful. I don't like beautiful things. Two little kids are playing football. Everything's good. I haven't stopped drinking every day. A few hours every morning, I start when the sun rises. Scattered light from the horizon passes through the two dust surfaces on my glasses and enters my addled head. The small yellow sun begins to emerge from behind the mountain, protruding little by little. Kidney-shaped droplets of blood come little by little from the small wound. The blood doesn't clot, it overflows the droplet and brightens every day. Later I go to sleep. Every day is bright; we go home sitting in the bus. We get to the city and take another bus. Everything's good. I want to go back. I sleep every day. Morning: class. When class is through I go to Gerel's. I live quite close by. A high yellow building. We ate, drank, slept. It was good with her folks. Everything was good with them.

Gerel: So why didn't you go to Baatar's?

Delger: I was afraid.

Geree: You weren't afraid. You've nothing to be afraid of.

Delger: I don't care about anyone. I have to be myself. I don't care about anyone.

Gerel: Even me?

Delger: Even you.

We fought.

My paintings, my pictures. I painted another. In the last three pictures, I just painted them—the sun's too big, there's no moon. A big dark red sun. I meet Gerel at school. We smoke together. I tell her I was wrong, we talk about many things. We talk about one thing.

Delger: It always seems to be one thing. We know nothing. I think sometimes it seems there's something. No need. Why? I need it. Why? I'm not Delger, I'm me. There are things hanging between being and nonbeing. *Between what and what? Being doesn't exist. Not being doesn't exist. Not at all. I know. Seems I know everything.*

Gerel: Always something. It doesn't appear so, there's no appearance. No need, just no need. You're always another person.

Delger: Yes.

Delger and Gerel are a couple again.

It's hot outside. My home. We watch TV. A movie. A man comes home from war; his friends welcome him. Laughter. Flowers. The end. When I watch such things, I laugh, I don't like it. Gerel likes it when films end like this. We're different. But we love each other. Everything's good now. It was good to be on my own, and it's good now. Everything. Constantly alive.

It looks like there's no class. We smoke in the corridor. We're smoking TU-134s. Zaya also doesn't have class. As soon as I see someone I know whether I'll be friends with them, or hate them. Mostly I don't care. Zaya's a nice guy. I look through the window, everything's the same. *Always one thing.* Gerel didn't go to work today. She has to come at one-thirty. Meanwhile I have a couple of classes. Class is okay.

Gerel and I watch a play here this evening. I really enjoy drama. Drama is artificial, deceitful; it doesn't hide itself, people talking but not talking, a painting full of clothes and faces that never leave the theater. I take Gerel home. Three men call out to me. Three drunk men. *Hey, come here . . . We just want to ask you something.* They're after money.

No. Don't talk to me. Those two are standing at a distance, watching the UB evening . . . *I'm just talking.* We should let them be. Two electric lights nearby. Some guys come out, want to walk quickly close by. I'm happy to leave work, my face and hand have gone hard. Those three head off in one direction, I go in another direction.

Mom: A girl came by yesterday with a bag for you. What is it?

Paints.

New paints. One earth, one sky, the red sun's too big. A picture—*You're free.* Another color. Red sun, blue sky, dark blue sky. Nothing more than this, there's too much happiness. I start wanting to run away from here, from this freedom. There's really nothing better than this excess of happiness: nothing better. If I get it before I pass away, I'll be charged for it. I know that nobody, nobody can get away from here, so do it, and don't be sad. That's how it is now. Everything's good. The oversized red sun. Everything. In the evening I go to Gerel's. Everything's good with her folks. This and that. Always. I was bringing a cassette for Gerel. I forgot it. Everything's good. Tomorrow—tomorrow doesn't matter. Everything.

In the morning, I wake from my dreams, I wake again and again. I sit up and look around. I don't want to see anything. It's hot outside. On the way to school, I think about how it's hot, walk fast. Don't think about anything.

I get close. I approach the school but I don't go inside. I know I'm being followed, so I don't turn around and look. I get close. It's hot outside; it's warm in the school too. There's a man in a white dressing gown selling *buuz*. Flies jostling one another.

Lots of people. *Delger, go to class.* I'll go. The teacher's saying things that are not interesting, not interesting and not true. I don't like things that are not true. So I don't like this. Something else. Everything else is the same. I realize, I perceive, that soon, right now, everything is mental vomit, and as soon as I realize this, it pours into me. Pour into me, pour into me! Watch. No matter. It clots and covers everything, this mental vomit; no point in believing in the old good. When everything's good, everything's not good. It must be, it must exist. You shouldn't chase the visitors away, the visitors are you yourself. You vomit, and you clean away the vomit.

I'm troubled that bad things are happening, I hope that things will be okay later, that they'll be good. There's nothing now, nothing's different. Just ashes: absorbed, inserted. So there's fluctuation. Back and forth. Everything back and forth, near and far away. Choking on vomit, covered in ashes.

I have no desire; nothing seems pleasant to me. As soon as I look, there's vomit, the eyes looking on are vomit. Whatever I do—I'm alive, I get money for being alive. It's a living. It's good that everything's been good. I had the desire for everything to remain good. If I have a desire, I have the desire and the enthusiasm and the pleasure that the desire be realized. Everything's good. *Ashes.* There must be a support for this desire. The support, that everything's good, a support for me, then I can say, "Everything's fine." It's not good now. They say, "Everything's good," right? Is it really fine? Not with this one. *I'm choking.* Good or bad don't exist. At all. Not at all. How am I to play with this not-at-all? *Vomit.* What does this existence do? Again. *Vomit.* What does this existence do? Again. *Ashes.* The cover of a book, the pages of a book. Karl Marx. Ernest Hemingway. Religion—the opium of the people. They need opium. Everything is opium.

The two pleasures. Alcohol and girls. According to Rinaldi, the one is an obstacle to work, the other takes only a half hour.

More than half an hour, then you're waiting for nature, for the natural process, to show itself. So you need two people. Two people—two pieces of trash—ashes—so only half an hour. One of them is wet. Happiness: again—more—again more, a few protracted moments. Warm ashes. Then I like to go outside, lean against a wall, and smoke. Ashes.

The other one's an obstacle to work. I have no work to be obstructed. The old people say that being around alcohol is paradise. Everything's a paradise, you don't need it. A few hours drinking, you really don't need it. What do the doctors say?

There are more powerful things than alcohol—heroin, morphine, opium, LSD . . . If you use them every day, every morning, then you can be freed from all this. Not completely after a few hours. (You need a lot of money—ashes.) If you smoke and drink and have sex every day you'll be free from all this, you'll have another life. Another man with another life. This other Delger's nothing to me. I want to be myself. So I'm not afraid of being an alcoholic, not that, there's no connection between the alcoholic Delger and today's Delger. Ashes. This is how it is now. In another life, they're not drunk, not happy with the best of the best, they have a normal life. Everything. Alcohol and tobacco free you from this life, and place you into another life.

It's not necessary anywhere, it's never necessary, it's never necessary. For everyone one thing, everything. *I'm choking.*

Gerel and I, smoking and listening to music in my room, saying nothing. Ashes. Cigarette in my right hand, I press it into my left hand and put it out. Vomit. Gerel's fear seems like laughter, her shocked look, her movement. Later there'll be many cigarettes, many days. Every morning, every day. Everything. Back and forth. I'll wear myself out, getting rid of the one thing that does not exist. Ashes. Nothing more than this. Everything exists. Always.

When you fast, there's food, and when you're satisfied, there's another thing. Another thing is too much.

Only cursing.

It was easy to write how everything is strangely stinking garbage. Easy and lovely. I like such things. I know it's garbage, I've experienced it. So what about this "garbage"? What about it? I have the power and the desire to say that it's fine. It doesn't exist now, doesn't need to. Hot ashes inside. It's always always constantly. Suffering is not suffering. Happiness is not happiness. Grieving is not even grieving.

I laugh and vomit up clots of blood. A sad corpse has died, the cadaver's dead. I'm alive.

Look then—

1993

25

ROOM FOR RENT

H. BOLOR-ERDENE

Nothing normal is truly normal. If you don't believe me, just
look at your eyes in the mirror.

That's what the student needed. A room at a cheap price. He
saw it in the announcements. Most of these announcements
were of a similar type. "For rent to a single person . . ."

There had been no real problems. The student had called a
few numbers from a pay phone. Sometimes the phone rang for
a while. Sometimes the room had been rented. The student was
thankful that his final hope picked up the phone. Somebody at
the other end of the line was breathing heavily. Their gender
wasn't obvious from their voice. Nonetheless, the two of them
spoke briefly, and effectively. . . . Apartment number such-
and-such on floor number such-and-such . . .

After classes the following day, the student went to the address.
An old, dark-colored wooden door. No bell. He knocked, and the
door opened silently. Barely a creak in the hinges. A young girl
turned and looked at the student with an icy glance. "What's a
little kid like you looking like that for?" But because the girl just
looked at him without making a sound, the student stepped

through the door. It was quite silent, as though nobody was living there. *The couch looks old*, he thought. Some kind of acrid, disturbing stench pervaded the place. When he saw the room into which the girl led him, the student was again shocked. The room was full of people. Middle-aged men and women. An old man too, and among these were two young men of about the same age and of similar appearance. They all looked at the student with precisely the same icy gaze as had the young girl. It was the student's job to say something first, so he modestly noted that he had come because of the announcement. The landlady didn't say much, but rose from her seat and took him to see his room. So it was that the student took the farthest room in this three-room apartment. Every time he left the room he would see the whole place, but all the doors were closed against him anyhow. Nor was his own room particularly suitable. The bed had an old iron spring, and the furniture that decorated the room comprised a peeling gray desk and its accompanying chair. But that was no problem. The main thing was that it was cheap.

That evening, then, the student moved into his new home. He brought a backpack. Inside it, he had a few changes of clothes, some books and notebooks, and a photo album that he always kept under his pillow. When he knocked on the door of his new life, nobody opened it. It opened as though of its own accord, and the student entered the apartment. Not a sound inside. In order to accustom himself to the thought that someone was in fact at home, he walked quietly along the corridor and entered his room. On his way there, he glanced into the other rooms and felt no sense of shock or surprise anymore. He was beginning to believe that those people who were sitting there, frozen like stones, were actually mourning someone. The acrid and disturbing stench, which didn't appear to be coming from anywhere in particular, made him uneasy.

The student's first night did not pass peacefully. It might have been because of the acrid smell, but he was beset by a

ROOM FOR RENT

243

succession of unpleasant dreams. There were so many people in the apartment, and yet he couldn't reconcile this with the fact that there was hardly any sound of movement. A few days passed, and still this quietness continued. At least the door facing his own room remained closed. The student began to wait for something untoward to happen. The end of the forty-nine days of mourning after someone's death, or a complaint from the landlady, or the clanking of a spoon in a mug, or of pails and buckets, some disturbance from the young girl, or a delicious smell of food—he didn't know what, but he was expecting something to change. He made some unsuccessful attempts to strike up conversation with the members of the household. The little girl didn't even glance at him when he said, "Here, have some chocolate." It wasn't clear to him when they ate meals, nor when they used the bathroom. Whenever he went out and whenever he returned, it seemed that the people were still sitting there, motionless. For the most part, he encountered in the corridor the old man, who had one eye that shone like glass, and the young girl, with her surprisingly venomous stare. But he couldn't clearly make out the faces of the others. And although he tried to recall the face of the landlady, he couldn't bring it to mind.

He had unpleasant dreams for the next few nights, and resolved to deal with the acrid and disturbing stench. He bought an air freshener from a store especially for this purpose. In the evening he sprayed the scent around his room and retired in the belief that he would find some comfort. But that night, he dreamed that the rest of the household had gathered next to his bed, a heaving mass gazing down upon him, and he woke up in a fluster. In the morning, it seemed that the smell was even stronger than it had been before.

One day, when the student came back from his classes, there was the old man, one of whose eyes shone like glass, sitting in his own room. He watched the old man for a long time before retiring, and in the old man's hands were the photos of the student's family, which the student had left pushed under his pillow. This unsettled the student, but all he could say, in the mildest of tones, was, "They're my family. . . ." He was pleased, though, that someone had shown interest in something of his. The student was extremely proud of the pictures that had been taken with his many friends and acquaintances. These photographs made whoever saw them gasp in amazement; on many occasions they had rendered him the most interesting of people. Suddenly the idea came to him to actually show them to the old man. He went over to the desk. "Take a look at these." He took some of the pictures from his bag, but when he turned around, the old man had disappeared. The door to the old man's room was shut. There was no indication that anyone had just been there. The corners of the photographs that had only just been in the hands of the old man were sticking out from under the student's pillow. The student regained his composure and removed the pictures. "Good God," he said with a sigh. Each of the pictures had but a single eye. He felt queasy when he saw that one eye in each of the pictures had been inked over. He rushed angrily from his room and went to the door of the old man's room. But the old man wasn't in the room where he always sat. Behind him, he heard the gentle creak of an old hinge, and when he turned around, a small crack had appeared in the door that had never before opened, and then it had closed again. The student felt that the old man must have had some kind of psychological problem, and went back to his room.

Nothing had changed by the following day, nor by the day after that, nor after a month, nor after several months. The people in the apartment lived, as before, like shades. In the end, the student even became used to their manner and stopped trying to get them to say anything. Occasionally his friends came to call and talked with him for a while, but they felt oppressed by the family's uneasy silence and hurried away in whispers. And so classes ended, and the student began to make ready to go on vacation to see relatives who lived nearby in the countryside. In the spring evening, he went back home along the street, intending to enter his room and sleep. He quietly unlocked the front door, but when he entered, the evening gloom outside was overwhelming, and all the rooms were dim and indistinct. The student took off his shoes, but when he entered his own room he came to a sudden stop. It was like the hairs on his back were standing on end; he stood there as though pinned to the door, and then slowly he turned around. The door that was never open had been opened, and in the gloom of evening, the lighted candles upon the shelf illuminated the room with a cold yellow glow. And there were perhaps six framed pictures draped with blue offering scarves, and the cold gazes he knew so well were piercing him. And yet there had been nobody in the apartment.

The student ran straight out into the street. He paid no attention to how or why he had gotten out. He ran on, wandering about in a cold fear, as though from behind the three windows of the apartment where he lived there was someone secretly and unceasingly watching him. After two weeks, the student suppressed all his fear, took four of his classmates, and went back to the apartment to collect his things. Apartment number such-and-such on floor number such-and-such. But as soon as he reached the door, he stiffened again. "Go on," said his friends, "knock!" He was scared, and he turned to them, revealing the pale color of his face, and said, "But this isn't the door." In place of the old wooden blue door, there was an iron door the color of brown leather. But it couldn't be that he had mistaken the door through which, over the course of five months, he had passed back and forth, so at the urging of his friends, he pressed the bell. . . .

After that day, because of the nature of the change that had overcome the student, his classmates had had no option but to have him placed in a psychiatric hospital for observation. But the student kept repeating, "Apartment number such-and-such on floor number such-and-such, that's right." That large angry woman had scolded them, "What are you all talking about? My family has been here for five years. What's this about framed pictures, the candles, the offering scarves? And a rented room? We're not the kind of family who would rent our rooms to someone like him!" And these angry words had been the last the student had heard before losing his mind.

2002–2007

26

WINGS

P. BATHUYAG

It seems that there is nobody in this world who has never flown in their dreams. They dream that they sprout wings and fly freely through the air. It could be that at one time, we humans did in fact fly, and perhaps when we dream we're thinking about that wonderful time.

There's a small town in a chain of high mountains on the roof of the world that nobody can leave in summer, nor indeed in winter. The inhabitants see themselves as being of a heavenly lineage, descended from eagles. The men eye one another angrily and watch their every move, so as not to sully their lineage. The town's police force and fire brigade, its few nondescript bars, its one and only school, and the places where its inhabitants go when they are sick and when they are hungry, this was the extent of the town: we might wonder whether there were many people there at all. And yet, if we imagine a large town with a bustling population, in fact it was a very peaceful place. If people ever fell out with one another somewhere in the town, within thirty minutes everyone would know and it would be

uploaded to the internet, their own special network of knowledge, and this would all be quickly placed on file almost everywhere in the world. Because a lot of snow falls in the winter, most people are unable to leave their homes and end up prisoners there. During the short days and long nights, the people only discuss their preparations for dreaming. Early in the morning, as they walk quickly to their various jobs, it seems that the men make their decisions half-heartedly, and that like us they have a great desire, the desire for freedom. Their wives wander through the stores, filling up their bags, but it appears that they are used to getting together to talk about nothing. There's a poor old man who makes his home along the alleys of the town, his being nothing like a regular life, and drowns his sorrows in drink, and a prostitute who stays out every night, brazenly selling herself around the bars, and we might think of these two as "superstars." We all talk badly of these two, yet deep inside, most of us are jealous of them, because through this old man and this prostitute we want to taste the freedom we have already forgotten. We can see that those two have truly tasted such freedom.

As winter passes and the snow gets lighter, we note an unusual festival in the town. I had not heard of such a festival anywhere. They choose the day during the first month of spring when the full moon shines, and spend the whole time in bed, celebrating the "festival of good dreams." They get up early the following morning, when the sun has risen, and gather in the central square of the town, and they talk together about what they dreamed the previous day and night during this "festival of good dreams," and the mayor selects the best dream and awards a monetary prize.

That year, they celebrated the "festival of good dreams" earlier than in previous years. But that night, when everyone had been taking care of their dreams, the old vagrant's body had been trembling; he'd not gotten a wink of sleep. The prostitute had forgotten about the festival; all night until dawn she had been out looking for customers. Everyone apart from these two had been sleeping, dreaming some extraordinarily good dreams. Even those who had no spare time, like the army and police, the medical service people, security guards, and officials who should have known better, had observed the festival. Although the old vagrant had ventured out into the alleys when dawn had barely appeared, he was shocked and most displeased to find each and every liquor store closed. He waited there, but nobody came. But once the lights came on and the babble of human voices continued in these warm and cozy homes, although the old man went after what he needed and kept on knocking at their doors, still nobody opened up. In his desperation, he rested against the statue of a horseman in the town square and fell into a sound and all-pervasive slumber.

It was in that time before the dawn, at about five or six in the morning, that the townspeople began to wake up. The first to wake screamed as though he was dying, and woke up the rest of his household, who also began screaming. Soon, the people in the surrounding buildings were crazily screaming. The things that could be written about how the mayor's fat wife screamed ended up in a couple dozen rather risqué jokes. Everyone was on the phone countless times with all the people they knew. There was a great deal of commotion inside their houses. Having the intention of going outside, everyone who had observed the night's festivities—apart, that is, from the prostitute and the old vagrant—had grown a pair of wings in place of their arms as they slept. These wings were the conch-white color of a swan's wings, and this was what they were screaming so loudly about. After a little while, though, their excitement subsided; they turned their wings and looked about, and some of the more determined ones began to experiment with flapping. As they stepped lightly on the ground, they couldn't feel their bodies; they all felt that something odd was holding them back. Soon they were looking out of their windows and hiding behind the curtains, and asking their neighbors about *their* bodies and what *they* had dreamed. What was amazing was that there had been but one dream dreamed throughout the whole town. They had flapped their wings and flown freely in the vast expanse of the sky. . . . But at first, nobody had thought that they might flap their wings and fly. But in fact they did.

There was a young businessman who had just gone bankrupt, but when he suddenly developed wings, in his misery he had leaped from a fourth-floor window. But before he was smashed to pieces on the ground, he had flapped his wings and soared upward. Boys from the high school hung about in the sky with their girlfriends, their sweat dripping without restraint over the statue of the horseman where the old vagrant was sleeping. He was awakened by something wet on his back, and this time, and for no reason, it was he who screamed loudly. So this was how the townspeople ended up flying in the sky. It was really quite sweet, how fathers and mothers had their children following behind them like a line of cranes. The town's mayor had his fat wife following him, and however much he flapped, his administration followed him in formation. By the afternoon, all those who had wings—that is, those other than the poor old vagrant and the prostitute—were out in the sky. Filled with happiness, they wondered at the misfortune that had befallen those two:

"Right—how could Heaven look favorably upon them?"

"Such beautiful wings are not for such sinful people."

"Destiny's really interesting! It really knows the difference between people, doesn't it?"

This was the sort of thing they said to sharpen their tongues. They were enjoying their life in the sky. Soon, though, the sun began to set, and a gusting wind cooled the sky, and the wings that had flapped all day, unaware of tiredness, grew slack, and the people began to think about coming back to earth. They had all learned to fly, but nobody had yet attempted a landing. The young businessman, who had been the first to try flying, came close to the ground and, although he made as soft a landing as he could, he still hit the ground with a crash, sending a few white feathers into the sky. When she saw this, the mayor's fat wife lost consciousness, and it was in such a state that she struck the ground. The things that could be written about how she screamed and fell unconscious from the sky ended up as a few stories bandied about the hospital. There was more commotion among the people in the sky than there had been among them on the ground. The cool kids from the high school out with their girlfriends and the little children flying after their fathers and mothers all began to come down to earth. The night continued with the sound of thudding. However they tried, nobody could manage a soft landing. Strong young people hung around for a while and finally hit the ground at dawn. For an entire week, the poor old vagrant took the winged people who had fallen from the sky and buried them in the countryside. The prostitute, however, didn't show her face outside, but spent ten days bundled up, all a-tremble. Finally she left home for something and walked the alleys as before. She saw the old vagrant, and she was so very happy that she was not alone. In a watering hole left without a barman they talked together, and remembered the people of the town.

"They all grew wings and lorded it over me," the prostitute said. "I didn't care. I'm a woman who's tired of living."

But the old vagrant said, "I've seen some things in my sixty years. A human might grow wings, but that doesn't make him a creature of the sky. When they die, everybody falls to earth. Greed and desire made the people of our town grow wings, they were flying toward Hell."

27

THE COMPOSER

M. UYANSÜH

H e sat in a small pericardium-like room. It was cramped, with a single window touched by the sun. It seemed to me as though the world was contained within this cramped room, just as the heart is contained within the pericardium, just as a human lives within their heart. A single low chair, a quiet old table, a piano covered with fine dust. The bones of the room were worn and warped, and the man who had come through the thin door, its sound like a frustrated screech, had taken a couple of steps, bowed, and sat down before the piano, which had been placed close to the wall. He was existing so close to us. But our relationship with him was so distant; we gave this "great composer" a drink and so made him lose his place. Later we would speak badly of this. He went this way and that. . . . This cramped room, in fact, was the studio of this "great composer," on the third story of a three-story building, in the shape of an ancient theater.

When I entered, he had sat for a while, touching the keys of the piano as though distinguishing the black from the white, and had abruptly played the final pair, and in a strange muddle he sang, "*That's just how it is inside*" and smiled darkly.

Someone had requested a song, and it was clear they had plied him with drink, so much that he almost fell. At that point, it was notable that he was unsettled. In his distress from being so inebriated, a real melody appeared. I want to say that this divine melody had come from his sadness.

We had known each other for a very long time. We had frequently enjoyed ourselves over a drink or a meal. When we drank together, I would hear the same stories from his mouth, such that I had almost memorized them. The hero of his stories was a drunk. This man, Saasag, was a man whose drinking disturbed the waters of his homeland. His only possession was a brown cloud horse that they talked about in places nearby. As he rode slowly through the rain clouds, his voice reached a family's doorstep from far away:

"My fine benefactors!" he shouted. "Come outside!" and a woman and her children ran out carrying a pitcher of *arhi*. Saasag didn't dismount. He bent down from his horse's withers and gulped the *arhi* down.

"Yes, I'll give a big prize to the person who goes off and brings the pitcher back full. These locals check the standard of the food here." The old people were saying that Saasag was a reincarnate Buddha who had cleared away the people's misery.

The night before Saasag left this world, he asked them to give him *arhi*, which he drank under the round moon of autumn, and he dug his heels into the saddlecloth like a wild man and galloped away, deep into the hills, the moon as bright as day.

After that night, when the old women had put their hands together, praying, "Oh, holy mountains, forgive me!," Saasag did not come back to this world from deep among the blue hills onto which the moon poured down. Such pain was his by nature.

He flattened out the pages that had become crinkled while he had been digging and digging away at those southern slopes. In front of those flattened sheets, on the music stand, he placed the score. He clicked his fingers and tried to sing. He tried to play the piano. But nothing came. Angry, he felt in his pocket and found a single crumpled cigarette, which he repaired with saliva and lit.

"They're coming to give me something very strange. It's difficult . . ." and he held out the papers to me. A poem, but a poem nonetheless. It could have been an old man's poem.

He looked out through the window. It was autumn. Beyond the window the leaves were tumbling; it was as though he had nothing left. Somewhere a bird was singing its response. I was tired of watching his behavior, and I poured from the bottle of *arhi* I had brought and placed it on the table. It was odd how he revived when he saw this. He was having difficulties, struggling with something, but not the poem; he gave the impression that he was angry that I had not come earlier.

The two of us drank, sharing the bottle equally between us. We managed to finish it all in three rounds. The first two went down with the clinking of our cups. And then we shared the final portion. I got up to leave. He was flushed, and his nose was covered in droplets of sweat.

"We're not going to the doctor. We're not going to the hospital. We're not losing our minds!" We shared this solemn vow, and went our separate ways.

As I went out the door, he scolded me affectionately.

"You don't care about me! You don't give me even a poem! It doesn't matter. . . ." I turned as I left; he was strangely bent over the piano, his hands over the keys, like a hunchback carrying an eternal burden. And yet . . . once I had gone out, it seems he got up. He got up and went over to the window; it was open wide and touched by the sun. There he sang a truly divine melody. And then he stretched out his arms and, falling forward from the third story, he flew, and I feel the gods supported the life that remained in him.

*   *   *

I went to visit him in the hospital. Through the window, the trees were already bare and the cold rain of the final month of autumn was raging. Soon the first snow would fall.

He looked at the things in the bag I was carrying.

"Did you bring—something?"

"What do you mean by 'something'? Have you forgotten how close you were to dying?"

"Who cares? My ripped flesh and my shattered bones will heal . . ."

I put the bag of things in the closet next to his pillow and slipped the small bottle of *arhi* I had hidden from the doctors beneath his covers. He touched it.

"With such a friend," he laughed, "I'll have no complaints even if I die."

"Ah . . . right . . ." I shook my head. "And then you'll go off to the next world."

But it wasn't long before he left the hospital. The doctors said there was no lasting damage. But I wondered whether the gods who'd supported him when he fell hadn't also worked to heal him. When he was in the hospital, he had sung me a song with a sharp and particular rhythm, like a spanking trot.

It was just like a horse's hoofbeat.

2008

AIMAG: an administrative unit roughly equivalent to an American state or an English county

AIRAG: fermented, slightly alcoholic mare's milk

ARHI: Mongolian vodka

DEEL: a long, traditional Mongolian jacket, worn by men and women, and tied by a belt at the waist

GARUDA: a legendary bird, or birdlike creature, in Hindu, Buddhist, and Jain mythology

GER: a portable circular tent, common to Mongolian nomads, constructed from felt draped over a wooden framework

HAAN: a ruler, used of the Manchu (Qing) Emperor, of Western monarchs, and of Chinggis Haan

HANGAI: mountainous, wooded landscape in the western region of Mongolia

HUURGA: a kind of pilaf made with rice and vegetables, sometimes including meat or eggs

IKARUS: a line of buses produced in Hungary, which dominated the bus market throughout the Soviet bloc during the Cold War period

KOMSOMOL: a Young Pioneer, a member of the MPRP's youth organization

LONG SONG: a genre of folk song marked by elongated and highly ornamented vowels, and sung in a wide variety of regional styles

MPRP: Mongolian People's Revolutionary Party

NAADAM: a festival at which Mongolia's "three manly sports"—archery, horse racing, and wrestling—take place. There is a national naadam held every July, and local and regional naadams are held throughout the summer.

OVOO: a cairn constructed from stones, used as a waymarker and as a propitiatory offering to local spirits

SANGHA: the community of Buddhist practitioners, although frequently used specifically of monastics

SHAMBHALA: a mythical and perfect land in Buddhist cosmology

SHIMIIN ARHI: the best quality of *arhi* (q.v.)

STUPA: a Buddhist reliquary built to house the remains of highly respected teachers

SUM: a local administrative unit, smaller than an *aimag* (q.v.)

TAIJI: a minor noble in the prerevolutionary period

TÖGRÖG: a unit of the Mongolian currency. A *tögrög* is divided into 100 *möngö*.

TORMA: a triangular offering cake, made of flour and butter, used in Buddhist rituals

TSAM: ritual dances performed by monks in the courtyards of monasteries

TU-134: A brand of cigarettes, named after the Soviet jet airliner the Tupolev 134, sponsored by the Soviet airline Aeroflot, produced in Bulgaria, and sold throughout the Soviet bloc during the 1970s and 1980s

WALL NEWSPAPER: during the Soviet period, newspapers pinned to walls in buildings or to hoardings in the street, as a way to inform people about recent events and the latest government directives

NOTES ON THE STORIES

S anjaasürengiin Anudar (1973–1995) was born in Ulaanbaatar and graduated with a degree in philosophy from the
Mongolian National University. His application for graduate
study in the same department was accepted, but soon afterward
he fell to his death from a window in a university dormitory. No
autopsy was held, and the cause of his death remains unclear.

Anudar left behind him just a few stories, of which three—
including "Everything"—were collected and published in a
book following his death. He was, however, considered the
most innovative and radical prose writer of his generation,
whose youth was defined by the social and political changes
brought about by the collapse of the Soviet Union. This was a
generation generally untroubled by censorship and able to read
freely nihilistic and anarchic writing, and to listen to heavy
rock and punk music emerging from Russia and Eastern Europe
during the late Soviet and post-Soviet periods.

"Everything" is a story in which nothing much happens, but
in which everything is somehow meaningful. The narrator
Delger goes to school, paints, hangs out with his friends, and
thinks about existence. Anudar's philosophical perspective

informs the tenor of the story, in which life happens to, rather than being lived by, Delger and his friends. Parallels can be drawn with the existentialism of Samuel Beckett, Jean-Paul Sartre, and Albert Camus, and with work from the Russian *chernukha* movement such as Vasili Pichil's 1988 film *Little Vera*. Of particular importance to Anudar was the rock poetry of Alexander Bashlachev, who himself had committed suicide in 1988 by jumping from a window, and whose work Anudar used as an epigraph for another story, "At Least Try, Then. . . ." However, for a Mongolian readership, Anudar's was a youthful and extraordinary new underground voice, and a harbinger for the development of a Mongolian literature free from restriction and open to everything.

Böhiin Baast (1921–2019) was born in Bayan-Ölgii, in the far west of Mongolia, and came to Ulaanbaatar in 1940. Over the course of his unusually long life, he produced poems as well as novels and short stories, and several plays. Although he started his career at a time when many of his contemporaries were writing highly politicized works, he tended to focus on the experience of individuals, mainly of herders, rather than on ideology, and his works, for children as well as for adults, became popular for their charm and humor as much as for their insight into human character.

Baast was trained as a veterinarian, and his writing—such as "Images from a Single Day"—shows a great sensitivity toward animals and the natural world. In this story, he describes the bombardment of cattle by insects and the suffering that can result from this. The commentary, common in Baast's stories, comes both from his characters and from the sayings of herders in the countryside, and gives his story a slightly old-fashioned and folksy tone. But the repetition of such wisdom, of course, is also how people keep safe on the wild and empty steppe.

*   *   *

Pürevhüügiin Bathuyag (b. 1975) was born in Ulaanbaatar and works as a writer of fiction, poetry, and drama, and as a literary critic. During the early 1990s, following Mongolia's democratic revolution, he was a founding member of the UB Boys literary group, whose focus was to explore tradition from new and unusual perspectives. He currently teaches Mongolian literature at the Mongolian University of Art and Culture.

Bathuyag has for a long time been fascinated by mythology and by human psychology, and in the story presented here, "Wings," he explores the frequent oneiric experience of dreaming. The identity of the setting is unclear, but the phrase "the roof of the world" will tend, most likely, to make readers think of Tibet and the many mysterious stories associated with the Himalayan region. But this story, in switching between light-hearted vignettes of people in flight and the more serious histories of the two individuals untouched by this new gift, might also be seen as a parable, not only of people but also of countries such as Mongolia in the wake of communism, who are happy to fly but unprepared for their inevitable descent to earth.

Haltarin Bolor-Erdene (b. 1975) was born in Ulaanbaatar and worked as a journalist on the city's free newspapers until 2007, since when she has lived in Paris, France, with her family. She writes short stories and novellas and published her first novel, *The Running Woman*, in 2019.

"Room for Rent" is an example of how Mongolian literature is responding to the horror and supernatural genres. More than the unnamed student, it is perhaps the claustrophobia of the eponymous room that is the central character of this story. Unlike the mystery in Tsend's "A Great Mystery" and Damdinsüren's "Two White Things," in Bolor-Erdene's story there is a presence, a tangible feeling of menace, which might call to mind the work of Edgar Allen Poe, which has been available in Mongolian translation since the 1930s.

* * *

Sonombaljurin Buyannemeh (1902–1937) was born in Dundgovi province. One of the high-profile intellectuals who came
of age around the time of the 1921 revolution, he joined the
Mongolian Revolutionary Party at the beginning of 1921 and
cofounded the Revolutionary Youth Union in 1922. It was
around this time that he began to write songs and poems,
including a Mongolian version of the Internationale. In 1924 he
went to Southern (Inner) Mongolia, where he remained for two
years, working as a journalist and campaigning for indepen-
dence for Southern (Inner) Mongolia. In 1929, under the auspices of the MPRP, Buyannemeh was one of the founders of the
Revolutionary Writers' Group, and he was both editor and primary contributor to the first anthology of Mongolian literature,
published later that year. Between 1930 and 1937 he worked as a
journalist, and he was director of the Mongolian Writers' Union
from 1934 until 1935. Buyannemeh was arrested, tried, and executed in September 1937 on false charges of counterrevolutionary activities on behalf of Japan.

"Something Wonderful" is an account of how one family
learned about the establishment of the people's government in
Mongolia on July 11, 1921. The story is simple, yet Buyannemeh's skill is to populate it with characters likely to benefit
most from the revolution—the old and the young, the unedu-
cated and illiterate, and those of religious faith. Within a few
years, writers would be discouraged from including the kind of
Buddhist imagery and fabulous narrative devices employed in
this story, but Buyannemeh's central message of social advancement promoted by the people's government would continue to
be reinforced.

As a young intellectual and a committed supporter of the
revolution, Buyannemeh was clearly excited by Mongolia's new
world of technology and industry. Building upon the kind of
narrative device used in "Something Wonderful," his works

include stories based on folk narratives in which cars, bicycles, and trains discuss socialist policy, and plays about the social reforms that defined the revolution. His execution was a loss felt especially hard by the literary community, and in 1962 he was rehabilitated by the MPRP.

Dungarin Chimid (1904–1932) was born in Selenge province. Educated at the University of the Toilers of the East in Moscow, he worked for the MPRP and coedited the first anthology of modern Mongolian literature, published in 1929 by the Revolutionary Writers' Group, of which he was one of the founding members. He also served as Minister of Livestock and Agriculture for eighteen months between 1930 and 1931. Following the repudiation of the "left deviationists" by the Ninth Party Congress in 1932, Chimid was called to Moscow, where it seems he was executed sometime during 1934.

Chimid was both a socially progressive writer—in that he embraced the ideas of social equality and of universal education promoted by the MPRP—and an intellectual whose works suggest sometimes the influence of European modernism. In the late 1920s, while writers such as D. Natsagdorj and D. Namdag (both represented in this collection) were being educated in Germany, Chimid himself went on a bicycle trip through Germany, which he wrote about in a short travelogue. His sensitivity to European culture led him to experiment with Europeanizing his name, and he frequently used "Chimid Dungarin" in place of the Mongolian "Dungarin Chimid."

"The Shelducks" offers an interesting take on the nineteenth-century *üge* (word) tradition, which itself was influenced by the fables of the Indian Pañcatantra. In an effort to appeal to both tradition and revolutionary ideals, the story tells of the overthrow of the despotic and thieving shelducks by a radicalized group of little birds. Stories such as these—including Buyannemeh's "Dispute Between the Trucks" (1929) and Dendev's

"Story of the Writing Brush, the Pen, and the Pencil" (1928)—
were popular with readers but fell out of favor in 1929, when the
Party started to encourage more realistic writing. Chimid's
work includes an account of a lovers' rendezvous ("Lovers
Kissing," 1929), written in strikingly frank language for the
time, some poems, and the story "Zandanpil the Serving Girl"
(1932).

Tsendiin Damdinsüren (1907–1986) was born in Dornod
province. As a writer, he came to prominence in 1929 with his
story "The Scorned Girl," arguably the first piece of socialist
fiction to be written in Mongolia. That same year he was one
of the founders of the Revolutionary Writers' Group.
Between 1934 and 1938 he studied at the Institute for Oriental
Studies in Leningrad and began at that time to translate Russian literature. Damdinsüren was arrested in April 1938 on
false charges, accused of being a Japanese spy. After two
years without trial, he was eventually sentenced to six years
in prison but was released in 1943, conditional on his working
to refine and implement the new Mongolian Cyrillic
alphabet.

Following the deaths of Stalin and Choibalsan, in the relative thaw of the late 1950s, Damdinsüren felt that he needed to
choose between writing and scholarship. He chose the latter
and began to carry out scholarly work on premodern Mongolian literature, and in 1959 produced what would become the
standard collection. He also researched Tibetan language and
literature, and wrote extensively on Tibetan literature in both
Tibet and Mongolia. In the same year he became director of the
Institute of Language and Literature, and he was head of the
Writers' Union for two brief spells in 1943 and 1954.

Although Damdinsüren's reputation was made through
"The Scorned Girl," many of his other stories also became popular. The two included here—"Two White Things" and "What

Changed Soli"—were written around the same time, but in their very different characters show the breadth of Damdinsüren's art. "What Changed Soli," moreover, was possibly the first attempt in Mongolian literature to address the idea of the transformative power of labor, a theme central to the doctrine of Socialist Realism, which would soon become a popular and politically expedient style among Mongolia's writers.

When "Two White Things" was first published, Damdinsüren was criticized for the portrayal of the abusive treatment of horses by a Mongolian. A debate, which remained unresolved, continued intermittently as to whether, given Damdinsüren's interest in Mongolian folk literature, this story might have been based on a story he had heard on a research trip to the Altai mountains in 1930. Despite the unfavorable characterization, this remains one of Damdinsüren's most anthologized stories.

Sormuunirshiin Dashdoorov (1936–1999) was born in Dundgovi province and trained as a teacher in Ulaanbaatar in the early 1950s. He taught for two years and was then admitted as a professional writer to the Mongolian Writers' Union. In 1969 he graduated from the Gorky Institute in Moscow.

In addition to fiction, Dashdoorov also wrote poetry and film scripts, and in the 1970s he was the general editor of Mongolia's film production company, Mongol Kino. He was particularly successful as a writer of narrative fiction and in 1975 was awarded the prestigious Writers' Union Prize for his novel *The Heights of the Gobi*.

Although not one of his best-known stories, "The Cricket" shows Dashdoorov's use of irony in creating the character of Jamiyanbuu. This minor operative, petty and frustrated and proud in equal measure, battles against bureaucracy, and against other petty, frustrated, and proud operatives, to carry out his appointed task. Alone among the stores in this anthology, "The Cricket" embodies the anxieties of Soviet-era bureaucracy, and reveals too the skill of Dashdoorov in his sympathetic portrayal of one of the men buried beneath it.

Sengiin Erdene (1929–2000) was born in Hentii province and studied medicine in Ulaanbaatar, eventually specializing in psychiatry. His early writing coincided with the period of the post-Stalinist thaw, and he was then able to explore his interest in human psychology in an atmosphere relatively free of censorship. And yet, as he developed as a writer, Erdene began to attract the attention of the authorities. His work was sharp and exacting, and his comments on the system in Mongolia, while not seditious, were nonetheless highly critical. During the 1970s in particular, his literary activity and personal conduct were examined in the media, and the official censor refused to allow several of his works to be published.

The popularity of Erdene's early work among critics and readers alike encouraged him to write prose of increasing subtlety, creating complex yet sympathetic characters, often faced with making morally complex personal choices. The "Hulan" trilogy is one such story. Written in three sections over a period of thirty years, it is one of Erdene's most popular and most striking works. It is also based on his own experience as a young man, and there has been much speculation on the identity of the enigmatic Hulan. While the characters' unrealized love transforms gradually into a deep affection, their changing lives and circumstances reflect the social changes in Mongolia during the period.

In "Suncranes," the narrator, in preparing to leave the following day to continue his education at the provincial school, considers the life he has lived thus far and how the places he has known have changed. In both of these stories, Erdene reveals how, through observing the transformation of the outside world, we can also understand the transformation of the world within, and so manage to move on with our lives, despite the pain such changes can bring.

Chinagiin Galsan (b. 1944) was born in the Altai mountains of Bayan-Ölgii province, the youngest son of a Tuvan shaman. During the 1960s, he studied German language and culture at the Karl Marx University in Leipzig, which at that time was in East Germany. He completed his doctoral studies and returned to teach German at the Mongolian National University. In 1976, due to his being regarded as "politically untrustworthy," his teaching license was withdrawn.

Four years later, Galsan was diagnosed with a severe heart condition. He attributes his subsequent recovery to shamanic powers, and since that point, he has sought to develop his connection with his shamanic roots. His books, written in both German and Mongolian, observe the world through the perspective of someone as much at home in the metaphysical as in the physical world, and Galsan has become popular among European audiences for his stories and memoirs about life in the far west of Mongolia.

In "Heaven's Daughter," a young girl mysteriously appears in an encampment. The sparse population and harsh terrain make it hard for children simply to appear in this way, and so the girl's identity and origins become a metaphysical riddle. This is, though, also a story about how Mongolia's nomads, realizing the dire consequences for those who might be turned away from an encampment, accept whomever might appear, allowing them to rest and offering them food and drink. The tradition by which abandoned children (who are known as "children of the hearth") are adopted is still a common way of honoring life and reinforcing the social fabric.

Dorjiin Garmaa (1937–2016) was born in Töv province and trained as an economist, overseeing the finances of both

Bayanhongor and Töv provinces during the late 1950s. In 1966 he studied at the Gorky Institute in Moscow, and subsequently at the Soviet Academy of Science, from which he graduated in 1980. During his career as a writer, he worked on the satirical magazine *Tonshuul* (Woodpecker) in 1961, and as the editor of the Party's literature journal, *Tsog* (Spark), between 1966 and 1973. He also held various posts at Mongolian Radio and Television and in the Writers' Union.

The intimacy of nomadic lives, lived essentially in and around the small enclosed space of the *ger*, has produced a singular set of family narratives. In the largely unregulated world of these families, the expressions of relationship waver between the claustrophobia of expectation (for instance in D. Namdag's "Waiting for What He Has Lost") and the fluidity of the emotional and physical space in which nomadic life takes place (for instance Ch. Galsan's "Heaven's Daughter"). "The Wolf's Lair" describes something in between these two extremes, showing how a father's blind devotion to his son can lead to social approbation and personal resentments.

Rites of passage such as entering the wolf's lair are important for young nomads learning how to live in the physically harsh Mongolian landscape. But Garmaa's story also shows how these hardships affect the emotional landscape, and the very real dangers of pride. And also, as with the majority of Mongolian stories dealing with the place of humans in the natural world, "The Wolf's Lair" leaves us keenly aware that humans are not a special part of nature and available to any animal to whom they fall prey.

Chadrabalin Lodoidamba (1917–1970) was born in Gobi-Altai province. As a young boy, he was a novice monk before leaving his monastery to pursue education. He graduated in 1958, with a degree in art history, from the Mongolian National University. Lodoidamba wrote fiction and literary essays, and served for a time as deputy minister of culture. His novel "In the Altai" (1954) was awarded a State Literature Prize, and "The Clear River Tamir" (1962) was made into a highly popular film.

Lodoidamba's fiction shows a great interest in the relationship between human society and the natural world. In "The Saiga" he meditates on hunting, and the two perspectives of the hunted saiga antelope and the hunter. The hunters here are detectives, supposed to uphold the law: one of them invokes the law, which made shooting certain wild animals an offense. The cruelty of the men and their casual attitude as they watch the saiga's death seem—like the violence toward horses in Ts. Damdinsüren's "Two White Things"—to contradict the respect for the natural world among Mongolian nomads. In writing this story, it is possible that Lodoidamba was using the thaw following the death of Stalin to criticize the increasingly popular belief, which reflected the attitude in the Soviet Union, in the need to dominate nature in the name of progress.

Perenlein Luvsantseren (1933–1972) was born in Bayanhongor province and for many years worked as a veterinarian in the Gobi. At the time when "Blue as Water" was written he was studying at the Gorky Institute in Moscow, from which he graduated in 1967. Among writers of his generation, his was considered one of the most lyrical and poetic prose styles, characteristics that are clear in this, possibly his best-loved story.

"Blue as Water" explores the life of an old camel caravaner, drawing on the kind of stories told by the elders as he was growing up in the Gobi. Jantsan's experience of love as a young man and his fraught relationship with his father underpin the narrative, and yet from this humorous backstory there emerges an old man who cannot accept that he is getting old. In Luvsantseren's poetic language, the memories of Jantsan's youth interweave with what he realizes might be his last opportunity to see his caravaner friends ride off in the autumn on their annual journey. Like D. Garmaa's "The Wolf's Lair," Luvsantseren's narrative is a poignant *memento mori*, as well as a homage to generations of caravaners who left their families to ride across the Gobi.

Gombojavyn Mend-Ooyo (b. 1952) was born in Sühbaatar province. He was educated as a teacher and then immediately took up a position in a community on the Chinese border, where he spent most of his time working on poetry. The source of much of his writing is his childhood in a nomadic family in the Gobi desert, listening to the stories and songs of the elders, and observing the constant changes in the natural world that surrounded him.

"The Ballad of the Unweaned Camel" is one of the stories included in what he describes as his "almanac novel," *Altan Ovoo*, which he wrote during the late 1980s, with the specific aim of rekindling Mongolians' interest in nomadic culture in the years of waning Soviet influence. It could be described as an example of Mongolian "magical realism," an innovative attempt to draw the mystical from traditional stories and present it in a contemporary form. While the camel's arrival might be otherworldly, his experiences in battle and his relationship with humans are described with a lightness that contrasts with the gravity of the situation.

The literature that began to appear during the period of *perestroika* and *glasnost* tended to look to Euro-American fiction for its models, contrasting the ideals of socialism with the realistic portrayal in Western literature. Mend-Ooyo, however, stands out for his use of traditional Mongolian forms and imagery to draw his readers back into what he considers an understanding of the world based upon ancient Mongolian nomadic culture.

*   *   *

Luvsandorjiin Ölziitögs (b. 1972) was born in the city of Darhan and came to prominence during the early 1990s as one of Mongolia's new generation of writers influenced by Western literature, and particularly by the new wave of Russian authors working at that time. She has consistently sought to expand the envelope of Mongolian fiction and is now one of very few Mongolians able to make a living from writing. Her work has been published outside Mongolia and is especially popular in South Korea.

Ölziitögs's style is a mixture of surrealism and dark comedy, but this combination, as in "Raul and Raul," seems to cover a compassionate sensitivity toward the plight of those who are simply trying to live a life in the world. Like S. Anudar's, her writing challenges Mongolian readers' ideas of what fiction should be, dealing with issues rarely addressed, such as sex and drugs and the problems of Mongolia's modern youth.

Byambin Rinchen (1905–1977) was born in Selenge province and studied under the Russian Mongolist Boris Vadimirtsov at the Institute for Oriental Languages in Leningrad. In 1927 he became director of a school in Ulaanbaatar, and two years later he was one of the founding members of the Revolutionary Writers' Union. He was sentenced to death in 1939, accused of being a Japanese spy, but in his sentence was commuted to ten years' imprisonment, of which he served only four months.

In 1944, now working as the literary advisor to the Mongolian People's Revolutionary Party, Rinchen wrote the screenplay for Mongolia's first feature film, *Tsogt Taij* (based on the life of a sixteenth-century nobleman), which won the Choibalsan Prize. His literary work included *Rays of Dawn* (1952), the first full-length novel to be written in Mongolian, which gained him popularity among readers, despite being attacked for what was perceived as antirevolutionary sentiment. "Bunia Takes Wing," written only a few years later but in a very different context following the deaths of Stalin and Choibalsan, is a celebration of a young man's struggle for individuality within the confines of Buddhist monastic society.

Rinchen developed a reputation as an urbane and erudite scholar, internationally regarded for his work on Mongolian culture and history, and especially on linguistics. In works such as *The Princess* (1962) he used his knowledge of early Mongolian language to create a historically credible context, just as Manchu sources give credibility to the story of Bunia. Through his historical fiction, Rinchen worked to restore a sense of history and tradition to Mongolian literature, continued in the fiction of writers such as G. Mend-Ooyo.

Oidovin Tsend (1929–1981) was born in Arhangai province and graduated from the Mongolian National University in Technical Communication, a field in which he worked until his death. He wrote poetry and plays as well as fiction, but is best remembered for his short stories.

Seen in the context of the political thaw of the late 1950s, "A Great Mystery," which gave the title to the first of Tsend's four books, published in 1959, concerns itself only with the complex nature of human relationships and the psychology of memory. What is an apparently simple mystery, regarding the origin of the dramatic scar on a man's face, reveals a story of many layers, its narrative entwined in a kind of unspoken love as well as in an earlier brief encounter. Tsend's characterization is a master class in the subtlety of human nature, while the main building of an agricultural collective in a winter landscape provides a claustrophobic setting, from which the characters separate at the close of the story.

Sonomin Udval (1921–1991) was born in Töv province. She studied at the University of the Toilers of the East in Moscow and subsequently at the Soviet Communist Party University.

She wrote poetry, plays, and fiction, and is especially famous for her novella *Odgerel* (1957) and for her many short stories. From 1961 until 1974, she was director of the Writers' Union, in which capacity she oversaw the rehabilitation of many writers executed under false charges during the Great Repression.

Udval's style is almost cinematic, and in many of her stories lines of dialogue predominate, seeming more like a film script. The style of "He Came with a Spare Horse," however, is more descriptive, albeit told in the first person by the principal character. It takes place at the lunar New Year, a time at which wishes are made for the future and old friendships are recalled. Udval's humor is seen in the interaction of Dogisüren with his friends, as well as in the clash between past and present, in the sign written in the traditional Mongolian script, barely remembered almost two decades after its replacement by Cyrillic, and in the new style of denim jeans.

Tserenjavin Ulambayar (1912–1976) was born in Arhangai province. He wrote only fiction and began to publish in the late 1930s. He later became the editor of the Mongolian Writers' Union journal *Tsog*.

Ulambayar was a master of very short fiction, generally only two or three pages. These vignettes, such as "The Morning of the First" and "The Green-painted Car," open up small and intimate pockets of daily life in Mongolia's newly industrialized urban areas. He was one of the first writers to focus almost entirely on these rather than the more traditional countryside settings, and in the postwar period, with Mongolia's relationship with the Soviet Union growing closer, he described the lives of workers—such as the members of Bidyalah's family—who were busy contributing to the improvement of the country.

Bidyalah's father is trying to complete the requirements of Mongolia's first five-year plan, projected for the period between 1948 and 1952. The idea of working hard to exceed what is required reflects the Stakhanovite attitude that had seized Mongolia since the end of the war and became more important in fiction until the death of Stalin.

With education at a premium, her father's attempt to enroll her in school a year early is thwarted by her name, meaning "we will be victorious," which would only have been given to a child born after June 1941, when Mongolia entered the war in support of the Soviets. This kind of irony—found also in the poignancy of "The Green-painted Car"—is a feature of Ulambayar's prose, and gives it a character belying what otherwise might seem to be a blind adherence to the political system of the MPRP and the Soviet Union.

M. Uyansüh, the pen name of Multsangiin Sühbaatar (1967), was born in Uvs province. He spent his childhood around Mount Harhiraa and was especially influenced by his uncle, a very famous storyteller in the region, who encouraged him to pursue a career in writing.

Uyansüh studied Russian and graduated from the National University of the Humanities in 1991, and became journalist and teacher of Russian in Uvs. Having earned a second degree in 2012, in business administration, he lives today in Darhan, Mongolia's second city, where he works as the director of libraries at the School of Agroecology and Business Institute of Plant and Agricultural Sciences.

As a writer of poetry as well as fiction, Uyansüh has received awards both in Mongolia and in Korea and is generally reckoned as one of the most skilled and influential writers of his generation. His dark short story "The Composer," with its dark, intertwined narratives and hints of black humor, reflects the influence of traditional Mongolian folktales and a more contemporary concern with the place of the artist in Mongolian society.

Mordendeviin Yadamsüren (1904–1937) was born in Ulaan-baatar. He studied at the University of the Toilers of the East in Moscow between 1924 and 1928 and on his return worked for the Justice Ministry and as a state procurator, and was director of ideology for the Central Committee of the Union of Revolutionary Youth. He was head of the Writers' Union from 1930 until 1933. At the time of his execution in 1937, on charges of being a Japanese spy, he was head of the Central Theater. He was rehabilitated in 1962.

Yamasüren wrote plays, stories, and poetry, and although it is believed that he probably wrote much more than what we have available today, what we do have is not only of high literary quality but also notable for its modernism. A striking example of this is "The Young Couple," with its urban setting and the love story of the factory worker Jaltsan and the modern young woman Adilbish. Written in 1937, it is both a fascinating admixture of high-flown prose and epistolary fiction and an illustration of how Mongolian writers were beginning to explore the modern world.

The other of Yadamsüren's two novellas, "Three Girls," is also set in Ulaanbaatar and tells the story of the experience of three very different young women—a teacher, a student, and a prostitute—whose relationships are played out against the clash between the promotion of education for women and the mistreatment of prostitutes by Chinese merchants. The psychological insights of these two stories, together with the mélange of sights and sounds in the descriptions of Ulaanbaatar, mark Yadamsüren as, perhaps even more than D. Natsagdorj, Mongolia's leading exponent of modernism in the European style.

ACKNOWLEDGMENTS

I would like to thank G. Mend-Ooyo, O. Munkhnaran, D. Tsedev, and P. Bathuyag for their help in securing the necessary permissions from the copyright holders of these stories. The initial impetus for this collection came from Morris Rossabi, and I would like to thank him for his role in connecting me with Columbia University Press. My thanks also to the anonymous reviewers and to Christine Dunbar and the editorial and production team at Columbia University Press, whose work has helped to make this a better book. Finally, I thank my wife, Sunmin Yoon, who encouraged me to find a secure home for my translations, and whose support and love sustains me.